DAUGHTER, SON, ASSASSIN

DAUGHTER, SON, ASSASSIN

A NOVEL

Steven Salaita

Brooklyn, NY
Philadelphia, PA
commonnotions.org

ISBN: 978-1-945335-08-2 | eBook ISBN: 978-1-945335-21-1
Library of Congress Number: 2024933985

10 9 8 7 6 5 4 3 2 1

Common Notions
c/o Interference Archive
314 7th St.
Brooklyn, NY 11215

Common Notions
c/o Making Worlds Bookstore
210 S. 45th St.
Philadelphia, PA 19104

www.commonnotions.org
info@commonnotions.org

Discounted bulk quantities of our books are available for organizing, educational, or fundraising purposes. Please contact Common Notions at the address above for more information.

Cover design by Josh MacPhee
Layout design and typesetting by Suba Murugan
Printed by union labor in Canada on acid-free paper

About the Nonaligned Series

Nonaligned is dedicated to fiction, literary nonfiction, and poetry that explores the historical and ongoing legacies of anticolonial politics, the evolving nature of imperialism, and the world-making freedom movements of our times. The series highlights vital and creative sources of internationalist imagination within the fractures and faultlines of the current world order. The name takes inspiration from the worldwide anticolonial and anti-imperialist self-determination movements that sparked a wave of decolonization in the 1960s and '70s across Africa, Latin America, Asia, and the Arab world.

In the Nonaligned Series

Daughter, Son, Assassin, Steven Salaita, 9781945335082
Ragás, because the sea has no place to grab, Sónia Vaz Borges and
  Maria Isabel Vaz, 9781945335099
Rojava: A Novel of Kurdish Freedom, Sharam Qawami (translated by
  Kiyoumars Zamani), 9781945335105

Fred

———

THE DUNES ROSE and fell like the knolls of an unfurled blanket. I could see only shades of beige in every direction. No trees. No grass. No shrubbery. I had been dropped into an ecosystem of microbes and subterranean animals.

Two concave wounds on my right cheek festered in the midday heat. My abdomen throbbed beneath fractured ribs. I sat in a drift of sand near the top of a dune, battered, pathetic, exhausted. Dehydration pushed my brain against the inside of my skull. I scanned the cloudless sky. No hope of curing the condition.

I took off my shirt and wrapped it around my scalp, trying to cover my shoulders and arms with the remaining fabric. My boxer-briefs were useless but for the slim hope that I would encounter another person. No leg bones were broken. My bare feet were an advantage in the sand.

The soldiers concealed my vision on the drive over. Once the sounds of civilization had disappeared, we were on a paved road for a long time, but I had no sense of scope or distance. We pulled off and then drove across unstable terrain for another long time. I figured I wasn't terribly far from a road, which would eventually lead to a curbside stall or a village. A battered man in underwear wouldn't entice any drivers to stop, but one of them might recognize my dire condition.

I stayed in place while considering my options. There really was no choice but to follow the tire tracks before the wind blew them away. They could lead me further into the desert, but I didn't imagine my captors to be so clever or patient. They would have wanted to get home and eat dinner. These were men guided not by method, but appetite.

The sun was high overhead. It scorched my wounds and gave my skin a papery texture. Nightfall would bring relief and a new set of problems. I always heard that stargazing from the desert is remarkable, that without light pollution the entire sky looks different, brighter, busier, but I'd never done it. Here I was in the desert and still wouldn't get the chance. I doubted I'd be alive by twilight.

I considered dying where I sat—it wouldn't take long—but I wasn't ready to give up the prospect of impossibility. So I got off my ass and started walking.

Nancy

NOBODY HAS EVER found my father's remains, so technically he could be alive. He's not yet legally dead but I haven't seen him for eleven years. I long ago accepted that he's gone but it's not like a normal death with a viewing and a funeral and then everyone gets on with things. Mom and I were in limbo for months, years, when we just sort of decided that he's not coming back. But because he was never found, there's always that tiny bit of uncertainty, that remote possibility he's somewhere in the world, locked in a dungeon or enjoying life with a new alias and a different family. I'll never know for sure, which I suppose is a way of saying he's dead even if he's physically alive.

I remember knowing something was wrong well before my mom confessed that he was missing. For weeks she was tense and temperamental, yelling on the phone and entertaining a parade of visitors who never smiled. A bunch of cameramen showed up at our house one morning. I came downstairs to find the living room crammed with soundboards and cameras, Mom off to the side whispering to some man with a fancy black suit and perfect hair. Teachers started being extra-gentle, to the point of annoyance. Friends no longer wanted to play with me. I felt dangerous, grotesque, like I had something contagious.

When she sat me down to explain that Dad might not be coming home for a while, I didn't cry or ask questions. I'd noticed his absence among the crowds glumly cluttering our space. I didn't know why he was gone, only that he traveled a lot and always came home, usually with a box of candy or a stuffed animal (which I figured out later in life he bought at the airport). I was concerned and all but it was almost a casual worry because I assumed he'd eventually show up. It never occurred to me that his absence would be permanent.

One morning after breakfast, Mom walked me to the formal living room, a faux French Country salon with floral wallpaper where my parents did their entertaining, and sat me on a tufted Ottoman. "Nancy, love," she said, wrapping her hands around mine, "I want to explain something to you and I need you to pay your best attention."

Moisture had formed around her eyes. "It's about Daddy." She paused for some deep breaths. By the time she finished explaining, she was inconsolable. I sat across from her, quiet and composed, wondering how to react. I believed what she was telling me, but the idea that Dad had simply disappeared was still unbelievable. He'd arrive anytime, a special gift in hand, and things would return to normal. Cry, I told myself, and he'll be gone forever.

I remember everything about this period. Gloom and insecurity disrupted our well-ordered life. Mom had taken leave from her job in the admissions office at George Washington to work fulltime on the search for Dad. She hosted a ton of quiet but intense conversations with stolid strangers and some former dinner guests I recognized. Eventually the glad-handers and hangers-on disappeared and we were left with piercing quiet and a shitload of confusion. Their departure coincided with the end of media coverage.

Mom and I didn't know how to behave around one another without Dad as an intermediary. He traveled frequently, but the simple fact of his existence buffered lots of tension. We wanted him back so badly because he couldn't absorb that tension in absentia. We figured things would only get tenser as the likelihood of death increased. Mom and I would spend the next decade thinking about the meaning of departure.

I used to sit on top of the stairwell, underneath the knob of the bannister, and eavesdrop on their conversations. "She's too boyish, Fred. What do you think is wrong with her?"

"I don't think anything's wrong with her."

"I was reading this article about peer communities in elementary school and she's just … I don't know … different?"

"She has friends. Her teachers love her. I don't see the problem."

"That's because you're more interested in spoiling her than raising her."

"That's unfair, Lara."

"I'm with her every day. You can't see what I do from Europe and the Middle East."

Mom always had the final word. She was present, something she apparently hated. He was the unfairly popular absentee parent bearing smiles and treats at his own convenience. But I barely recall his absences, the defining feature of our relationship.

We used to spend hours in Rock Creek Park, exploring the woods alongside Beach Drive and the National Zoo. "Watch out for escaped animals," he'd warn whenever we stepped off the trail.

"Nuh uh. You're trying to trick me."

"Of course not. For all we know, there could be tigers and crocodiles and elephants running loose."

I would stare at him, trying to find some indication that he was lying. The longer his face remained stoic, the more mine filled with apprehension. Then he'd burst into laughter and kiss the top of my head. I could never stay angry longer than a few seconds. His tales of dangerous wildlife probably had something to do with my impatience. Nothing seemed more exciting than eluding predators with my father. Sitting in classrooms with monolithic walls, or around dinner tables with Mom's friends, fewer by the year, only strengthened my formative memories of spontaneity and freedom. In college, I'd read much of Dad's work and saw a wonkish thinker trying too hard to be incisive, a person committed to satisfying the elite while flattering the rank-and-file. His work was conventional, but actually required imagination. It's not easy to write a paper that's inoffensive to all sides of a conflict.

My life would come to be defined by threats of lurking danger. In Rock Creek Park, we had nobody to impress. Bullshitting wasn't a livelihood; we did it for fun, for a sense of intimacy. It established our smallness in the world—fantasy as a reminder of the boring environment we actually inhabit. We could wander through the park for hours. We were stationary only when visiting what I called our Secret Place.

I must have been five or six when we found it. Up a hillside from the main path was an undisturbed patch of oak trees (and even a rock maple) close enough to the perimeter of the forest to hear whooshing from the Avenues. While exploring the patch, looking upward for barred owls, we ran into a drainage gulch feeding the creek. A thick tree had fallen across the gulch and we decided it was a good place to rest. We stayed for almost an hour, sharing a bag of plain M&Ms.

"Do other people come here?" I asked.

"I doubt it," he said. "It's a secret place right in the middle of a big city."

So it became the Secret Place. A regular destination. Dad filled a backpack with snacks and bottles of water and we'd picnic on the log, searching for frogs when the gulch was damp. He'd ask about school and I'd give him one-word responses. I'd ask kindergarten stuff no adult could possibly answer. The point was to be in one another's company, within and beyond the center of civilization. I realize now that he probably saw the visits as an obligation.

"Please, Daddy, can we go to the Secret Place?" I nagged every weekend.

"I can't today, darling. Daddy has a lot of work to finish."

Standard answer.

I wouldn't drop it, though, and more often than not he relented. Every time we reached the downed tree, his sense of hurry dissipated. Springtime made for optimal hiking, with vines and saplings sprouting from the slime of last autumn's leaves. Without a developed underbrush, it was easy to move around off-trail. Here, amid the pre-Columbian flora, we could negate the lethal inertia of civility, relax amid the clatter of isolation. Being there was easy. Arriving was the problem.

I was always in competition with Dad's work. It was impossible for me to win, for anyone but his patrons to win, really. Mom accepted his absences because they were necessary to the kind of world she desired, the same one she inherited. I commanded dad's attention only by guilting him into fulfilling some idealized version of responsible parenthood. He was otherwise the property of foreigners. I was always in battle with busyness, a word I didn't understand. Busyness was sacred, ubiquitous. It governed my little world with cruel efficiency.

Once home, he'd disappear for hours, holed up in his basement office. We lived in an updated craftsman in Cleveland Park with a thin, deep lawn. Like most of Northwest DC's residential streets, ours had pretentions of urbanity overlaid onto suburban design. The houses were close together, most of them boasting additions, with busy sidewalks stretching beneath the gloom of citified foliage. Other kids lived on my street, but we were rarely outside. Ours was a good neighborhood, but still dangerous. Cars drove too fast. The streets were confusing. And the Metro brought God-knows-what-kind-of-people. My social life consisted of playdates with classmates from the International School and various children of Dad's colleagues, most of whom I'd never met before and would never see again. The adults would sit around bottles of wine and cold cuts and couldn't be bothered with our noise, so we decamped in bedrooms with vintage hardwood beneath rugs boasting more aesthetic than practical value.

I wasn't too bothered by our move to Virginia. Mom, on the other hand, was glum the entire time. I guess she didn't like what the move represented. We had pretty much been kicked out of our social circle. Dad's disappearance was originally this huge attraction. Everyone wanted to be an insider, a friend of the family, but after a while, when interest died down, people treated us like we had some kind of disease transmitted through social contact. Even worse, we didn't have enough money to stay. Mom wasn't ready to return to work and had no insurance payment coming because Dad wasn't officially dead. She could have asked my grandparents for money—they had plenty—but what was the point of staying? To our neighbors, we already ceased to exist.

Before we moved, I visited the Secret Place. I don't know why. Maybe I thought I'd find Dad's spirit there or maybe I just wanted to see it one last time. I was only ten, but wise enough to know that it would probably make me sad. I ended up being wrong. The bark on the log was starting to rot and other trees had fallen in the vicinity, but otherwise it was exactly the same. I didn't sense Dad's aura or whatever. He could have been anywhere. But he wasn't at the Secret Place. I sat atop the log for a while and stared into the gulch. It was filled with deep, thin grooves hardened by a mini-drought. A tiny desert hidden among the greenery.

I stayed until the sun went low on the horizon and light poured through the trees in shades of orange. I knew it would be the last time I saw this place. I don't remember feeling sad or lonely, just tranquil, like I was experiencing a preview of adulthood. It didn't take long to realize that Dad wasn't showing up. Not here, anyway. I trudged back into civilization before Mom had a chance to call the police.

"Where have you been?" she screamed.

I sat at the table without talking and began eating dinner. Mom was relentless.

"Staying out till dark. Already I've lost your father. Now I have to worry about you. Are you trying to kill me?"

"Mama, I've been to the park a million times."

"So selfish, just like your father." She's repeated the accusation my entire life. The thing is, I'm not much like Dad, at least based on what I know of him from other people. And that's how I know him, really, through stories mostly told by strangers, parents by proxy, which made the entire world feel strange.

When Mom said we were going to Virginia, I pictured horses and red barns and rolling mountains, but instead found strip malls and highways and office parks. Our new place was actually smaller than the house in DC. We had a middle unit in a huge complex of townhouses encircled by parking lots with numbers painted on the curb. The fenced-in garden out back had a toolshed and flagstone porch. "The schools here are excellent," Mom kept saying. It meant nothing to me. I went to a good school in DC—"one of the best"—and was glad to leave. Mom insisted that the quality of schools and not the twenty-year limbo of Dad's life insurance was the reason we left Cleveland Park. She'd never recover from the indignity Dad had caused—not his disappearance, per se, but the behavior that made it possible in the first place.

One afternoon, a few weeks before the start of fifth grade, I was helping Mom plant flowers along the front walk when a girl rode up on her bike. She straddled the crossbar, wavy black hair tumbling from beneath a pink helmet. I glanced at her a few times, but she didn't move. Mom was having none of it. "Can I help you?" The girl shook her head.

"Well, if you want to help," Mom panted, slapping the dirt with the back of a trowel, "come and help, then."

The girl laid her bike on the sidewalk and walked over, stopping a few feet away from me.

"I'm Elena," she said.

"I'm Ms. Baker," Mom interjected before I could respond. "This is Nancy."

"I'll be in fifth grade," Elena said after a momentary silence.

"Is that so?" Mom looked Elena up and down. "Here, help Nancy," she said, handing over a glove.

I finally spoke. "I'll be in fifth grade, too."

"Are you new?"

"We've been in the area her entire life," Mom said.

"There's a cool playground up the road," Elena said. "Wanna ride bikes there?"

I was fascinated by this person who had appeared out of nowhere and wanted nothing more than to travel up the road with her. Elena seemed magical: lithe and spirited, with hair like a lion's mane and skin the color of saturated earth. Mom continued sizing up Elena. "I don't think it's a good idea," she said. I wanted to argue but Mom glared at me before I could start.

"Oh, okay," Elena said, dropping the glove. "I'd better get home."

"Yes, dear. You wouldn't want to worry your mother."

After Elena rode off, I began to pout. "Why didn't you let me go?"

"We have to finish the house. School starts in two weeks."

"I won't have any friends. I don't wanna go to school," I shouted before running inside. I laid on my bed and wished Dad were around to intervene. He would have said yes. If he had been at home, even hidden in his office, Mom also would have said yes. Back then I didn't understand the fear of loss, the fact that Mom's existence was indivisible from my well-being. But I understood that Mom had immediately found dozens of reasons to disapprove of Elena. Her disapproval materialized the moment Elena appeared. We lived in the same complex, but, unlike Elena's family, we weren't of the place. Virginia offered a place to reside, but it wasn't a permanent condition. Mom was accustomed to a different breed of diversity.

She finished planting and tinkered in the kitchen before coming upstairs. I flipped over and faced the wall when she tapped on the door. "Oh stop the bullshit, Nancy," she said, sitting on the edge of the mattress. I pressed my knees into my stomach. "We know nothing about that child, or this neighborhood, and I won't have you running off with strangers."

I glanced over my shoulder so she could see my face. "We were just going to the playground."

"Next time."

It would become a lifelong struggle with Mom. Her overprotectiveness and suspicion were forever in conflict with my impulse to freedom. Time was something to put off until another epoch. We were supposed to just exist in the meanwhile. Next time was always the unfulfilled promise of the present.

The following day she took me to Tyson's Galleria to get school clothes. While we cruised along the Beltway, she was unusually chipper, listing all the things she'd buy for me and how they'd form an excellent first impression among classmates and teachers. I wasn't as confident. The idea sickened me, anyway. My emerging sense of style was at odds with Mom's designer taste. She'd have me dolled up like the urban girl I was at heart so I could distinguish myself from the yokels in the metropolitan hinterland.

I passed the time thinking about Elena. She wasn't like the kids I'd known in Cleveland Park and at the International School. My former classmates accepted the version of the world their parents imposed; even as children they understood that the arrangement was good for them. They were the winners. They could take food and shelter for granted, be around the world's movers and shakers without feeling out of place. For their families, the status quo was precious, a way of life to be anxiously secured in both froth and minutia. Even their occasional shock about this or that injustice was calibrated to its preservation.

But Elena.... I could tell she was different. Nobody at the International School would have been so spontaneous, so brazen. Elena operated within a different set of rules. She was governed by the kind of instinct my mother considered a duty to erode. I wasn't raised to be celestial. In the days after I met Elena, I repeatedly asked Mom if I could go outside and find the girl who helped us garden, but Mom stayed true to the never-ending itinerary of next time.

Now at the mall, Mom was stricken by affluenza. "No," she said, speedwalking past Gap; "not this one" as Abercrombie melted into a haze; "keep going" she snapped even before we arrived in front of Forever 21; Banana Republic got a glance before Mom decided that it's too New Money; we lasted five minutes inside LL Bean. We completed a lap of the mall before ending up at Lord & Taylor. Mom requested a personal shopper and for the next two hours I tried on blouses and pants and accessories the saleswoman passed over the door to a dressing room that smelled like Old Woman lotion. After putting on each item, I walked outside to get assessed, Mom's index finger on one cheek, her thumb on the other. Nobody asked my opinion. Mom made a declaration, the saleswoman agreed, the garment went onto the keep or discard rack, and finally we finished, barreling toward the parking garage with four puffy bags slapping our legs.

The clothes didn't make me any more excited about school. Neither did the school's supposedly excellent quality. There was one attraction, though: Elena. I had seen her a few more times, walking to her parents' car or biking toward the playground. She was graceful, regal, the kind of person Mom spent lavishly to make me. I understand now that one reason for Mom's wariness was a suspicion that Elena would illustrate how class isn't synonymous with money, or how elegance can be uneconomical. Mom wasn't ready for that kind of epiphany.

Not so for me. Mom couldn't control my choices in school and the teachers were delighted by my friendship with Elena. I saw her the first morning. A bunch of kids were waiting for the main doors to open. Elena was in the middle of the action, giving direction to kindergarteners and lecturing a group of rowdies about their behavior. I found an opening and, inspired by her example, pushed through the crowd. Fifteen minutes later we were sitting together in the cafeteria. We were assigned to the same class and chose desks up front. Soon we'd be spending all our time in school together. Unperturbed by Mom's coldness, Elena would scamper down her front stoop and join us on the walk to school. Mom couldn't very well make her stay behind us. And if she increased the pace, Elena kept up easily.

When Mom accepted a job at George Mason, she could no longer walk me to school. Elena took on the responsibility. Eventually she let me and Elena socialize in the afternoon. There had been no change of heart; Mom simply wasn't in a position to banish Elena from my life. My having a place to go at the end of the school day saved Mom the trouble of enrolling me in aftercare. Her parenting time was severely restricted. Anyway, Mom didn't have the patience to entertain an only child. I needed a playmate. My friendship with Elena became essential to the household economy.

Strangely, Elena liked Mom. "She's so beautiful," she'd gush. "Like so smart and tough." Elena didn't understand why I apologized for Mom's attitude. She regarded it as something to emulate. Her own mother's disposition had a lot to do with it. She was a hugger who fussed and dickered and always served snacks. Elena thought it was lame. I wondered if her mother was secretly a shitty person. It didn't seem possible.

I'd never heard anyone judge my family from an insider's perspective. It was a useful but scary way to make sense of my unusual life. I learned that in many ways both of my parents were a mystery. They raised me without belief in exceptional qualities.

"What are you guys, anyway?" Elena asked one day.

"What do you mean?"

"Like, my parents are from Eritrea. Where are yours from?"

"Um, I don't really know. America, I guess."

"Hmmm. Your mom doesn't look American."

Mom had never discussed with me where she and Dad were from. Dad's parents died before I was born. Mom's parents lived in some faraway country she never mentioned. I wouldn't meet them until I was a teenager. By then I had a sense of history, but at age ten I was just a vaguely brown figurine in suburban anonymity. Those faraway places, so mysterious and momentous, absent but ubiquitous, would come to define my young adulthood. They already defined my childhood, although I didn't know at the time that I possessed a wide and varied internal topography.

When I told Mom what Elena had said, she narrowed her eyes. "And just what does she mean by that?"

"I don't know. Are you from America?"

"Of course I'm from America," she said.

"Where are Grandma and Grandpa from?"

"They lived in America for a very long time, so they're American, too."

"But Elena says that—"

"I don't give a damn what Elena says. She's the foreigner. Let her worry about who is or isn't American."

"But—"

"But nothing. Khalas."

I was almost in college before I realized that *khalas* isn't an English word. Mom sometimes employed it to end an argument. I thought it was slang from the days of yore. I used it a few times in high school to confused looks before it hit me that nobody knew what the fuck I was saying. I have vague memories of Dad and Mom speaking in another language, but they're not dynamic images—more like hazy stills with incomprehensible thought bubbles. Individually, they only spoke to me in English. And they only used the foreign language in occasional spurts, when they didn't want me to know what they were saying. They typically sounded like every other parent in Cleveland Park.

Mom had made me more confused. I didn't understand how Elena could be a foreigner if she was from Virginia. I asked Elena to be sure and she told me that she was born in Alexandria. She'd been to Eritrea three times, though, she announced proudly. "Haven't you been to wherever you're from?"

"I went to California once," I said.

Elena rolled around her bed in a fit of giggling. "You're so funny, Nan."

I wanted to join Elena in laughter, but I didn't understand the joke, just like I didn't understand all this where-are-you-from business. The world was getting weirder by the day. Dad had vanished, Mom was bitchy, and everyone seemed to know stuff about me that I couldn't comprehend. So I giggled along with Elena. It was the moment I realized that fakery is an indispensable skill.

For a while, Elena didn't inquire about Dad. Neither did her mother. Her father wasn't so shy. He drove us to Chick-fil-A one evening. We loved riding in his car, a red Prius with ARLINGTON TAXI COMPANY in block letters on both side doors. The car smelled like dryer sheets and had a knotted cloth rosary hanging from the rearview mirror. Elena made him turn on the television in the back of the front seat even though it didn't show anything but commercials and stock prices. After we pulled away from the drive-thru, he caught my eye in the rearview mirror.

"Nancy, is your father still alive?"

"Baba!" Elena screamed, "Mama said we're not supposed to bring that up."

"What?" he said with exaggerated naivete. "It's important question, no?"

I tried to avoid a response, but he held my gaze in the mirror.

"I…I don't know," I said.

"You don't know? How can this be?"

"Baba stop it!"

"Okay, okay," he said, patting the steering wheel. After a few seconds of silence, he added, "I want your friend just to know that we also can be her family."

"Whatever, Baba."

Elena held my hand, but I wasn't upset. Maybe it was the gloppy odor of fried food or the novelty of riding in a taxi that kept me calm. Or maybe it's because I was seriously considering the offer.

The year passed quickly. My walks to school with Elena began amid mature trees bursting with greenery and then transitioned into colorful rot and the eerie cleft of bare branches before exploding with dogwood flowers and cherry blossoms. I acclimated to a life that would have been impossible in the city. In good weather, large groups of children stayed outside until dark. We roamed the innards of our complex, those hundreds of spaces hidden between brick abodes meant to replicate Georgetown's rowhouses. The people who design these places probably never imagine anyone will discover their dereliction, but children have a knack for cataloguing every decaying fencepost, every ungraded drainage grate, every jagged patch of asphalt. We never went into the adjoining woods. Grown-ups didn't forbid us from doing it. We kept away by silent agreement, as if programmed into some ineffable knowledge that civilization provides everything we needed.

Mom was usually home when playtime ended. I'd come inside to find her puttering about the kitchen, halfway out of her work clothes. No kiss or hug, just a slow walk to the adjoining dining nook. She'd set out leftovers along with some fresh dishes. (Mom was fanatical about eating homecooked food; restaurants were for socializing.) She'd ask about my day and I'd offer halfhearted responses. I'd then ask about her day and she'd complain for thirty minutes about ungrateful students and all the idiotic people she has to work with, finishing with the same coda, "You're different, thank God." It was the closest thing I'd get to an open show of affection.

One evening a reporter from the *Washington Post* called. It had been a year since Dad's disappearance and she was curious to know how we were doing. Mom was agitated when she hung up the phone.

"She wants to do a stupid human-interest story," Mom said.

"What's that?"

"She wants to make people feel sorry for us."

In time, I'd come to understand Mom's stubbornness, which I view now with admiration, even warmth. Our friends had abandoned us. People who had made careers from trading on Dad's name scrubbed him from their biographies. It took years of painstaking work to ascend DC society and only one baffling misstep to be expunged. Mom didn't want anyone to enjoy a feel-good moment at our expense. And no matter how much the reporter embellished, she'd never be able to make a triumphant narrative of our story. Not while Dad was locked in a box somewhere on or beneath this earth. Mom wanted the kind of reportage that might reveal what happened to him, not the kind that rendered our suffering a corny tale of perseverance.

In the next few years and on into high school, Mom and I repeated the patterns established during that first year in Virginia—sadness mitigated by tacit, almost ritual, affection—with Elena becoming a fixture of our relationship. I can't say that Mom warmed up to Elena, but she accepted Elena as a safe alternative to despair. Elena's mother doubled the warmth absent from my household, genuinely thrilled that I was her daughter's friend or else the greatest actor in a region filled with pretense. Years later, she was the only person I considered telling about my plans, but I kept quiet for fear of putting her in danger.

Elena and I placed into a gifted track for middle school, she for science, me for language arts. We'd both get accepted to Thomas Jefferson High, the nerd school of Northern Virginia and a guaranteed path into a good college if we didn't fail out. I felt guilty in young adulthood because I didn't often think of Dad. When I did, he was an abstraction. I couldn't really tell whether his existence was something I had dreamed or an event that actually happened. Only when visitors told stories would his memory become palpable. I struggled to remember him as a creature of my own experience.

And that was my childhood, basically. When I was nine, my father disappeared in a foreign country and was never seen again. Facing financial hardship and social ostracism, my mother moved us to Northern Virginia. Various interlocutors cleared up some mysteries about the past despite my mother's disapproval. I made a friend in elementary school and we would follow one another all the way to college, from which I too abruptly disappeared. I excelled at a magnet school, although without real pleasure, and tried on various identities before deciding that in order to achieve a sense of belonging in this decomposing world I would have to commit a murder.

Fred

I DIDN'T TECHNICALLY work for the Kingdom, but I was certainly in its employ. It was a circuitous route that led me to the directorship of the Geostrategic Partners Institute, but it was the kind of job a person with my resume usually lands sometime before retirement, or accepts in old age as a ceremonial position.

The Institute was a few blocks from Dupont Circle, two Metro stops from my house, in a box of glass and concrete modernism. Office amenities belied the exterior's dour appearance. We boasted a library, state-of-the-art AV equipment, a Breville espresso machine, a wet bar, and a humidor for visiting dignitaries. My office, appropriately spacious for a man of my position, looked across Massachusetts Avenue at a rival think tank financed by an adjoining kingdom. It really was my dream job. Every time I walked into my office, I took a second to relish the gold-plated inscription on the wall: "Dr. Fred M. Baker." I never doubted that I would retire in good standing.

We sold reports to private contractors and government agencies, but most of our funding came from the Kingdom's Ministry of Information. The Kingdom supported various outfits; the Institute was its flagship. Our trustees and affiliates had served governments on four continents. Fluffing the ego of people accustomed to special attention was a critical part of my job. Some of those people were content to flaunt the affiliation (and pocket the honorarium), others wanted to run the place. These were men of power; running things was in their breeding. For them, it was impossible to be neutral because an outcome was never without personal consequence.

The meddling could cause serious problems, though. Or solve them, depending on where you stood.

In my second year as director, I received a phone call from the Kingdom's ambassador to the United States. "We must meet, clear your calendar," he said with typical brusqueness, though I could tell by his inflections that he was panicked.

I tidied the office and set out an ashtray. The Ambassador was a stress smoker. I rarely interacted with him, but he was a significant presence in my daily existence. If he was around, something bad had happened, which meant he was most on our minds when we were ignoring him. When I began, he was slowing down, but remained one of the most connected men in the District. I set a bowl of dates next to the ashtray and waited.

The Institute's security guard left him at my door. He skipped the usual elaborate greeting and sat on the couch, removing a pack of Dunhills from his starchy white robe.

"There's a problem," he said, pointing a cigarette at my face.

"Some dates, Mr. Ambassador?"

"One of our guys has been arrested." I raised my eyebrows. "It's Amjad," he continued. "He got picked up this morning. No cameras."

I knew it would be Amjad, the imbecile of a brainless family. The embassy had fished him out of trouble before, but this time the problem seemed serious. I prayed that he hadn't been nabbed by one of the federal agencies. "Who got him?"

"The DC Police."

Okay, we could work with this. The DCPD tended to be reasonable. It was accustomed to donations. "What for?"

The Ambassador sighed and glowered at the wall behind me. "Rape. The girl is a teenager. Sixteen, as I understand."

I kept my composure, but inside I was screaming obscenities. Amjad was determined to fuck up all our lives, but he was the King's half-brother, a captain of our industry. "Who knows about this?"

"You and the police. I contacted you directly."

"I'll call the Mayor and set up a meeting. Mr. Ambassador, have you planned for what to do if this comes out?"

"This cannot come out. Do you understand?"

But it can, I thought to myself. There were hundreds of ways that the arrest could end up on the airwaves. The Ambassador knew it. He wasn't in denial. He was threatening me.

Two hours later we were in the Mayor's office. The Ambassador had brought his son, a tall, impressive young man in designer jeans and a blazer. Amjad, in Wayfarers and a disheveled red hatta, sat back from the wooden conference table, his beefy cheeks puffed with annoyance. Every time it looked as if he'd speak, the Ambassador glared at him. The Mayor began.

"Gentlemen, it seems we have a bit of a problem."

The Ambassador jumped in before the Mayor could continue. "It is a very small thing. Very small. We do not wish to inconvenience our American hosts. The King believes that it would be beneficial to all parties for his brother to return home, immediately, of course."

"Be that as it may, Mr. Ambassador, and with all due respect, there's the matter of a pending criminal investigation."

"We have not come here to be insulted. It is our position that—"

Amjad, spittle on his bottom lip, began to protest, but the Ambassador cut him off. "Shut up, you donkey," he yelled in Arabic, before returning to English. "As you can see, our colleague is quite distressed by these accusations. He is a good citizen, involved in many charities. Surely you recognize the serious problems of an investigation."

"Not really," the Chief said. "It's an open and shut case. Fucki—um, having relations with a sixteen-year-old is illegal, never mind the accusation that it was without consent."

The Ambassador's eyes darkened beneath the rim of his hatta. His son leaned into him and began whispering. The Ambassador nodded.

"Mr. Mayor, Mr. Chief," the son said, extending both hands in an exaggerated gesture of humility. "We appreciate the sensitivity of your position. We share the same concern, in fact. If this incident were to make the news, it would be … *disquieting* for all of us. This is a general point of agreement, no?"

The Chief: "So what are you saying, kid?"

"Well, let's imagine that our distinguished guest"—he nodded toward Amjad—"were to suddenly visit his brother, the King. That would be easy enough. Nobody can fault a man for visiting family. The concern is with the young lady and ensuring that she doesn't feel she's been treated unfairly."

The Mayor: "That young lady is fixin' to fuck us six ways to Sunday."

"But she's not, Mr. Mayor. Our people are speaking with her family at this very moment, making sure that all her needs are met."

The Mayor chuckled and leaned back in his seat. "And if they ain't?"

"Given the sensitivity of the matter, I'm quite certain that the family will come to realize the value of keeping quiet."

"And it is the value of a lifetime, shall we say," the Ambassador added.

The Mayor and the Chief glanced at one another.

The Mayor: "So either way we're not gonna be hearing from the girl? Is that what you're telling me?"

"I have the utmost confidence in the embassy staff to diffuse the situation," I said. I knew I would need to speak sooner or later. After all, I was there to provide credibility as an independent observer.

The Mayor seemed satisfied, but the Chief was unconvinced. "We have certain obligations to the people of this District," he said. "Those obligations include vigorous investigations of criminal offenses."

"Absolutely," said the Ambassador's son. "As it should be. And it is for this reason that we have expedited a meeting with our embassy's philanthropic arm. I'm sure you'll find the meeting highly conducive to the long-term pursuit of your obligations."

That evening, a private jet taxied down the runway at Andrews Air Force Base. Amjad, drunk from the preflight entertainment, was sprawled out on one of its leather couches, convulsing and snoring contentedly.

I should have been mortified by my role in his escape, but, truth is, I wasn't even conflicted. Maintaining order was part of my job. Every white-collar schlub in the capital understands the great unwritten rule of professional etiquette: protect the institution. In my case, the institution requiring protection happened to be democracy. Don't laugh. I'm quite serious, even in my current state of apostasy. Democracy lives and breathes in darkness, in obscure, unclean corners of civic life. It requires furtive malfeasance, wall-to-wall conniving, the everywhere violence of civility. Men of education maintain an ecosystem of seedy relationships that allows a democratic economy to function. No matter how much Amjad deserved to be tossed into prison, if it came to pass thousands of innocent people would also suffer.

Only my daughter, a baby at the time, gave me pause. I tried to fight the image of Amjad, sweaty and insatiable, overwhelming the teenager, and the graver prospect of an unmatured corpse somewhere in Rock Creek Park. I sometimes took Nancy into the park in her stroller. Being away from hubbub made her relaxed. Even as a tiny creature, she was introverted and cerebral. I suppose she got it from me. Lara, my wife, would never take a nature walk. It was one of the few things unrelated to work that I made time for, and even so it was a pretty rare event. I wanted Nancy to be happy. Delivering her into the woods was the easiest way to do it.

Nancy was a strange imposition onto my life. Don't get me wrong. I adored her. I *liked* her, too, beyond filial obligation. I just couldn't wrap my mind around the phenomenon of a child, of a creature so physically inconsequential that at the same time required intense attention to survive. She was the entire world reduced to a noisy package of epithelial cells. Only now, in my dying moments, has it occurred to me that Nancy was the apotheosis of my professional life.

That's why after the meeting in the Mayor's office I thought about quitting, maybe get into consulting (a thriving industry), or transition into academe, some other aspect of the machinery that demanded less nurturing. But truth be told (and what else does a dying man have but freedom to tell the truth?), I liked the prestige of being director, the social and financial benefits of the Institute. It gave me clout, the most valuable currency in Washington.

That clout in turn got me access to cable news. I'd tell Nancy to watch CNN at 7:30 or C-SPAN at 8:00 or whatever and then do my talking, always with charm and composure. I was a master of earpieces and lapel mics and teleprompters, at home in liberal doses of skin-lightening foundation that eventually cracked into tiny hexagons and left yellowish stains on my pillow the following morning. I wanted to get home and see Nancy's reaction, but I had to chat up the hosts and producers and often stayed out late in hotel bars peopled by the cognoscenti. If I happened to see Nancy the next day, I'd ask how Daddy did on television.

"You sounded funny," she'd normally answer, which I took to mean that she didn't understand what I had been saying. I didn't want to admit that her response might have been literal.

These appearances came with conditions. There was no freedom of expression, no free speech (what a joke, any half-honest pundit will tell you). Part of my purpose was to inform the public, sure, but my main responsibility was to gratify the Kingdom. It could be done tacitly or through artful selectivity. A person adept at sectarianism through the appearance of objectivity can command a high salary. Anyway, I had plenty of leeway. Nobody told me what not to say. I could speak my beliefs because the Kingdom wasn't doing anything that bothered me. I thought it a happy coincidence that my opinion happened to align with the Kingdom's interests.

All good education is about finding that happy coincidence. It wasn't really on my mind when I studied for my PhD—at the Hopkins shop in DC, just down the street from the Institute—but looking back I can see the importance of informal learning, the stuff that happens off the books, networking, socializing, hustling, anything, really, that illustrates a willingness to acculturation, to don the right clothes, deploy the right vocabulary, dine at the right restaurants, display the right body language. Success required diligence and timing. You had to identify the most opportune viewpoint amid vicious competition and then figure out the best moment to deploy it.

It wasn't the vision of education I grew up around in Blacksburg. My father was an engineering professor, but with a humanist soul. My mother was what we called in those days a homemaker. I never went to school without an elaborate lunch or returned home to a sparse pantry. Her devotion to mothering was almost mechanical and yet it was deeply serious and I think that without the pretext of a child she may well have become anything from a CEO to a disembodied consumer of daytime TV. She came to life when her parents visited, which my mother treated

as an event because of difficult logistics and lack of money. Their visits
lasted for months at a time and in those periods my mother was loud
and confrontational, extra attentive to me, but at the same time strangely
detached from her usual domesticity. It's from them that I learned my
halting but functional Arabic. Their English was poor and they never
struck me as having been inclined to use it even if they had the option.

I never met my father's parents. His mother was alive until I was
around ten or eleven, but they never visited and my father made no effort
to return home. I always had a sense that he couldn't, but the topic went
undiscussed. When she died, which I remember mostly because my father
was on the phone for two days straight in animated conversation, he didn't
go to her funeral. A lot of "eh but." Expense. Time. Work. Health. The
Situation. She'll be buried long before I arrive, he pointed out. Comically
effusive in typical circumstances, he was plainspoken in shirking a return.
Nor did we mourn in exile. No somber dinner. No storytelling. No special
prayer. Just normal life, haunted by one man's perplexing denial.

My mother's parents told me a bit about my other grandfather. He
was some kind of leader, a war hero, they said, captured by the enemy and
sentenced to death. But he escaped and was never seen again.

"He sneaked away and lived in hiding until he was an old man," my
grandfather said.

"Don't be stupid," my grandmother snapped. "He died in the Valley
trying to cross the border."

"No, that makes no sense."

"And living out his life in London pretending to be a Pakistani grocer
or an Ecuadorian taxi driver makes sense?" my grandmother yelled.

"Not London. Somewhere closer. Where he could watch his family."

"My God, always with your ridiculous theories. He died, God rest his
soul. The end."

"I don't believe it."

"Go ask Mahmoud. Go on, ask him. He'll tell you."

"What does he know?" my grandfather said, making a dismissive
gesture with both hands. "He was a baby when it happened."

My grandmother turned to me, "Don't listen to your seedo. He's out
of his mind."

That's how I learned about my father's father: through loud arguments about an unknowable past. (My grandparents were something of a model for my academic career.) Nobody asked my father for his opinion, because we knew it would only increase the mystery and put him in a foul mood, a rare occurrence that felt like a pandemic when it happened.

Whatever predilection I had to spoil Nancy came from my father, although I shunned his professional habits. Whereas I aspired to transcend my Appalachian upbringing, my father was content with a life of small-town security. Whereas I prioritized work over family time, my father loved to play hooky, one of his favorite phrases. He was forever playing hooky, as if hooky were a competition that required vigorous training. He was hooky's most devoted contestant.

As soon as I was old enough to say "Baba," my father filled me with stories about falcons, hyenas, leopards, hares, sand cats, and other creatures of his childhood in a fantastical geography coveted by all the world's powers. He shared tales of transit and college and the beautiful woman who would become mama. The narratives were never consistent, but they were always true, histories I wouldn't quite remember but would anyway know. I remember tapping at his cheek, sometimes putting my fingers in his mouth. If he wore a sweatshirt, I would pull on the strings until each end halted the other's momentum. I sometimes slept on his lap, immobilizing my father with the untold weight of innocence until he had no choice but to also sleep.

"Good morning, yaba, wakey-wakey, yaba" he would sing when I gurgled into consciousness, stroking my cheeks and tickling my ears. "Happy to see you again." He knew to quickly feed me to preempt grumpiness, a trait I carried into adulthood, kissing my forehead every few seconds as I chewed bread doused in olive oil, having graduated from bowls of homemade puree.

When the weather was adequate, he loaded me into a stroller and took long walks, often without a destination. He gave me plastic spoons and action figures for entertainment as we explored the town's recreation trails. If there were errands to run, he parked the stroller outside and wheeled me about in shopping carts, explaining the utility of everything we bought—milk for calcium, bread for calories, eggs for protein, potato chips for pleasure. People in the store smiled as we noisily traversed the aisles. My father couldn't have survived without the approval of strangers.

As a kid, I was up to the challenge of my father's nonstop conversation. I never knew I knew so little about knowing things until I became a parent and was suddenly faced with an insistent question: "Why?" I imagine my father faced the same reckoning. When Nancy was little, my answer to "why?," even a good answer, was invariably followed by, "But why?" I found it nearly unbearable, if only because I knew it was never a bad way to react to an explanation. But why? Like my daughter, I demanded an answer from my father. Like my father's son, Nancy heard plenty of horseshit in return. The paternalism would serve me well in halls of power.

Despite his folksy affectations, my father could be pointed and sometimes provocative. I suppressed these inclinations with Nancy. It was so easy I figured I could do it forever.

"I have to pee-pee," I said one afternoon when we were in the middle of the woods.

"We shall pee on a tree, yaba."

"No, Baba, no." I was screaming. "I want a potty."

"There is no potty, my son-son. As you can see, there are only trees."

"But pee-pee goes in a potty."

"Sometimes pee-pee goes outside. It will help the trees grow."

I was intrigued, taking my time to select the anointed trunk. My father held me by the armpits and leaned me forward so I wouldn't dribble on the underwear bunched around my ankles. After my pants were buttoned, I walked back to the trail and looked upward, my hand shielding my eyes.

"Look, Baba! Look how big I made the tree!"

I helped an entire forest mature that summer, sometimes amid the disapproving glare of other parents. My father was already a curiosity at playgrounds, libraries, and puppet shows, a swarthy governess with an accent and a liberal interpretation of tact. Conversation with fellow caretakers could be awkward.

"So, yes, what do you do, um, what was it?"

"Mahmoud."

"Oh, what an interesting name. Is it Indian?"

"Yes." He didn't technically lie. The name belonged to many nations.

"Are you, like, his nanny?"

"Yes."

"You guys look kind of alike."

"That's probably because we share genes." This could result in a look of confused hostility.

"I stay home with Skylar and Ellis. My husband is in sales. What does your, um…?"

"Wife."

"Yes, what does she do?"

"I am a professor."

Every time, my father was unimpressed by the strangers' desperation to escape. They were the ones who insisted on making small talk.

"Oh, that's nice. What do you teach?"

"Free speech and geopolitics, that sort of thing." He could never whip up any enthusiasm for engineering.

An extended lower lip, a slow nod, followed by a sudden excitement.

"I'm really interested in free speech. It's going extinct. Everybody is always getting offended by any little thing."

"Is that so? Like what, for instance?"

"Race stuff and women's stuff, you know, stuff like that."

"And who are those taking offense?"

A quizzical expression acknowledging the miscalculation. "All these minorities who are too sensitive about everything. I mean, you have to admit."

My father gazed at the play area. "Come on, my son-son," he yelled, "we're leaving."

I ambled over. "Why, Baba?"

"This woman," he said, indicating the free speech activist with his chin, "is the reason Baba is always confused."

In reality, my father didn't write much about anything. He exhausted his creativity in parenthood. He spent his years as a lower-level senior scholar and was surely the subject of private complaints about deadwood among his younger colleagues. Far from being lazy, though, my father was almost maniacally energetic. He was terrified of ennui and wanted nothing of my life to be constricted. Sentience was his main vocation.

In summer, we spent long days at the community pool. My father tried to make the visits educational. "Kick, yaba, kick," he would yell, holding me by my stomach in a futile attempt to keep me horizontal. "Cup your hands, pull the water. Pull the water!" Various spectators paid more attention than I did. They were alternately bemused and mortified by the strange, hairy man doing something (educating? berating? instructing? abusing?) they couldn't quite understand. Once, he let me go on purpose so my head could be submerged under the water, something I refused to do voluntarily. He pulled me up in less than a second but immediately recognized the mistake. I gasped for breath, made more difficult by my impulse to scream. I must have sounded like an injured seal, grabbing desperately for my father's neck.

"It's okay, my love. It's okay, my son-son. Baba's here. I'm here."

And then he wasn't.

I have no recollection of my father being anything but composed. Internally, though, he must have been a mess. He probably saved his manic episodes for my mother, though to this day I can't picture him breaking down. He coped by acting even more like himself.

I remember playing video games in my room one afternoon when my father knocked. I was annoyed when he peeked in and said, "Come on, let's go."

"Where to?"

"Yalla, just come."

He wouldn't say where we were going as the town petered out. When we reached the countryside, treetops frosted with the first colors of autumn, he pulled the car to the side of the road and gestured to my door. "Okay, get out."

"Are we going on a hike?"

"No, my boy. We're going to learn to drive."

"Dad, I won't get my license for like two years."

"That's right. You better start practicing."

I was excited, but something felt weird about the whole thing. Why did my father suddenly want to teach me to drive? We'd never discussed it. But once I sat in the driver's seat, these thoughts disappeared. I grinned and looked at my father as if to ask "really?"

He poked my shoulder. "First things first, yaba. Put on your seatbelt. You never move the car without being buckled in. Don't play with the radio or the window or anything else until you've done the seatbelt, okay?"

"Yeah, sure, Dad." I maneuvered the clasp into the latch.

"Adjust the seat."

I could see over the steering wheel, but had to stretch to reach the pedals. I pulled the lever and moved the seat forward with my butt until it clicked into place.

"Now the mirrors. You want the side mirrors to show everything from the car to the other side of the road. You should see the entire back windshield in the rearview mirror."

I tinkered with them until meeting my father's specifications. "I think I'm ready."

"Ready?" my father bellowed. "Ready? No no no. You still need to check the fuel gauge."

"But, Dad, you just filled up half an hour ago."

"Will I always have filled up half an hour ago when you drive? You need to learn good habits now. You don't want to end up running out of gas in the middle of nowhere. God knows what kind of people you'll find. Haven't you seen *Deliverance*?"

I stared at him in confusion.

"Khalas, don't watch it. It's disgusting."

"Okay, *now* I'm ready."

"Put on your turn signal. Down is left. Great job. You're a natural. Now press the brake, firmly. Use your right foot for both pedals. You only need both feet for driving a donkey, not a car. Very good, very good. Put it into drive, see that D down here? Perfect. Let go of the brake, slowly. Slowly. Slowly. Check your mirror. Now, fast, look over your left shoulder. There's a blind spot over there. You always have to check your blind spot. All kinds of horrible things in the blind spot. But be quick about it. You look at the blind spot too long and you begin to miss what's in front of you."

My father was right: I was a natural. I gradually gained confidence, taking curves without crossing yellow lines, slowing and accelerating in smooth increments, keeping a safe distance from oncoming traffic, hitting the turn signal and checking blind spots in fluid, unfettered motions as we motored past fields of soy and tobacco with unpainted barns and old stone shelters, all while my father delivered needless instruction and shouted frenetic encouragement. After a few hilly stretches, I realized my father had gone quiet. I slowed the car and looked over to find that he had fallen asleep, the back of his skull against the headrest and his mouth slightly ajar. I drove for fifteen more minutes before pulling over and shaking his arm. He jolted into consciousness and looked side to side. "Ah, yes. Very good, yaba, very good. You're like Richard Betty."

"Who?"

"He's an old race car driver, back in your father's day. Anyway, never mind. I don't want you racing. Promise me you won't race."

"I promise."

"Good man. I love you, yaba. I'm proud of you. Let's go tell your mother what we just did. She'll probably beat me with a rolling pin."

"Dad, do you know where we are?"

"I haven't a clue, my boy. But we're alive and we're together. Everything else is easy to solve."

Two days later, I was helping my father cook dinner when he said, "Let's take a break." He told me to sit at the dining room table and came over with two bottles of Bud Light.

"Dad, are you, like, gonna get drunk?"

"Not at all, son, not at all. I don't plan on drinking both of these."

"Oh-kay. Um, then why do you have them?"

My father slid one of the bottles across the table. "For you," he said, smiling. He twisted open his bottle using the bottom of his shirt. As usual, I was confused.

"Go ahead."

"I don't understand."

"Open it."

"I'm supposed to drink this?"

"Tell your father the truth: have you ever had a beer?"

"No."

"Terrific. What a fine son you are. Half the kids your age are alcoholics. Today we're going to enjoy ourselves, bas we're going to learn to drink responsibly."

I reluctantly twisted the cap. I wasn't sure I wanted a beer, but I didn't want to disappoint my father. This situation had never come up in all the lectures we got in school about peer pressure.

My father raised his bottle. "Cheers. Sahtayn." I clinked my bottle against his and stared into the round opening at the pissy liquid. My father drank four loud gulps. He looked at me. "What's the matter? You don't like?"

"I don't know, Dad, this is kind of weird."

"What weird? Every boy should have his first beer with his father. Your grandfather, God rest his soul, used to make his own wine, right on the roof of our house. Me and you? We only need to go to the 7-Eleven. What a country."

"What if I don't like it?"

"I will be very happy if you don't like it. But one of these days you'll want to try. I'd rather you satisfy your curiosity at home with me than with God-knows-who, drinking God-knows-what. If you don't want to try it now, khalas, fine. I respect your decision. Just promise me that when you decide to try, you'll come to me or your mother."

"I think Mom would kill you if she knew what we were doing."

"Your mother?" he roared, transitioning into exaggerated laughter. "She's a million times more permissive than you think. I'm like a Bedouin compared to her."

"Mom?"

"Yes, Mom. She just wants to make sure you're safe and healthy. You don't know how lucky you are to have her."

"I know."

"No you don't. It's okay. No boy does. You'll appreciate her after you have your own child. But I do want you to always respect her and trust her. Will you do that?"

It was stranger than the driving lesson, but I assured my father that I would be a good son. I took a gulp of the beer. At my tender age I already understood what drives people to drink. It tasted like liquefied body odor.

I almost spat it out, but steadied myself and swallowed all at once. My father laughed at my scrunchy expression. "It's good, huh?"

"Oh my God, it's terrible."

"Drink another sip. By the third or fourth one you'll have grown accustomed to it."

My second sip tasted as bad as the first. "I don't think so, Dad."

"You've always been picky. When you were a child, I had to lie and beg to get you to eat anything that wasn't pizza or a hot dog."

"I like all kinds of stuff now."

"Yes, cheeseburgers and chicken wings and frozen lasagna." He chuckled. "Whatever you're eating, you've grown into a big, strong young man and that's my greatest accomplishment in this life." He paused. "Yalla, finish your beer."

A few days later, my father had another surprise. He sat me at the dining room table with typically cryptic solemnity. "We need to have a serious conversation, son. I need you to promise to be honest. Can you do that?"

"Yes," I said, unsure if I was agreeing to the promise or to the honesty.

"Have you had sex?"

I couldn't tell if he was joking. He looked serious, which on its own was disconcerting. All I wanted was a bag of chips and a game console. "Uh, Dad, you're kind of freaking me out."

"Don't be such a puritan, yaba. I asked a simple question."

I didn't think there was anything simple about it. "It's just a really weird question."

"I swear, this country has such crazy hang-ups about sex. The question only seems weird because the culture here is dysfunctional. We talked about sex all the time when I was growing up."

"Why are you even bringing this up? Can I go back to my room?"

"No. Be patient, my boy. This is important. Now, I ask again: have you had sex?"

"No." I had no idea if this would make my father happy or sad.

"Okay, good. Now, then, we have time to plan."

"Plan what?"

"For you to have sex responsibly, of course."

"Dad, I really don't know what to say."

"Just listen, then." He reached into his pocket and removed a small black packet with a circular protrusion, placing it on the table in front of me. "You know what this is, correct?"

I put my forehead into my palms. "Yes," I grumbled.

"What is it?"

"Dad, do we really have to do this?" My father tapped the packet. "It's a rubber," I managed.

"That's correct. Also known as a condom, which, quite frankly, is a much better word. It will help you to avoid contracting and spreading disease and greatly reduces the risk of pregnancy."

"I know all this. We talked about it in health class, remember?"

"I remember half the parents acting like idiots and complaining to the principal."

"Anyway, I know what a condom's for."

"Carry it with you. If anything comes up, promise me you'll use it."

"Okay."

"No. Promise me."

"Oh my God, I promise."

"This isn't a joke, Farid. I want you to one day have children, many healthy, beautiful children. But not when you're a teenager. I'm asking you to understand that sex is wonderful, but it has consequences. Many of those consequences are great, but many are also very bad."

"I know, Dad."

"Take the condom. Put it in your wallet. If you need more, let me know. If you need to talk about anything, don't be shy. I won't judge you. You can always come to your father. Or your mother, for that matter."

The conversation with my father was bad, but I couldn't imagine talking about sex with my mother. I really didn't like to discuss anything with her. I crammed the condom into my wallet and pushed out my seat.

"Wait a minute," my father said. "We're not finished."

I wanted to complain, but figured the quicker he finished the quicker I'd be free.

"I want to talk to you about moral responsibility," he continued. I nodded, though I had no clue what "moral responsibility" meant when it came to condoms. My foot flitted back and forth as if shaking off mosquitoes. "Wanting to have sex," my father said, no change in his tone, "is perfectly natural and I believe it's stupid to teach young people to suppress those feelings. However, it must always be consensual. Do you know what that means?"

"Yes."

"Tell me what it means."

"That both people, like, want to do it."

"Good enough. If you hear no, you stop. Understand?"

"Yes."

"And, remember to always treat your partners with respect. Ask what they like. Ask about their feelings. Listen to them. Make sure the terms of the relationship are understood. Got it?"

"Come on, Dad. I'm not some, like, rapist. I know how to act."

"I know, yaba. I just want to prepare you for this world the best I can. I want you to continue growing into a good, honest man."

"I will."

Moisture appeared in the bottom of my father's eyelids. He sniffled and coughed. "I know you will, my boy. Your old man will always be proud of you."

"Can I go now?"

"Yalla, get out of here."

Three or four days later, my father called me into the living room and told me to sit down. He took my hand and kissed it. "Let's talk, yaba." I had come to expect his surprises, but the hand kiss was weird even by my father's ambitious standards. Who knows what it would be this time? Still, I had grown from dread to grudging appreciation of our unusual routine. I smiled until the moment my father explained he was dying of cancer.

Nancy

ADOLESCENCE WITHOUT MY father could be blinding, as if the world existed in a series of disconnected simulations, blobby or furtive or out of focus. It sometimes felt like I wasn't of my surroundings, just a bit player in some grand theatrical production with an unlimited run. Lots of kids lose parents, but I didn't handle it in what was supposed to be a normal way. I was constantly disoriented by my father's death, a non-death, really, an event fully of the imagination. That's why it was so difficult, because his life had no comprehensible arc, his death no sense of finality. Mom and I didn't even get the satisfaction of a tragic ending. I don't know how to explain it. I always felt like a spectacle, whether subject to attention or ignorance. It's what happens to people so capable of eliciting pity. My reticence was motivated by a fierce desire to undo conventions that seemed to cause pain in all my surroundings. I grew up with stories nobody dared to tell me. My ancestry had vanished and so my birthright was dispossession. From an early age, I lacked all sense of kinship, but at the same time I knew, down to the ripple of my capillaries, that blood wasn't a neutral substance.

Fred

———

"IT'S NOT SO bad after all," Lara said one night as we shared a pint of ice cream. Nancy had the croup and couldn't sleep longer than twenty minutes at a time. In our circles, kids were more an accoutrement than a commitment, but Lara was fussy about Nancy even while maintaining pretenses of proper parental distance.

"Have you thought of it as bad?"

"No." She considered the question. "Just different than how I imagined it."

"In youth, everybody's future is a utopia."

"But the happy parts, you can never imagine them when you're young."

I had stopped imagining spectacular futures. At the time, I couldn't have imagined the event that put me in the news cycle. I had spent too much time fantasizing about the glory of influence, the impact of prestige. And yet it was the doldrums of filial duty that most influenced me when it mattered.

In her final days, my mother told me everything. About my father's life of expulsion, his experience of confinement, his fits of malaise, his memories of prison. How all he wanted was for me to be a good man, an honest man, somebody whose daily kindnesses rebuked the indecency of this world. She said she was proud of me, her successful intellectual, for I had fulfilled my father's desire, made it further than he could have imagined, further than he ever made it.

That's when I knew I had succeeded as a man of the capital, had succeeded in my dream of becoming a scholar of institutional distinction. It was a horrible recognition.

Nancy

I WAS ALWAYS attracted to the boy's section. Mom would dress me in clothes appropriate for a proper girl, but I wanted to hang around the clearance racks with button-down shirts, the square shelves stacked with blue jeans, the bins of crewneck tees wrapped in cardboard and plastic. The idea was ridiculous, Mom assured me. Girls have different bodies and need items that fit. Until I bought my own clothes, she'd be the one in charge. I wasn't really afflicted by dysphoria so much as a curiosity about the utilitarian potential of fashion. Mom made the simplest things sound momentous and sacred. All I wanted was some comfy outerwear.

Once I spotted a pair of aqua green slacks displayed in a J. Crew window. I don't know why I found them so beautiful—they were standard khakis in a pretty color—but I fell in love. I daydreamed about those slacks. They would look perfect on me. I was certain of it. My imperfections would disappear into visions of swimming pools and ocean water, or maybe a thin flower stem with a leafy crown and creamy petals. I wanted to articulate feelings of difference, to assert discomfort with uniformity, with utterly conventional habits of individual expression. I finally summoned enough courage to ask Mom about buying those beautiful green slacks.

"No."

"Why?"

"Because I said so."

"But why?"

"Your father secretly wanted you to be a boy. I won't give him the pleasure."

Fred

I HAD TWO dolls, one a stretchy sock puppet and the other a plastic baby in a turquoise onesie. The baby was Cheesy and the puppet Cheeto. I screamed for them in moments of distress, well past the appropriate age for houseplay.

"Baba, I want Cheeto," I would protest at naptime. "Cheesy, too," I added after the puppet had been delivered. I squeezed one in each arm and curled into a fetal position. When Cheesy misbehaved, I put her in timeout. "Sit here, Cheesy," I commanded, placing her in the corner next to the couch. "No moving. Stay for the whole timeout." Adequately chastened, Cheesy would apologize in my high-pitched inflection, having been subject to a stern lecture about her bad behavior. Cheeto never misbehaved, but he spent many hours, sometimes days, in a state of neglect. I had learned by the age of three how to manage the precarious balance of discipline and affection.

"What did Cheesy do this time?" my father sometimes asked.

"She didn't listen to my words."

"Ah, my son-son. Not everything needs a punishment. Some rebellion should be rewarded."

In those years, life was a bounty of monkeys and beds, mountains and white horses, apples and bananas, bushels and pecks, spiders and waterspouts, wheels and buses, rings and rosies. My father wasn't censorious, but he banned "You Are My Sunshine," a lullaby he found incredibly sad. His dislike of the song reflected the brutal possibilities of fear. So many things in the world can be taken away. His selfhood was a tenuous node of fatherly nerves. If nothing else worked, he at least wanted to be sure that his son would be indemnified from any type of confiscation. No, he wouldn't allow himself to imagine that level of violation.

The song probably ran through his head as he walked me to the bus stop on the first day of kindergarten. I was prepared for school. My father had taught me simple arithmetic and basic reading comprehension. I could write both my names. My father was less prepared. We held hands while waiting for the bus to arrive, my father offering a mishmash of neurotic suggestions: it's beautiful to be out on your own; don't be afraid without me, I'm only a phone call away. I was aware that the advice wasn't meant for me. As the bus came into view, my father unsuccessfully feigned composure.

"Bye Baba," I said after the doors opened.

"Behave at school, okay."

Before I reached the second step, I scrambled back to my father, pressing my face against his stomach. He too had been pretending. He massaged the back of my head. "Don't be afraid, yaba, don't be afraid. Baba will be waiting for you right here after school." As I climbed back onto the bus, my father called out to me: "I'm proud of you, my son-son."

I grew wiry and turbulent, losing interest in workbooks and instead taking up video games. I regularly upbraided my father for being so weird. "My teachers all hate you," I once told him. He had developed a reputation as a meddler, giving the principal hours of unsolicited feedback. He complained about the Thanksgiving lesson, social studies, and world history, especially world history. "These hillbillies," he liked to say, "couldn't find my country even if you stapled a compass to their asses and introduced them to Jesus." Until very recently, I was deeply embarrassed by his style of humanism.

One year, I forget the exact grade, I became sullen and aggressive, reacting harshly to either admonishment or affection. My father knew what was happening. One afternoon he took he took me out for pizza.

"Punch back," he said abruptly after ordering.

"What do you mean?"

"Don't ever accept somebody putting his hands on you."

"But I don't want to get suspended."

"It's okay to get punished for standing up for yourself. Do you understand, yaba?"

I nodded. We ate happily and heartily that evening.

My mother was mortified when he recounted the scene. I creeped out of my bedroom to eavesdrop on their conversation.

"How could you teach our son violence," she said.

"I didn't teach him violence. I taught him self-respect."

"For fuck's sake, Mahmoud, he's going to get in trouble. Or beat up. Is that what you want?"

My father was unmoved. He could tolerate a wide range of qualities, but he refused to assent in the face of aggression. Whatever consequences accrued from punching back would be offset by the rewards of fortitude. He didn't gloat in the coming months when it became clear that their son had adjusted to the rigors of adolescent socialization. He was long dead by the time I turned his pride into parody.

After his diagnosis, he officially retired, although he was only an employee of the university according to HR documents and paystubs. I doubt many people on campus missed him. I never met anyone so adept at being simultaneously reserved and exuberant until Nancy went to school. For my part, I was absorbed in the secluded life typical of male American teenagers. When I asked to eat dinner at a friend's house or holed up in my bedroom listening to heavy metal, my mother would yell for me to visit with my father.

"It's okay, habibty," my father would say. "Let him live."

"Mahmoud, he's going to regret not spending more time with you for the rest of his life."

"Who doesn't have that regret with their parents? It's good for him to enjoy freedom while it's still available."

I sometimes came around. I think my father found it easier to talk knowing my presence was voluntary.

"You know, I don't like the name Fred," he said one afternoon.

"Dude, Farid is like an old-man name."

"It is," he said. "But it's a name of great pride. You should remember that. Call yourself what you like, but know where your name comes from."

"Yeah, I know, Dad, from your father."

"He died fighting." After a brief silence, he continued, "In my own way, I lost my life fighting, too. Anyway, it's a name of honor, that's all I want you to remember."

"I'll always remember that, dad, don't worry. I know more about you than you think."

"Your mother wanted to name you John or Joseph, something American. She had a hard time with her name, you see. But after I told her the story of my father, she wanted to keep him alive through you. I think he'd be very proud that you carry his name. You're a good boy."

"I'll live up to it, dad." It seemed like the appropriate thing to say.

"I don't want you to be any kind of symbol, yaba. Being a symbol is hard. Symbols don't have feelings. But people who are symbolic do."

"I don't get it."

"Very good, very good. I hope you never do."

My father's physical deterioration was rapid. His once-luminous hair became wispy and gray, his neck a bunchy sack of flesh. He still managed to command space, coughing more frequently than speaking, but his theories of life always got an airing. He left time for my mother's stories about the gardens of her childhood.

On his final day, he summoned me to his bedroom. I entered slowly. I didn't want to go in at all.

"Don't be scared, yaba," he croaked. "Is there anything you want to tell your old man before I go?"

I looked at my feet, shook my head.

"It's okay. I hear all kinds of beautiful words in your silence." After a coughing fit, he continued, "I just wanted to tell you one thing."

"Dad, you're not really going to die, are you?"

"I am. Soon."

"But why?"

"Don't be too sad, yaba, okay? I did everything I wanted to do."

"What will I do without you?"

"Great things. I know it. I know it." We limply held hands. "When you were a boy, you used to come to my bedside, crying for me to sleep with you. Your mother said I was spoiling you. You pattered back to your little bed with your dolls and I would lie next to you and sing the Sesame Street song until you fell asleep. It was the safest place in the entire world." His breathing became strained. His voice trailed off into incomprehensible hoarseness.

I sensed the moment's passing. "What did you want to tell me?"

"The greatest moments of joy I had in my life are because of you."

"I love you, Baba."

My father used the last of his energy to squeeze my hand. "I love you, too, my son-son."

Nancy

ELENA AND I sat on a bench set back from the parking lot. Traces of smoke blew skyward from the rooftops of the townhouses across the road. An orange-red haze spread out behind the bare treetops. We leaned against one another for warmth. When the bus came into view, we stood and walked toward the sidewalk with penguin steps, still pressed together.

The bus picked us up and dropped us off at our old elementary school. TJ (as everybody called it) was way on the eastern side of the county, around a mile from Alexandria City, and the trip took almost half an hour. I had everything about the route memorized. Once we passed over the Beltway on Braddock Road, there were only three stoplights until we got to school. The light at the intersection with Backlick was a mess, but after passing through it the ride was uninterrupted. In the afternoon, Braddock became a crawl once we passed over the Beltway. It usually took three cycles of the stoplight before we could turn onto Burke Lake Road. We had it better than the kids from surrounding counties, though. Some of them were forever stuck in traffic on 95 and 66.

"Morn," the driver greeted us. I grumbled in acknowledgment. "Good morning!" Elena sang out. We took a seat in opposite rows—the bus didn't have many passengers—and leaned into the aisle.

"You gonna see Priya today?" Elena whispered.

I smiled. I had no way to see Priya outside of school, but Priya owned a car, which meant alone time between classes. I reclined, my knees pressed into the seatback in front of me, and watched the modest houses of North Springfield fly past. Elena had her own excitement at school, but I didn't feel like hearing about it. I wanted to fantasize about the day's possibilities.

After puberty, my skin darkened and my hair grew kinkier. The transformation did nothing to make me look more feminine. Mom was unhappy about the changes, but I pointed out that my features came from her side of the family. I most resembled her father, whom I finally met at age fourteen when he and my grandmother visited. Mom didn't want them to come, so she was impossible from the moment they announced the visit until they arrived.

It was weird for me, too. Mom never talked about them. She never talked *to* them, either. I knew they had money and had once been refugees. Dad had said so in a venomous tone during one of the conversations I overheard in Cleveland Park—"They used to live in a fucking tent, so I don't see why they should act so high and mighty"—but otherwise they were a black hole. I was nervous before they came. I felt pretty sure that if they hated Mom, they'd hate me, too. Then I worried that I wouldn't like them. What kind of people hate their grandchild? I had no choice but to hate them back.

I asked Mom why they were coming. "I guess they feel like there's no chance of your father coming back," she said.

"Did they really not like Dad that much?"

"They had a different husband in mind for me."

"Why?"

She became aggravated. "I don't know, Nancy. Instead of being so nosy, you should thank me for protecting you from this shit."

"What shit?"

"Watch your language. You don't need anymore boyish habits."

"I was just repeating what you said!"

"Hmm, you don't listen to anything else I say. How convenient."

Despite the foreboding, my grandparents turned out to be awesome. To begin with, they gave me a thousand bucks. Ten fresh bills. Mom hit the roof, but she was powerless to stop the transaction. Her parents didn't look at all like I pictured them. I'd seen photos, but nothing specific about them stuck in my mind. I was expecting my grandmother to be a carbon of Mom but with gray hair or something, maybe a headscarf or a walker, and my grandfather to be a combination of Aladdin and the Monopoly guy—thick eyebrows, a potbelly, funny shoes, and a million-dollar blazer. He reminded me of Dad, though, clean-cut, polite, casual almost to the point of carefree. His hair was gray on the side, shaved close to the scalp before emerging up top into a coppice of tight black curls. I knew he was taken aback by our resemblance the first time he saw me.

They took me to hip neighborhoods and my favorite restaurants. Mom refused to come. She mostly stayed out of sight, content to let her parents make up for lost time. When present, she made small talk and regularly suffered from loss of hearing. Surely she knew that turning me over to her parents ceded her version of familial reality to theirs. Competing narratives form the unity of every family around the globe and Mom adamantly preserved a singular identity. She probably figured that she had made me impervious to meddling—that, or she no longer cared to guide me through ignorance.

After I was comfortable enough with my grandparents, I asked if it was true that they hated Dad. They looked at each other. My grandfather—*seedo*, as I came to call him—gestured for my grandmother (*teyta*) to answer. They were in a booth across from me at Silver Diner. Teyta turned up the mini-jukebox at the end of the table.

"Where did you hear this from?" she said in her heavy but formal English.

"I don't know. It's just, like, common knowledge."

"Your mother, I see."

"Not really," I said. "It's, I don't know, a thing. Mom doesn't talk about you guys, to be honest."

"We did not hate your father," Seedo said, and I could suddenly tell why Mom and Dad talked of him as an intimidating presence. "Your mother thought we did and then ran off with him. We would have accepted him, but she never gave us a chance." (Later she would grudgingly agree with their version of the story, noting that she ran off for many reasons.)

"We were very upset by what those people did to him," Teyta said.

"Bastards," Seedo added.

What people? What did they do to him?

They didn't know. They were hoping I could tell them. But in the years since Dad's disappearance, Mom and I had received no information. No agency ever discovered a body. No arrests. No suspects. The congresspeople who had been concerned about the situation never again mentioned his name. If Mom had heard anything, she didn't pass the news to me.

We went to the Air and Space Museum near Dulles. Teyta looked along with me in excitement, but Seedo wasn't impressed. At an installation of military jets, he said, "These planes carried napalm." I hadn't thought about what the planes actually did; they were just cool displays hanging from the ceiling. "That one there," he said, pointing at the Enola Gay, "dropped a bomb that killed thousands and thousands of people." Suddenly the museum wasn't so fun.

Afterward, at Ledo Pizza, I was quiet and fidgety.

"Shoo? What's wrong, habibty?" Seedo said.

"I don't know, I wish you didn't tell me about the napalm and the bombs."

"I know about the napalm from firsthand experience. Your mother, too. She doesn't remember. She was a baby."

"Oh. Umm—"

"She's not wanting you to know this information because she thinks America is a place to forget."

"Will she be mad that you told me?"

He shrugged. Teyta laughed. "Your mother tells us you're a gifted student," she said.

"I guess."

"That's all you should worry about. We crossed the river with practically nothing. Now we have a big house in the fanciest neighborhood ['Abdoun,' Seedo interjected] and our children are all successful."

"My teacher said I could change the world."

"Forget all that nonsense," Seedo said. "Concentrate on your grades and making a decent life for yourself. Your father, God rest his soul, learned this lesson the hard way."

"I don't get it."

"Just do well in school, dear. Now eat your pizza."

Anyway, back to Priya. She raved about my tight curls and the ochre skin covering my cheekbones. I was tall and thick and she liked both of those qualities, too. Priya reduced me to my physical components, which I found liberating. She was my anti-mother. I texted her as the bus pulled into school.

park during lunch break? she texted back.

Static prickled throughout my chest. It was setting up to be a fun day. I was flattered that Priya wanted to sneak off despite the cold. I wouldn't get to enjoy her company next year. Priya was determined to leave Virginia. She was deciding between Cal Tech and Stanford, but for sure it would be some place in California. (A few years later, I'd see a Facebook post celebrating her engagement to some culturally appropriate guy working in Silicon Valley.)

Before lunch, we had to survive English. It was presentation day. Because of my unfortunate last name, I was always one of the first to go. I had put good effort into my topic, "Why the Humanities are Important to a Scientific Education." When I practiced the speech in front of Mom, she said I was being too analytical. "The mark of a good speech is telling the audience what they want to hear." Her advice confused me. I thought I was making a strong case based on the merits of my argument. It seemed lazy to pander rather than persuade. After I finished, only a few of my classmates attempted to look enthused. Fuck me. Mom was probably right.

They perked up when Elena hit the dais. All year she'd been agitating to change TJ's nickname, the Colonials, and everyone knew her speech would be a fiery call to action. "A Colonial," she began, "is nothing to be proud of." Wearing a thigh-length pullover dress atop black spandex, her hair bunched atop her scalp, Elena commanded the room with both elegance and force of personality. She walked side to side after reading her introduction, notes left behind on the lectern. My classmates, awake and engaged, deflated Mom's theory of speechmaking.

Elena explained the ravages of colonization, calling on classmates by name to describe how it probably affected their ancestors and then explaining how it affected hers. She railed against the genocide of America's Indigenous peoples and the ongoing trauma of slavery. Thomas Jefferson himself was implicated. The school board should change the entire name of the school, in fact. Why not rename it for Sally Hemings? How cool would it be to attend the Sally Hemings Institute of Technology? Get it? Just kidding. But Sally Hemings Magnet School sounds great, doesn't it? Or just Sally Hemings High. The Sally Hemings Heroines. The SHMS Legends. The SHH Insurgents. Wouldn't that be great? Shouldn't we honor the people who really built this country? Haven't the dead white guys been privileged enough already? At the very least they need to get rid of the harmful nickname, which is constant violence to all the students of color at the school, not to mention the bus drivers, cleaning staff, and kitchen crew. Furthermore, she concluded, the aftereffects of colonization can be seen every single day in TJ. Where are all the Black students? The Latinas? Most of the few Black students are from Africa. Black Americans are structurally excluded. Something needs to change. Let's start with the name. Elena took her seat to a hearty ovation.

I served as Elena's assistant throughout the year as she gathered signatures on a petition to change the name. Mom thought the entire thing was ridiculous, but she didn't care as long as I maintained high grades and kept good relations with the school's administration. I didn't care much, either. Or maybe I should say I wasn't passionate like Elena. She regularly asked for my input, but I had none. I just wanted to support her and enjoyed the drama, something in rare supply at TJ. I didn't have much of a choice, anyhow. In TJ's racial ecosystem, I was clearly something—Indian, Afghan, Salvadoran, Arab, Persian—that obliged me to the cause. Most of our peers were indifferent, but lots of kids could be persuaded to sign the petition if I convinced them that it wouldn't affect their academic standing. I didn't have to lie. The students at TJ were the county's pride and joy. Administrators would never punish us for doing exactly what they pretended to encourage: think critically, be leaders, make a difference.

Not all students went along with Elena's activism. Some, hyperaware of our school's nerdy reputation, acted too cool or disaffected to care about politics. Or they couldn't understand how a term like "colonials" was objectionable. Others were hostile, arguing that the name was fine and the attempt to change it was a bunch of PC bullshit. Most teachers encouraged us, although it felt kind of mechanical, like they were sensitive about being good educators. I guess they were hyperaware of reputation, too. Elena had a way of making it feel like saying no was tantamount to supporting Donald Trump. She regularly met with the principal and various teachers. The meetings were friendly. They were always looking into it. They took everything very seriously. The matter would be brought to the attention of the curriculum committee. It would be discussed at the next school board meeting.

A few weeks after her speech, for which she earned an A, Elena's campaign got a mention in the *Washington Post*. Her mom cooked a celebration dinner and invited us. I went alone. ("That child doesn't need any more encouragement," Mom declared.) Elena's mom had a stack of papers on the kitchen island and beamed as she served various stews and flatbread. Halfway through the meal, Elena's dad, thin and lurching, with a Nationals ball cap on his head, came in and immediately tore into the food. Elena's mom filled his ears with praise of their daughter, each line beginning with "Our baby." Her father shrugged and kept on eating.

Elena finally intervened. "That's enough, Mama. It's just a line in the paper. There's so much more to do."

"What do you hope to accomplish?" her father wanted to know. The question had a ring of accusation.

"I want justice for our people, Daddy."

"Our people? Who's that?"

"Okay, Robel," Elena's mother said before Elena could answer. "She means all the people of the world. Our baby has a compassionate soul."

Elena's father grunted and patted her hand. She snatched it away. "You don't get it. You think this country is free, but look at you, busting your butt for twelve hours every day and we're still broke all the time."

"I'm proud of my work," he said sharply. "Me and your mother have given our life for you to go to this fancy school. And instead of being grateful, you attack the place."

"Ugh, you're so clueless," Elena said, smacking the table. "You really don't see the racism everywhere in this country?"

"I see what I see."

"What does that mean?"

"I keep my head down. I work."

"That's the problem. You should put your head up."

"Let me tell you about life, my daughter. The people you defend, they will never do for you in return. Believe me on this."

Elena's mom barked at him in Tigrinya and soon all three of them were yelling. I slumped in my seat, wondering if it would be rude to sneak out. When I was about to make a move, Elena grabbed my arm and pulled me upstairs. "Can you believe him?" she said after shutting her bedroom door. "What an asshole."

I didn't know what to say. Should I validate her? If I did, would she be insulted? She spared me the decision with a long rant about her annoying dad. "He's, like, so internally colonized," she concluded.

"What's that?"

"Oh my God, Nan, for somebody with your background, you're as clueless as Baba."

I bristled. Being clueless wasn't my fault. Since birth, my parents withheld vital information. I was raised to be ignorant, my mind fed by generic blood. Even the most significant event in my life was a mystery. The pain of that event was attached to something abstract, which made closure impossible. It intensified all other forms of uncertainty. Elena was supposed to be my haven from this stuff, my one normal relationship.

Did I experience some racism? Yeah. Like the time a driver with a rebel flag affixed to his bumper screamed at me to get out of his country when he thought I had jumped a four-way stop. And the military paraphernalia all over the region always made me uneasy, as if I were purposefully being made to feel unwelcome, although I couldn't explain why. I understood that racism felt shitty. But racism wouldn't become real to me until I embraced the healing properties of violence.

"Sorry," Elena said. "I didn't mean that, Nan."

"It's alright. I *am* clueless. I just wish I could help you more."

"I need it."

"I mean, I don't think your dad's trying to be a dick. He's just worried about school and stuff. Everybody at TJ's parents are the same way."

"But not everybody's parents are Black. The thing is, he knows better. I've heard him tell my mom about some racist fuckery he experienced a million times."

"Yeah. I guess he's just worried."

"He needs to worry more about white people." By this point she was mumbling because she had taken to Twitter. Her thumbs danced furiously across the surface of her smart phone as she recounted the dinnertime drama with her dad. She had around 4000 followers. The internet would make up for the support I didn't provide.

During her speech at TJ, Elena suffered no problems. She was too confident, too commanding, for any high schooler to challenge. Everyone wanted to be her friend, or at least to have her on their side. She was gracious and beautiful and being her best friend was my biggest source of self-esteem. After English, we were in different classes. Normally we'd meet for lunch, but on that day I had my rendezvous with Priya.

She was waiting for me in her car. We went to Green Spring Garden, a regular spot because of its free parking and isolated crannies. Just up Braddock from TJ, the park boasted a stately brick colonial with green shutters and white dormers. Beds of witch hazel, spring beauty, and blue violet covered the grounds, dotted with oak and dogwood. Even in the middle of winter, the garden seemed to buzz with life, offering a respite from the desolation of surrounding shopping centers and subdivisions. Wooded trails led to a pond with a pitiful little fountain. Priya and I usually hung out near the pond.

After we sat on a bench and felt sure the place was empty, Priya pulled my face toward hers and kissed me, taking my bottom lip into her mouth. We went on that way for a few minutes and then stopped to talk. It was too cold for any kind of nudity. Soon we were kissing again, trying to touch body parts beneath bulging jackets. I'll never forget the gravity of winter that morning, the branches around us like cracks in a gray canvas. Crows yawped across the surface of frozen water. Our tryst felt like the flash of cold that precedes a scalding. I could never shake the sense that desolation was the upshot of our tryst.

Many people at TJ knew about me and Priya, but it was still a strictly secret pairing. We weren't an official couple, though mutuals knew us to be more than regular friends. Mainly we wanted to keep our parents in the dark. Mom suspected that I liked girls. I could tell by her snide comments about my fashion choices and masculine habits. To my ear, the comments had a distinctly carnal undertone. Priya's folks had no idea. She looked like any other good girl in her community.

(In college, I would find out that Mom knew, had known since I was ten or eleven, and had no problem with it. She simply didn't like my fashion choices and masculine habits.)

Priya rested her head against my shoulder. Trucks and buses groaned through the intersection at Braddock and Little River, but otherwise the air was still. Two squirrels crunching through the brush interrupted our reverie and we decided to head back to school. I told Priya about how my speech sucked compared to Elena's. Priya said that trying to change the school nickname was dumb. I kept quiet. I didn't want to remember a fight every time I smelled her hair on my coat sleeve. Mostly I was afraid Priya would win the argument and then I'd have her reproach in my head whenever I saw Elena. Priya was gifted like that. She could deem something lame or uncool and instantly it would lose luster. At TJ, that sort of gift gave a person considerable power.

For her part, Elena considered Priya a basic bougie girl from McLean who lived in a new-money eyesore rebuilt atop the ruins of a midcentury rambler. The appearance of prosperity was paramount to that class of people. Elena didn't say it out loud, but I can read her thoughts by the shading of her eyes. In reality, Priya didn't give a shit what the school was called. For her, TJ was defined solely by the value of its reputation. Nothing personal against Elena. It didn't occur to her that Elena might take rejection personally. Protecting TJ's honor was a business decision.

When we returned to school, Priya kissed my cheek and then glanced into the parking lot before digging her mouth into my neck. I squirmed with pleasure and pretended to be mortified. "Catch you later, darling," she said in a faux aristocratic cadence and walked quickly into the building, leaving me to lag behind.

With a few minutes before the bell, I hung out in the lobby, an open space with couches and tables in its back half. An HD video board down the hall displayed various student accomplishments. I figured to graduate without making an appearance. I was mostly anonymous at TJ, which put me in the majority, but, like other unknowns, educators led me to believe that I possessed a special capacity to do great things. I'm not sure if I've proved my teachers right or wrong.

The bell rang and I headed off to computer lab. It wasn't really my thing, but I learned a lot in the course, most of it outside the classroom. There were areas of the internet where you could buy pretty much anything. At the time, the thought terrified me. I had anxiety about all the strangers I saw every day having easy access to guns, drugs, underage girls (or boys), slave labor, military-grade weapons, black-market currency. Technology was supposed to make life easier, make us more civilized, but it felt to me like it facilitated danger. I'm sure Dad would have laughed off my fear. Then again, Dad wasn't around to reassure me.

I joined up with Elena in seventh period. At the final bell, we loitered near the cafeteria with friends and then walk-jogged across the school to catch the bus. The driver was sideways on his seat with his legs stretched in the aisle. He looked up from his book. "Come on in, cold out there." Before either of us could respond, he turtled his head into the downy hood of his jacket and began reading again.

Soon we were among a procession of thirty buses cruising down Braddock. Our bus stayed in the left lane, whizzing past those to the right at a distance of only inches. I kept recalling the tryst with Priya, which filled my stomach with glints of bliss.

Elena interrupted the memory: "Coming over today? We can work on the campaign."

I was a bit tired of the campaign, but wanted to stay with Elena. Before we could start talking about it, a voice piped up from behind us. "If a child refuses to sleep during nap time, are they guilty of resisting a rest?" The joke elicited a few chuckles. "*Uh* rest. Get it?"

It was Fang, a freshman who regularly read dad jokes from the internet during the ride home.

"Oh my God, Fang, not again," a girl in front of us said. Sousan, quiet except to upbraid Fang for being annoying.

"What did the pirate say on his eightieth birthday?" Fang continued, ignoring her. "Aye Matey." The bus filled with chuckles and groans.

"Where do you keep finding this stuff?" Matthew, another freshman. "There are like a hundred websites filled with them."

Sousan: "And you've already gone through every single one."

Fang: "What's the best part about living in Switzerland?"

Sousan: "Shut up already!"

"I don't know, but the flag is a big plus."

I laughed. Most of the time, I didn't get the pun until it was too late.

"Be careful," Elena said, "Sousan's about to flip her shit."

"Do you blame me? It would be nice to ride home in peace for once."

Elena shrugged.

"Hello, bus driver," Sousan yelled. "Can you make him stop?" The driver smiled at us in the rearview mirror and continued in silence.

Matthew: "I don't think he cares."

Sousan: "Obviously not."

"The fattest knight at King Arthur's roundtable was Sir Cumference," Fang pressed on. "He acquired his size from too much pi." Only Matthew and a few other boys laughed. "Get it? Circumference? *Sir*...Cumference?"

Elena: "Yes, we get it."

Fang: "Pie, as in, like, the desert, versus pi, the number. Too much p—"

"We get it, Fang," Elena interrupted. "It's just not funny."

"Yeah, it kinda sucks," I added.

"It's sexist," Sousan said.

Fang and Matthew looked scared and would have gladly left it at that, but another boy, Alex (a senior), leaned into the aisle and said, "How can it be sexist? Sir Cumference is a guy."

Sousan: "Because it just is."

Alex: "BUT HE'S A GUY."

Sousan: "And who always gets made fun of for being fat? Girls."

Alex: "But in this case it's not a girl being made fun of. It's a dude and he's not even real."

Elena: "Fine. The joke is ableist, though."

Alex: "That's bullshit. You're just making stuff up."

Fang: "Guys, I'm sorry. I didn't mean to make anyone mad."

Alex: "You shouldn't have to apologize. All you did was tell a joke. They're just looking for a reason to be mad."

Fang was on the verge of crying. "Anyway, I'm sorry."

Elena wasn't about to drop it. "Ableism is actually a thing."

Alex: "He's in ninth grade. He doesn't know anything about anything."

Elena: "So do you think ableism exists or not?"

Sousan: "He knows how to keep telling jokes nobody wants to hear."

Alex: "Whatever. You're just throwing shit at the wall to see what sticks."

Elena: "You're not answering. Is it ableist or not to make fun of large-bodied people?"

Alex: "No."

Elena: "What do you think, Nan?"

I didn't know. It was kind of hurtful being made into the expert. "I agree with you," I said.

Matthew: "What's ableist?"

Elena: "That terrible joke."

Matthew: "No, what's *ableist*?"

Alex: "He knows you think the joke is ableist. He doesn't know what ableist means."

Elena: "Neither do you."

Alex: "There's no such thing. Jesus Christ, it was a *dad joke*."

Matthew: "I still don't get it."

Fang: "I think it means making fun of fat people."

Elena: "Shut up, Fang. You're being ableist again."

Matthew: "Oh, I understand now."

Bus driver: "Cardinal Forest! Next stop White Oaks."

Elena muttered "douchebag" in Alex's direction as we stood up. After the bus pulled away, she said, "Can you believe that guy?"

I could. Alex enjoyed arguing. He really enjoyed arguing with Elena. For him, it was like a sport, but Elena never shared an opinion just to provoke people. Her provocations were absolutely sincere. I could make sense of her passion—I knew her at an atomic level—but her rhetoric usually confused me. She had no patience for people who couldn't keep up, even hapless freshmen, so I tried never to let my ignorance show. She must have known, though. Her patience was an expression of love. I still needed to try. No kind of love is unconditional.

I always felt that Dad could have helped me with this stuff. (Even if Mom made sense of Elena's social justice concepts, she wasn't inclined to provide clarification.) He would have understood Elena's vocabulary. But I never got to ask for his wisdom. It felt like my ignorance of meaningful issues arose from his disappearance. Elena and I were like sisters and not simply because of our closeness. I was the quietly ambitious student and she was the maven of ideas, each a stranger in our father's house.

I could smell curry and yoghurt before we walked into the door of Elena's townhouse, and knew her mother would be in the kitchen amid pots emitting trails of steam and little jars of spice peppering the countertop. She would smile and hug us both, ask about our speeches. She'd make me feel as if I had done as well as her daughter. And there would be nothing passive-aggressive about it. I only had to accept her love. That was her condition.

When I look back on those days, I mourn the sense of safety, the simple comfort of being alive, that existed in Elena's house, laid out exactly like mine but so different in décor and spirit. We were thinking a lot about college, what it would mean to leave home in another year. The planning excited us to no end, but it took barely any time once gone for us to recognize that a sense of asylum would be forever impossible to recover. The authority we wanted to escape provided the very independence we anticipated. We enjoyed certain guarantees: food and shelter and medicine, but more than that, endless visions of a happy and prosperous future. Once the future materializes, anticipation, the lifeblood of freedom, recedes into nostalgia.

My nostalgia is ambiguous. I yearn for moments that never happened, for a past doubly imagined. Always it's Dad in flashback and yet Mom is the real source of my sentimental eulogies. What I remember of Dad is abstract and I rarely know if a specific event actually happened. I recall the sensual aspects of his existence more than anything. The acrid scent of coffee on his breath. Traces of floral cologne on his weekend sweatshirts. Brooding eyes and wavy black hair. Halting displays of physical affection.

A clipped, mechanical laugh. The clicking of worry beads at the dinner table.

Beyond our weekend hikes to the Special Place, which only happened after hours of nagging, he wasn't around. Mom delivered me to playdates. She was my representative at the International School. She prepped my breakfast and checked my homework. Somehow I don't much remember her presence, either. Everything we did was measured and programmed according to the imagery of a normal life. My time in DC was a production unfit for memory.

But what I do remember of Dad is enough to fill me with anger for all that I missed. When I was six or seven, he took me to a DC United game. I don't recall the opponent or the outcome, only his unusually carefree disposition. Instead of telling me to be quiet and composed, he allowed me to bound through groups of people in the Metro station and during the walk to RFK Stadium. It was October and the weather was starting to turn. I had fought with Mom because she wanted me to wear a jacket. Dad took my side: "She'll be fine."

"Well, if she catches cold, then you can miss work to take care of her."

The air was brisk and I kept rubbing my arms. When we got into the stadium, Dad took me to the team store and bought a sweatshirt. He didn't have to admit Mom was right; he was simply treating his daughter to a souvenir. We held hands and walked to our seats. I jumped up and down the first time I saw the field through the tunnel leading to the stands. It was impossibly big, with perfect white lines crisscrossing a lavish expanse of grass. Our seats were near midfield. Dad could get good tickets through work. He bought me hot dogs and nachos and let me drink Sprite even though Mom forbade soda. In the second half, I grew bored of the action and cuddled next to Dad. He kissed the top of my head. I remember that kiss because he said, "My father took me to a football game in this stadium once. I was just about your age. I hope you'll remember today when you grow up."

On the ride home, the Metro car was crowded with fans. We had to stand most of the way to L'Enfant and then found two seats next to the door on the second train. My stomach was upset from all the junk food and I could barely keep awake. The new sweatshirt was stained with Sprite and mustard.

"Lay down, my love," Dad said, shifting his hip to the end of his seat. I put my knees against the plastic barricade and rested my head on his thigh. He stroked my forehead until I fell asleep and then carried me home on his back. After walking me upstairs, he sat at the edge of my bed.

"Are you gonna keep me company, Daddy?"

"Would you like me to stay?"

"Yes."

He stretched out and rubbed my back. "Ah, it feels safe in here. The safest place in the entire world."

That strange observation has stayed with me throughout the years. Maybe I had already fallen asleep and dreamed it. I'll never know. But the notion of safety would become a constant in my life, something I would come to see as indivisible from violence.

Fred

I WAS RELAXING in my hotel room just before midnight when they snatched me. I had stripped down to boxer-briefs and a white tee and was leaning against the headboard of my bed with my laptop in front of me. Someone knocked sharply. I knew it was bad news.

"Who's there?" I yelled, praying that my aggravated tone would send away the visitor. No miracle was forthcoming.

Another knock, sharper, more urgent. I put my laptop to the side and walked to the door, quietly, although whoever was on the other side would know I had moved. Through the eyehole I could see a man in a suit flanked by two soldiers in berets and olive fatigues. I was so arrogant, so naïve, that I thought I could talk them down, send them away with a bit of charm and diplomacy. So I opened the door. I should have tried to climb down the side of the building from the balcony.

"Mr. Baker," the man in the suit said. It wasn't a question.

"Can I help you?"

"Perhaps. Aren't you going to invite us in?"

I stepped aside and let them pass. They stood between the TV and the bed and cleared a path for me to walk past them so I couldn't run to the door. They gave no verbal orders, yet I had no choice. The man in the suit stood about two feet in front of me. "That was a very interesting speech you gave this evening."

"Thank you." I could see the hint of an angry twitch on his upper lip.

"There are some people who would like to speak with you about it. Perhaps get a clearer sense of your meaning. You used many large words. As you know, we're a simple people."

"I'm happy to explain it to you right now. And I'd be happy to drop by your office tomorrow."

"You must come with us."

"I respectfully decline. Now if you'll excuse me, I should probably phone my good friend, your ambassador."

One of the soldiers stepped forward and slapped me with such force that I lost balance.

The man in the suit said, "It is the Ambassador who requested our visit."

In my final days, I had plenty of time to wonder what exactly led to that moment. There's no confusion about the immediate reason for the man's visit, but I wanted to know the long trajectory of my downfall. Where did it start? Probably in some innocuous moment as a child in Blacksburg, perhaps with one of my father's apocryphal stories or an experience of bullying in school.

A clearer origin is graduate school, when I was making the connections that would facilitate my career as a public intellectual. Lara had finished her master's and was beginning her rounds in the administrative circuit of academe. I stayed on through my doctorate and landed a job as a media liaison in a PAC supporting liberal congressional candidates. In time I was the director of communications and vying for the top spot in the organization. The longtime CEO, a choleric man close to the Kennedy family, was nearing retirement just as a rift opened within the organization about which slate of candidates to support. The rift was largely generational. Most of the younger employees, myself included, pushed for a more progressive agenda, but the old guard wanted to stay the course. We organized into a half-dozen mini-tribes and did everything short of outright sabotage to outflank our colleagues. The office in those days was a hive of whispers.

As an up-and-comer with an influential position, I became de facto leader of the reformers. My main rival was the head of outreach, Michael Slotkin, who looked like a journalist in a 1970s sitcom with his disheveled hair and rolled-up shirtsleeves. He had been with the organization years before my arrival and was known to chew the eraser end of a pencil to signal deep concentration. Slotkin favored a pragmatic approach: appease party bosses and keep donors happy. He and I were the obvious candidates for succession. Slotkin was a company man with an extensive network around DC; I had youthful energy and a boatload of new ideas, which ultimately were a detriment. New ideas that don't recycle old conventions are frowned upon in the industry.

We managed to keep a civil relationship, but in private we vigorously fought for control of the organization. Slotkin had the upper hand in terms of experience and connections, but I had better social skills. Slotkin was competent, but people didn't like him very much. He was a born sycophant with an abrasive personality, meek or bullish depending on his status in any given moment. These were beneficial qualities except in struggles for power, when charisma could be decisive. I had the ear of the CEO, but it was impossible to know how he was trending. Slotkin had his ear, as well. We both dreaded the possibility of the CEO staying on to weather the storm. Drama is opportunity; tranquility is a curse on ambition.

Some major donors and party bosses demanded that the organization maintain its traditional orientation, but the CEO didn't want the losing side to splinter into its own group. He needn't have worried, for career is the town's universal devotion, but unity became an obsession that prolonged the infighting. Having the big-timers on his side was a serious advantage for Slotkin, but that's not what ultimately won him the position. The organization was concerned with optics and tradition. I was optically ambiguous in ways that worried the party leadership. There were concerns about my ability to be dispassionate about certain sensitive issues.

People around town knew what was happening in the organization. These things make the rounds. The culture of networking is nothing more than lucrative gossip. Everybody was begging to be poached. Two weeks after Slotkin became CEO, I was in the Kingdom at the behest of the Minister of Information. A month later, the Institute's Board of Advisors had tabbed me as director.

"We like that you are forward-thinking," the Minister told me. "This is exactly the image we wish to project."

My starting salary far exceeded anything my father had earned. I was determined not to repeat his example of minimum effort, which for him was a source of pride. My father had a powerful interior life, but little desire to intervene in a broader world of ideas. I was stuck on the idea of intervention. I had no particular affinity for the Kingdom. It was merely an entity that allowed me to pursue what I viewed as an important educational vision. Ideas require money. The Kingdom had plenty of it. We seemed to be a perfect match.

For many years, the relationship was mutually beneficial. I spent lots of time giving lectures at campuses and professional gatherings. Demand was high enough that I could be picky. A large honorarium was always a strong attraction, of course, but I also paid attention to the ideology of would-be hosts. I avoided partisan student groups, especially if they were focused on the Kingdom's region. Likewise NGOs and lobbying firms with a reputation for narrow thinking. I sought a hearing in respectable, bipartisan spaces.

The benefits for the Kingdom were manifold. The Institute helped the Kingdom cultivate a reputation of open-mindedness and moderation. The King and his advisors were keen on being viewed as exemplars of modernity—or at least as worthy of inhabiting the category. With my perfect English and devotion to the ideals of liberal democracy, I embodied the perception to which they aspired. I could serve as an emissary without ever mentioning the Kingdom. The money came in, the ideas went out, a thoroughly modern transaction. Whenever pundits or politicians expressed skepticism about the backward or tribal or hermitic Kingdom, I would show up to reassure the populace that despite surface differences we were all the same in the end.

I must again stress that my commitment to this arrangement was sincere. I never thought of myself as a lackey or a functionary. I was a man of letters free to speak my mind. Universities are seen as beacons of inquiry, but there's a ton of dirty money on campus, some of it from the Kingdom, which has departments and professorships named after its ruling family. Writers fancy themselves sovereign, but they're limited by the tastes of corporate publishers and the book-buying public. So the Institute had a funding source. No big deal. As long as I didn't feel restricted, that irksome fact didn't matter.

But I knew deep inside that it mattered plenty, that the entire arrangement relied on a certain kind of discretion. Breaking character would betray decorum, perhaps even morality. I viewed rebellion as childish.

At first, dissent was a strange undertaking, but it soon became a preoccupation. I found it exhilarating, a way to discover frustrations and then exorcise them with impetuous, ferocious keystrokes. Dissent made me feel positioned within a mystical world of descendants and ancestors. It removed me from a lifetime of obligation. That small prelude to incarceration was my second and final taste of freedom.

The change was sudden and seemingly spontaneous. The Kingdom was moving into alliances that could prove controversial among surrounding countries and its own citizens. Various agencies commissioned Institute studies that would downplay or deny those alliances. But they were an open secret. Pretending they didn't exist would damage the Institute's reputation as an independent source of analysis. As protests spread throughout the Kingdom's region and the imperial powers aggressively preached stability, our work assumed a desperate character. We were made to understand that we served as a frontline deterrent against the prospect of a third world war. I increasingly thought about my father and grandfather, my namesake, those vague, perplexing emblems of my own flesh and bones. They denied me the pleasures of struggle because they had been overwhelmed by anxiety and fatigue, but their sensibilities endured.

I especially thought about the callous inheritance I would one day pass along to Nancy. My work no longer seemed to match the incredible lessons available through conventions of fatherhood. Her existence was my only real sense of the public good.

Before her first-grade year, I had taken a day off so we could go swimming at a country club in Bethesda, a longtime promise that Nancy wouldn't drop. After a few hours at the pool, we drove home, where I planned to cook a healthy dinner. Nancy sat in the backseat, strapped into her booster, chattering about the roadway, the flora, the traffic, the music on the radio. Near home, on Connecticut Avenue, we saw a pizza parlor at the same time. I caught her gaze in the rearview mirror and we both giggled.

"We shouldn't," I said.

"Come on, let's do it, Daddy."

I couldn't argue and didn't want to push back, anyway. I double-parked and we ran inside, watching portly men play ping-pong as we waited for our pie. Once home, we stuffed ourselves, leaving the empty box on the table along with an uncapped bottle of Sprite. We played a few games of Uno in the living room before putting on the TV and falling asleep on the couch to Sponge Bob. The day's events were sudden and spontaneous. Each off-script act ended up being a perfect decision.

I rediscovered a dormant vivacity in the disorder. And I discovered that despite its myriad responsibilities, my job in its purest essence was applying order to humanity's vivacious impulses. I suppressed that awful discovery until the silence became intolerable.

When I first criticized the Kingdom—haltingly, delicately—nobody seemed to notice. It was in a tweet that got little engagement: "Remember, the Kingdom's foreign policy evolved over decades of careful planning." A tacit rebuke obscured by an apparent compliment. My life might have been saved if somebody affiliated with the Kingdom had noticed my displeasure and stamped it out then and there. I escalated my rhetoric until the displeasure became noticeable. Various employees and friends of the Institute suggested I tone it down; there was a definite change in people's vibes around me.

I could survive while my criticism was limited to social media and a tart comment here and there in lectures and op-eds, but my dissent reached crisis stage when I took to news programs and lambasted the Kingdom's new policy of accommodating historical aggressors. After I gave a scathing interview to CNN about the need for unity among our people, a category that didn't include Americans, the Ambassador's son reached out to me.

We should meet, he texted.

Things are very hectic at the moment, let me look at my calendar.

No immediately.

Within the hour, I was having lunch at the Ambassador's residence in Georgetown. The son, tall and courtly, welcomed me.

"Where's your father?" I asked after the exchange of pleasantries.

"He has another engagement. Please join me for lunch."

I followed him into the dining room, a deep and slender space with an ornate crystal chandelier and a teak hutch with exquisite carvings, displaying a bronze tea urn meant to illuminate the family's humble beginnings. The walls were striped in green-and-gold wallpaper. I tried to figure out why the ambassador had delegated the meeting to his son. It could have been a show of faith in his successor or a signal that my defiance wasn't yet a top priority. A Filipina woman in a white smock served pita bread and lentil soup before returning to the kitchen.

"Is everything okay, Fred?" the Ambassador's son said. "Or you might prefer Farid these days?"

"Fred is fine."

"Of course. Are there problems at home? With the Institute? If anything is troubling you, I hope you know that you can bring it to us."

"Things are going quite well, actually."

"Thanks be to God."

"Naturally."

He pushed his bowl away and rested his forearms on the table. "Let's speak frankly, shall we?"

"I would appreciate it, yes."

"There's some apprehension, even displeasure, among important policymakers with your recent... talking points."

"Why ever would anybody be worried or displeased?" I intended to make him verbalize his objection.

"Many people feel that your comments have been misrepresenting the Kingdom's priorities," he said.

"I would contest that impression," I said.

"As a sitting member of the government, I can tell you that you're wrong. There are diplomatic considerations above your understanding."

I chortled and dropped my spoon into the empty bowl. "Thank you for your concern, but I understand quite well."

"We know your background, Fred. If you don't feel like you can be objective, then we're happy to arrange for a temporary leave of responsibility. Just until you feel reinvigorated, of course."

"That's the thing. I'm feeling very invigorated these days."

"Yes." He stared at me and for the first time I could detect the brutality beneath the polish. His dark-brown pupils pulsated with anger, a sharp contrast to his manicured brows and lashes.

"I really ought to be going," I said.

"Please stay. Angeline is about to serve the main course."

"Thank you, but I must get back to the Institute."

"Before you go," he said, pushing back his chair and resting his chin on the knuckles of both hands, "I'd like a bit of clarity. Are you telling me that you intend to continue publicly criticizing the Kingdom?"

"I'm telling you that I'll do what I've always done, which is to raise questions that are pertinent to the public interest, as my job description requires."

"Then I am obliged to warn you that your recalcitrance might result in severe consequences."

"Are you threatening me?"

"I am fulfilling an obligation to my government by informing you of displeasure with your job performance. The displeasure reaches the highest level."

"The Institute is technically independent. We have a nonsectarian mission, for God's sake."

"Yes, but our interest in it provides us a certain amount of leeway. The King is very proud of the Institute. He follows your work closely."

"Fine. Duly noted."

I stood and he extended his hand. I shook it limply and hurried out. The Ambassador's son remained in the dining room, his head angled toward the floor, eyeballs halfway inside his upper sockets. Now, amid the last great event of my life, I deeply regret accepting the bastard's offer of a handshake. For decades, centuries, Europeans and Americans have made pilgrimages of self-realization to the kind of barren landscape that will soon become my coffin. It was always a frivolous endeavor. They knew exactly what they intended to realize before making the journey.

Me? Only after my body is picked apart by scavengers will I have derived real meaning from my odyssey into the desert.

I don't know whether the gala was an excuse to lure me to the Kingdom for an act of abduction or if authorities decided to abduct me after I had given my speech. Either way, I knew that I was courting danger. I suppose I was too arrogant to believe that a typical outcome would apply to me. Why did I push forward, then? I can't say. That's the strangest thing about a bizarre situation. I don't really know why I did it, not precisely, anyway. I'm relying on others to figure it out.

The annual gala in the Kingdom was a big deal. I went every year. The extravagance was a huge attraction. The organizers required my attendance. Representatives of the Kingdom's various business and scholarly holdings came together for a week of gluttony, luxury tours, and policymaking. Plenty of salaciousness was available despite the pious façade. The attendees traveled in tiers. I was among the group that enjoyed first-class airfare and lodging in one of the capital's ritziest hotels.

There were plenty of speeches, but I had enough clout to skip most of them. If a senior member of the government was at the podium, then I was in the audience. Otherwise I enjoyed the privileges of the Kingdom's underground pleasure industry, made possible by a tremendous demand for carousal and an oversaturated pool of foreign workers. Despite my altered consciousness, I would die as the kind of person I had been my entire adult life: a man of no appreciable constraint, a moral degenerate who in his final days was unable to manage a proper arc of redemption.

But the speech I delivered to a luncheon of princes and consultants was the high point of my career. That it also served as a prelude to murder is simply a matter of bad timing. The room was tense when I took the microphone. When I effusively greeted esteemed members of the audience, the energy of the room relaxed a bit. For a moment, the second-tier leaders of the Kingdom assumed they would avert the discomfort of a rogue speaker. I quickly disabused them of that assumption.

In other circumstances, it would have been a touching presentation. I spoke of my father and grandfather, a bit of my in-laws, too. I traced a recent history of pain and loss from my grandparents' generation into the very room where the beneficiaries of this misfortune were enjoying steak and lobster. I explained how the Kingdom had always been complicit, but used to at least feign concern for the dispossessed. Now it operated in open complicity, its pretenses of concern rare and unconvincing. I spared nobody in my origin story-cum-diatribe. I would unite all factions against me. My words were enough to upset the audience, but it was the humiliation that really enraged them. Nobody clapped. Nobody shook my hand. They rushed another speaker to the podium, somebody more conducive to excess.

I didn't wait for my driver. I left the banquet hall through a side exit and took a taxi to my hotel. Billed as a "seven star" resort, with gold featured in places likely to be covered by particles of shit, it was an Oriental dreamscape for travelers who want to pretend that luxury doesn't preclude them from being adventurous. Once in my room, I opened my computer. I didn't turn on the TV. I avoided email and social media. I read about sports and transcribed the main points of my speech. I had gone fully unhinged and never felt so in control of my intellect. I phoned Lara twice without getting an answer. Did she know about the speech? Were people talking about it? Or was I needlessly making a big deal out of it? It could have been one of those things that seems much bigger to the speaker than to the audience. The entire world may have forgotten it already, I reassured myself. Or maybe it was very much on the minds of important people. Over and over I returned to the feeling that I wasn't exaggerating the magnitude of my actions. I opened the door to the balcony. The warm breeze felt out of place in the darkness, like it was hoarding remnants of the day's sunshine. I stayed on the bed well into the night, with no intention of sleeping. Each passing moment heightened my fear and sense of safety in equal measure.

Then the knock.

After I had regained composure from the slap, I stared at the man in the suit, gasping, wide-eyed, incredulous.

"Come with us," he said.

"I'll do no such thing."

"I am not making a request, Mr. Baker. This is an order."

"I demand to call my embassy." Surely my colleagues there would get me out of this trouble. Surely the people who had ordered my arrest knew how bad it would look to detain a prominent American who had done nothing more than criticize the Kingdom's policies. They had to realize the trouble they were bringing on themselves. This was insanity. They'd never survive the news cycle.

I recognized the flaw in my thinking even before the soldier stepped forward and slapped me again, on the same cheek: I had already inoculated the Kingdom from whatever complaint I would manage to lodge with the embassy. I fell to my knees, trying to sort my double vision. Just as I was regaining composure, they put a dark sack on my head and tightened the opening around my neck with a pullstring. The soldiers grabbed me by the elbows and lifted me to my feet.

"Wait," I yelled from beneath the sack. "Can I at least get dressed? Please."

"Let's go," the man said to the soldiers in Arabic. "Walk him out quickly."

I let them drag me out of the room, but I started walking of my own accord after they burrowed their thumbs into my armpits with such force that pain traveled up my neck and down to my fingers. The hallway was quiet. I was praying for other people to appear, a drunken group of frat boys, a couple on their way to a hookup, a tourist dad in socks and Tevas, anybody. It remained quiet until they shoved me into what I figured was a service elevator. (No carpeting, slow, rickety.) They directed me through some hallways and what seemed to be a kitchen and then we were outside, in a spot without foot traffic. They led me to a vehicle—an SUV, I assumed—and pushed me into the middle of the back seat, a soldier on either side. The man in the suit sat in the front passenger seat.

I was beginning to suffocate, my face deathly hot beneath the hood. The soldiers took note of my wheezing.

"I think he's running out of air," one of them said.

A pause. A shuffle. The man in front had turned around to look at me. Another pause. "Let him sweat a little longer," he said.

I don't think they knew I could understand them. I wanted them to keep talking, but they returned to silence. The left side of my face throbbed from the slaps I'd received; my head felt mushy and swollen. Every breath increased the heat, life expediting death, the Kingdom's sweltering atmosphere condensed into a tiny enclosure. "What if Lara could see me now?" I wondered. She'd call me an idiot, upbraid me for being egotistical and irresponsible. "You have a child, Fred." I could hear her saying it with perfect clarity.

And I wanted to tell her that I was suffocating in the backseat of a government vehicle in a strange country precisely because I have a child. Lara would ask what the fuck that was supposed to mean and I'd have no answer, only an incongruous plea that I once had parents and remember how wonderful it felt to be proud of them, how we never truly escape the potency of innocence even at our most cynical. She would be furious, of course, tell me to stop with the intellectual babbling and focus on the real world. I still would have no answer. It's not that Lara couldn't understand. We had a tacit agreement that we'd navigate the world as it actually exists. She would see my descent into emotion as a betrayal.

And Nancy? I found it too painful to consider the effect of my behavior on her. All I know is that I was determined to leave her an inheritance. I was in no position to second-guess my decisions while strangers carted me into the unknown.

"Sir," one of the soldiers said, "I think he's sick. He's starting to go limp."

A pause. "Take it off."

When they loosened the rope around my neck and pulled off the hood, it felt as if I had plunged my head into a freezing river. I gasped and contorted. The soldiers grabbed my forearms. "Settle down or it goes back on," said the man in the suit.

We were on the outskirts of the city. The neighborhoods weren't well lit. Small apartment buildings surrounded single blocks of commerce: mobile phone stores, spice shops, food stands. The few people I saw on the streets appeared to be foreign. My captors knew it didn't matter if I could see. I wasn't going anywhere without them. Eventually we passed all civilization and pulled up to a gate patrolled by clones of the men next to me. Behind it sat a massive concrete building without identifying markers. We passed through a few security checkpoints and then down two flights of stairs.

The man in the suit whispered to a couple of guards in a drab anteroom. One of them unlocked a steel door and we passed through into a narrow hallway about twenty yards deep with symmetric doors on either side. The place felt empty. It was quiet but for our footsteps. We stopped in front of a door. One of the guards walked over and unlocked it.

They pushed me into a dark room and slammed the door behind me. No instructions, no suggestions. I sat on the floor and numbed my mind. After my eyes adjusted, I got a sense of my new environment. The room was about eight feet wide by twelve feet deep. A plastic bucket sat in one corner, a rolled-up bamboo mat in the other. No pillow. No sink. No toilet. I looked at the bucket. It was large enough to hold plenty of fluid, but I almost wretched just thinking about the smell. Maybe they were holding me here only for a short period. If they had in mind a long confinement, then a more proper cell, in a proper prison, would be more logical.

I learned quickly to do away with logic.

It was late and the day had been intense, but I couldn't sleep. Physical discomfort didn't help, but it was anxiety that kept me awake. I laid stomach-up on the bamboo mat with my hands clasped behind my head. The cell was cold, with stagnant air and no insulation. I had to piss, but wasn't ready to start filling the bucket. I also worried I'd get into trouble for using it. Mostly I tried to keep my mind numb by repelling ominous or wistful thoughts. I was suspended in a state of unreality and knew that any serious recognition of the surroundings would send me into panic.

I slept eventually and woke up to the same darkness. I had no way of knowing the time. My hip and shoulder were sore and I could barely turn my head, but felt surprisingly well-rested. I sat against the wall and resumed my vacant contemplation. Sometime later—five minutes? two hours?—I heard a key jiggling in the door. Two soldiers walked on. One of them smacked my arm and motioned for me to follow him. They led me upstairs to an interrogation room. It looked like something from a cop show: table bolted to the floor, single lightbulb hanging from a string, metal chairs, two-way mirror. I was unshackled but didn't dare walk around. Fear kept me from appreciating the irony.

Nancy

"YEAH, SO, I'M not sure what to do," I said to Elena, who was laying sideways on the edge of her bed.

"You have to go."

"It'll be really fucking weird," I said, leaning forward in my beanbag to hand her the blunt.

She inhaled heavily and held the smoke for three or four seconds before coughing it out in bursts of sallow vapor. "Nan," she wheezed, "you can ask him a question. That would be phenomenal."

"They're not gonna let people just ask him anything."

"Go up to him afterward, pretend you want to shake his hand or whatever. Then tell him to fuck off."

"Just what we need. Another person in my family getting into trouble for messing with these people."

Over the years, I had told Elena about my unusual family history and by the time we were sophomores at UVA she knew our story as intimately as I was capable of telling it.

She took another toke, less dramatically this time, and handed the blunt to me. "Look, Nan, you have to do something, right? The guy is repping the country that killed your father. Like, what the fuck? You can't let him roll through here without saying anything."

I tried to puff rings, my head dangling off the edge of the beanbag. "We don't know that they killed him. We don't even know he's dead. Technically."

"Jesus, Nan." She was about to rant, but thought better of it. Elena had grown into that type of friend: fiery, undeterred, but sensitive enough to accommodate my need for denial. Others didn't enjoy such grace. "Okay, look, just go to the lecture and see what happens. I'll go with you, don't worry. I swear you won't get into trouble."

And so she convinced me to attend the Ambassador's lecture. Maybe the plan I would carry out a year later began with some childhood event I don't remember. Maybe it began when Dad disappeared. Maybe it began when we left Cleveland Park. Maybe it began in one of the random days when Dad didn't return. But I'm pretty sure the beginning, the real beginning, was when I laid eyes on the Ambassador.

I suppose Elena hoped that going to the lecture would fire me up. From the moment we got to Charlottesville, she kept busy with organizing. Things were quiet when we arrived, but the street battle of the prior year still affected the town and campus. Elena immediately began preparing for the sequel. She considered any shifty white person a potential Nazi. I didn't interfere with her judgments. There were lots of shifty white people at UVA. Elena had always been a good social guide. "Believe me, they hate you, too," she had explained, both for my own background and my choice of friends.

She licked her finger and tapped it against the lit end of the blunt until it fizzled out. "Let's go," she said, swinging her legs onto the floor and extending her hand to me. I grumbled as I stood, the THC making my eyes feel buggy. We were off to a gathering of international students, one of the many clubs with which Elena was involved. I was pretty sure the gathering included a lecture. By that point, I was pleased with my social life at college, but it didn't correspond to Elena's mixture of purpose and extroversion. I liked fugitive spaces off campus where vice was customary. I fucked lots of women and a few guys, tried all kinds of drugs, but to Elena hedonism wasn't useful or sustainable. It wasn't my grades she worried over. I was a model student. I could keep pleasures separate from work. She worried over the condition of my soul, instead.

In late-night chats, cocooned in the intimacy of a poorly-lit dorm room, she explained that I was repressed, that my crazy background didn't match my political apathy. I told her that repression wasn't my thing.

My self-indulgent appetite was proof of adjustment. I accused her of puritanism, but she sucked in her lips and shook her head somberly. No, Nan, just no. Hadn't she too indulged the freedoms of college? Wasn't her behavior enough to mortify her parents and create a transatlantic scandal? For Elena, physical gratification and a fertile civic life were indivisible. She wasn't judging my promiscuity or my experimentation, or even my apathy. She was simply certain that I was allowing something important, something chronic to my quintessence, to metastasize in my subconscious.

She was talking about Dad, of course, but also the family histories inside of me that served as dead space because they lacked substance, had no words to give them shape. I thought often of my grandparents' visit and how wonderful it felt to hear them talk about mom's childhood and their experiences of the world, like they were painting landscapes inside my body. They were amused by my questions because they saw their answers as useless information, but for me it was a life I didn't know I had lived before memory limited me to my current incarnation, the empty afterlife of an unknown existence. I relied on strangers to make me knowable. Through bits of trivia and banality I managed to become whole. I needed superficial contact to maintain the condition.

Whenever I acquired new information, I passed it along to Elena, who then read it back to me with a clairvoyant's aplomb. I tried to reciprocate, but Elena didn't exist in shadows. She knew both of her parents and a transcontinental extended family numbering in the thousands. Her father was a sweetheart and antagonist, her mother a cheerleader and sage. Even the problems she had with her parents arose from familiarity. She'd been to Eritrea many times, spoke two of its languages, could negotiate its customs and peculiarities. And she fully understood her place in the United States. She wouldn't have been as passionate and determined otherwise. Elena had no business with ambivalence.

Maybe that's why she found me to be an interesting project. I guess I was always a curiosity to Elena. She needed my ambiguity as a counterpoint to her fortitude. We loved each other through both empathy and convenience. I never worried about Elena abandoning me for superficial reasons. Now, I'm forced to confront the impossible. If I tell her what I did, then she'll no longer want to be friends (at a minimum; she could do much worse than ignore me). If I don't tell her, then I'm setting an unprecedented limit on our friendship.

We left our room that evening with no disquiet. Elena linked her arm into mine and allowed me to set the pace. We arrived at the cultural center, a repurposed Victorian on the edge of campus. Inside, students and professors mingled in an open space with a view to the backyard lined with magnolia and holly. Elena introduced me to various friends, Americans and internationals of varying ages. The speaker, a professor of Global Studies, stood next to the lectern and waited for quiet. A younger man—a grad student?—joined him and began clearing his throat with exaggerated persistence. Finally, he dropped the act and rapped the lectern. When we took our seats, the young guy gave an introduction about both the professor and the evening's topic, economic development on the Horn of Africa. His introduction was so thorough I didn't see any point in the main speaker.

Elena listened closely and took notes. If she thought the professor got something wrong, she'd ask him about it afterward, credentials be damned. (In that moment Elena possessed the greatest credential on campus: an authentic identity in relation to the topic.) I daydreamed about new hairstyles (maybe letting my curls grow), what kind of food would be served at the reception, my creative writing assignment, the girl I recently met on Grindr. Suddenly I heard the speaker mention the Kingdom. Snapping back to attention, I glanced at Elena. She raised her eyebrows as if to say, "See, aren't you glad we came?"

The speaker explained that the Kingdom was a terrific proponent of development in East Africa. It was investing heavily in the region, which had potential to transform once-stagnant nations into real players in the global economy, a model for an impoverished continent. He cited figures from the Institute where Dad used to work. "He's on their payroll," Elena whispered.

Immediately after the speaker stopped talking, Elena raised her hand. The grad student, who had hopped up to moderate, ignored her and called on a man with gray streaks in his hair, obviously a professor, followed by

other audience members the moderator sought to please. Elena kept her
hand in the air and eventually the moderator pointed at her.

"Yes, I have a few questions, actually," she said. "I'm curious about the
nature of investment from the Gulf into East Africa. Isn't it just another
way to extract resources and enrich local elites? How has this investment
actually helped the people? Also, I'd like to hear more about your research.
Who funds it, for example?"

"Well, I've received numerous grants for my research," the speaker
said, a hint of defensiveness in his tone, "as is normal for—"

"Where are the grants from?" Elena interrupted.

"Various sources, most from the university itself. As to your other
questions, the nations of the Gulf that are investing in East Africa are
certainly motivated by self-interest, as are all state actors, but in many
cases throughout history we've seen mutual benefit in these arrangements.
The upshot for the people will be job creation and therefore an emerging
middle class, which, as you surely know, is virtually absent in the deeply-
stratified economies of the Horn."

Elena began to respond, but the moderator said, "Sorry, we have
other questions to get to." She waited for the end with crossed arms and
a half-smile.

Afterward, most of the audience stayed for refreshments. I stood in a
group with Elena and another girl from our dorm. She was telling Elena
about a killer consignment shop while I munched on carrot sticks and
hummus. I could see the speaker across the room. He nodded his head
as somebody I tabbed as a townie talked intently, waving both hands in
concert. The speaker peeked in our direction and escaped with a pat of
the townie's shoulder. He approached our group and then gently touched
Elena's arm. She stiffened and moved over to let him into our circle.

"Those were very provocative questions, young lady," he said.

"I'm sorry but—"

"Please don't apologize," he said, unaware that Elena wasn't
apologizing. "It's good to see our students engaging with international
affairs. And shall I presume that you are from the continent?"

"Eritrea."

"We're practically neighbors. I'm from Kenya."

"You never really had an opportunity to answer my questions," she said.

The speaker still hadn't acknowledged me and our other friend. He was fixated on Elena. It didn't seem like he was hitting on her, exactly, but he wasn't making harmless chitchat, either. There was something aggressive about his politeness. He was surprised that she had expressed no interest in his background, as is customary when somebody volunteers biographical information. Instead of directly answering her question, he boasted about his many associates and collaborators, one of which was the Institute.

"Nan, Nancy's dad used to be director there."

"Is that so?" His eyes widened and he smiled at me. "And what is your father's name?"

When I told him, the smile went away. He stuttered something about the unfortunate situation and then excused himself to refill his wine. He never returned.

"What's his problem?" our friend said.

"I think Elena scared him," I said. She didn't correct me, but we both knew the real source of his fear. Elena was probably offended, but my heart was beating in rhythms of intense pleasure.

We stopped for tea on the way home. Elena was busy tweeting about the lecture. I checked her feed on my phone and showed it to our friend, who stomped her feet and giggled.

"Damn, girl, you have like ten thousand followers."

"Elena is a Twitter star," I said.

"Just wait until he logs on," Elena said. "I tagged his ass."

"In more ways than one."

Elena furiously typed replies to her mentions. She knew how to leverage social media for validation. Anyone dumb enough to disagree would be castigated. Her followers liked her brand of audacity and emulated it on her behalf. Being harshly critical didn't alienate people. It accounted for her popularity.

"What if you end up in one of his classes?" our friend said.

"Don't worry about that," Elena laughed. "I just guaranteed myself an easy A."

Once back in our room, Elena and I got lost in the internet. The encounter with the speaker fresh in my mind, I googled him and didn't find anything noteworthy. He seemed like a typical professor: all his accomplishments, no matter how obscure or miniscule, were draped in self-importance. He didn't appear to be visibly liberal or conservative, but one of those analysts above the fray of partisanship. Just a man after truth, wherever it leads him. The fact that it led him to the Institute made me distrustful of his neutrality. I started questioning the notion altogether.

Realizing that I'd find nothing interesting about the professor, I searched Dad, something I did occasionally to see if there was any new information. Nothing useful came up, just a spate of dull articles about the ten-year anniversary of his disappearance. Otherwise the search produced thousands of decade-old results. Despite the outrage at the time— the newspaper columns, the vigils, the video clips, the congressional investigations—the story died quickly, seemingly all at once, right around the time Mom started seriously entertaining the possibility that he was dead. By now, Dad had been virtually forgotten. Consumers of the story got on with their lives. Normalcy reasserted itself for everyone but us. Dad's most vocal champions went back to hobnobbing with the same dignitaries they swore to renounce. It made me terribly sad, but I would come to see the forgetfulness as an advantage.

"What are you doing?" Elena said, slamming shut her laptop.

"Nothing. Just the same boring shit." I put my computer aside and got ready for bed.

The next week, we trundled across campus to witness the Ambassador's speech. The auditorium held around five or six hundred and it was pretty crowded, even without counting the poly-sci students there for extra credit. Elena tried to drag me to the front, but I refused. We settled on aisle seats two-thirds of the way to the rear exit. As we watched the AV guy test the microphone, I wondered who would voluntarily turn up to this kind of event. What would we get out of the man beyond clichés already available on his Twitter feed? He wasn't going to tell us any trade secrets or describe his government's real policies. He would say what he says every other time he speaks. I felt like I was the only person with a legitimate reason to be there.

After people stopped filing in, the provost took to the stage and yammered about the great opportunities available at UVA. Then a professor with an ill-fitting suit gushingly introduced the Ambassador. When invited to the microphone, the Ambassador sipped from a bottle of Voss, set it on the edge of the lectern, and began talking. I have to admit, it wasn't what I expected. He recited platitudes about democracy and innovation, but the delivery was powerful. Or maybe it was just the Ambassador himself, young, charismatic, well-spoken. He could have dispelled hundreds of stereotypes without saying a word. The professor had described the Ambassador as one of the most powerful men in Washington. And I understood that it was true even in the absence of politics. It was all there on the stage.

So I began listening. There was a terrible beauty in his platitudes. Fulfill your visions, he told the audience. Embrace the promise of technology. Aspire to transform the world. Start with your own mind. What, in the end, is democracy but self-realization? The Ambassador was saying everything my father would have taught me.

"Ugh, this guy is so full of shit," Elena said, unlocking her phone so she could announce that opinion on Twitter.

I was fascinated, though. He didn't speak much about the Kingdom's foreign or domestic affairs, but what he did say was predictable: it's a great ally of the United States, which is a great ally in return. The Kingdom was proud to be on the right side of the global struggle between barbarity and civilization. With terrorism threatening both countries, it's crucial to develop the best defense systems and preemptive capabilities. It's not just a matter of strategy and preparation, but of values. And who better to model those values than our great nations? The United States of America built the world's greatest democracy from sweat and toil, in the austerity of a harsh, unforgiving land. The Kingdom went from mud huts to skyscrapers, tribalism to modernity, in just a few generations. And we, the students of this fine university, could each make a similar evolution. All it takes is a strong work ethic applied to a creative vision.

And I knew then, knew with an alien certainty, that I would follow the Ambassador's recommendation. I needed to remake the world, form it into a place that could make sense for people deprived of kinship and inclusion, into a place that might even save me from lifelong deprivation.

As the crowd applauded, Elena told me I should say something. I shook my head. We didn't get a chance, anyway. The person who had given the introduction asked a question and then whisked the Ambassador backstage. Elena suggested sticking around afterward to see if we could meet him. "Come on, Elena, no way we even get near him." She agreed, but her lips were puffed out and she toyed with her hair. I could tell she thought I was chickening out.

"Let's go," I said, touching her forearm.

"What's the hurry?" Elena kept scanning the room, hoping for the Ambassador to reappear. He was probably already in the back of a black Suburban on its way to Washington.

"I need to get out of here. I have lots to think about." Even though Elena figured I was trying to forget the evening, it had already colonized my perception of the world. I didn't need to stick around. I'd be seeing the Ambassador later.

"We can talk about it if you like," Elena said, her voice gentle.

I loved Elena with a painful devotion in this kind of moment. I wanted to hug her, escape into the idyll of her lavender perfume, a beautiful environment for somebody ten years deprived of filial affection. We would talk, as we always did, but this time I wouldn't need Elena to ease my deprivation. I needed to protect her from my sudden lack of ambivalence.

Back at the room, Elena kept giving me looks as if to say "go on, get started," but I had nothing to talk about. Something had changed in my view of the world and suddenly I was inspired to drastic action.

Elena couldn't hold back any longer. "What a fucking tool, huh?"

"Totally."

"I mean, I almost died when he started talking about making the desert bloom and all that shit."

"Right?"

"Look, Nan, it's okay if you don't want to talk. Whatever. But you're not the only one affected by that guy. Remember, his country is fucking with mine."

I took a long look at Elena. She was right, of course. I didn't have exclusive ownership of the pain the Ambassador had so eloquently concealed. I pressed my forehead against her shoulder. "I love you, Elena. I just want to say that."

"Um, okay." A pause, a moment of tension, and then she rested her cheek on the top of my head. "I love you, too, Nan."

We decided to visit our parents a few days later. Although we lived less than two hours from home, we rarely made the trip. Weekends were important to the rhythm of life at college. Elena spoke with her mom every day, but I only checked in once or twice a week (Mom never did the checking in). We didn't have anything significant to discuss and Mom was never into chitchat. She was different this visit, though, stony and emotional at the same time. Her demeanor worried me. At first I thought she was upset because I ate with Elena's family before walking home, but she muted the television my first night there and started making small talk.

After a few minutes of her mindless observations, I lost my temper. "What the hell, Mom? Can I go back to my show?" I braced for her temper in return, but she just sighed and handed me the remote. I put it on the coffee table and asked what's wrong. If I couldn't bring us life through fighting, then I'd try to do it with calm.

"Nothing's wrong. I don't get to see you anymore. I thought it would be nice to talk."

"Okay."

"But I don't want to interrupt your important appointment."

I could handle this more recognizable version of Mom. "Some diplomat that Dad knew gave a speech on campus last week."

"I saw that. I wondered if you'd go."

"You knew? And you didn't say anything?"

"What was I supposed to say? 'Hey, this guy from the Kingdom will be nearby. Be sure to bring him roses. And maybe bake him a cake while you're at it.'"

"Don't be like that, Mom."

She shrugged and stared at the muted television. I looked at her closely for the first time in forever. Loose skin was beginning to gather below her jawline. She had a network of new wrinkles on her forehead. "I wanted to protect you from people like that," she said. Her accent had somehow grown thicker with time. "I never wanted you to inherit my baggage. Or your father's."

"I understand that. But you also deprived me of a culture."

She considered the accusation. "I tried my best."

"I'm not saying you didn't try."

"You don't know how good you have it, Nancy, how much bullshit I spared you from. You have no idea."

"Come on, that's so ridiculous. You have no idea what it's like to be Brown in this country."

She laughed. "What color am I? What country do I live in? And I have a foreign voice and worked in jobs where half the people thought I'm a terrorist."

"It's different."

"Take your friend. Elena."

"Mom, don't even start. You've always hated her for no reason. Or maybe there is a reason."

She caught my implication. "You're wrong. Don't insult me. If you want the truth, I was worried that you'd learn from her family everything I tried to protect you from."

"Like what? Support? Encouragement? Basic fucking warmth?"

"Elena can't pick her nose without a first cousin somewhere in the world gossiping about it. Or a fifth cousin. Or a twenty-fifth cousin. That's not support. Believe me. You're free to act without judgment. It's the best thing about this *khara* country."

"Only an immigrant would say something so ridiculous."

"You have no idea how different your life would be back home, or in this country with a big extended family. You're a lesbian, right?"

"I mean, it's kind of a complicated identity."

"You like girls, that's what I mean. This 'identity' shit doesn't matter in the real world. Well, you can't even imagine how much gossiping you'd have to hear. Nobody would ever shut up about it. And all those nice gatherings that seem so fun for Elena would be a nightmare for you. Elena likes that stuff because she fits in. But everything she does is being judged.

Trust me on this. Wait until she brings home a boy who's not Eritrean or Christian or rich. Just wait."

"I still don't think it was your choice to make. It's my life."

"Go do what you want. Who's stopping you?"

"That's not the point," I said. "You're just repeating a bunch of Orientalist shit."

"You know the man who wrote that book hated your father."

"What? Why?"

"That's what I'm trying to tell you, Nancy. All this stuff you think you missed out on is horrible. Everybody in our community hates everybody else in our community."

I guess Mom was fed up with the conversation, too, because suddenly the topic of Dad's disappearance didn't seem so awful.

"Anyway, so you went to the speech, I take it?"

"Yeah."

"And?"

"It was ... weird."

"He's a son of a bitch."

"That's what I gathered."

"He threatened your father once."

"He did? How?"

"I don't remember the details. He wanted Fred fired over a disagreement. I'm certain he was involved in whatever happened later."

"Jesus."

"If he wasn't involved, then he knows what happened. But I'll bet he was involved."

"Why?"

"I don't know. He's just that type. Your father never trusted him. Or his father, who was the ambassador back then."

"Do you know something, Mom?"

She looked more tired than sad. Years of stress accumulated in her expression. Finally she said, "Not really. Nobody ever got concrete information. I can only guess."

"What's your guess?"

"Honey, I want you to know that I tried. Do you understand that? Do you believe me?"

"I know, Mom. But he was my father and I have a right to know."

"He was there for some gala or conference, whatever. I think they kidnapped him and killed him. Who exactly I don't know. But I think people in both governments knew about it. A lot of politician friends talked about finding him and getting justice, but nobody really did anything about it. Just a lot of big-talk in front of the cameras. After a while it was very hush-hush."

"I know all that."

"Then you know about as much as I know."

"Why did dad go there? Didn't he know he was in danger?"

"Yes. He was stubborn about it. I told him to stay home, find a new job. He could have done it easily. He knew everyone in town. But he was hell-bent on going, like he was possessed. I told him he was being self-destructive. He wouldn't listen to me. I'm still upset about it."

I didn't tell Mom, couldn't tell her, but Dad's attitude made sense to me. I was terrified by the realization, but there was no mistaking the sympathy I felt for his foolishness. "I don't get it," I said. "What was he so hell-bent about?"

"I wish he were here to answer that question, because I don't know what in God's name he was thinking."

"Can you try? I really want to know."

"Maybe he was on some male ego trip, maybe he thought he could charm his way out of trouble. The only specific thing he ever said is that he wanted to do right by his namesake. 'Goddammit, Fred,' I told him, 'You don't even use the man's name. You never met him. What is this shit?' I really don't know what was in his brain. I told him of course his grandfather would be proud of him, a successful, important professional in the capital of America. He couldn't be convinced, though. Well, I hope his grandfather is proud of him for getting killed and leaving a wife and child behind."

I could understand Mom's bitterness, a condition we shared, but I also knew exactly what was in Dad's brain. I had inherited the same impulse to destruction. I felt it when seeing the Ambassador, and felt it earlier in life without recognizing its nature, and now I could attach words to the sensibility. I had loved writing since I was a kid, but never had I fully understood how dangerous it can be to articulate a feeling.

"Anyway, khalas," Mom said, interrupting my epiphany, "I'm going to bed."

I never told Mom, but the Ambassador's speech wasn't my first run-in with Dad's past at UVA. In a freshman course on modern Middle Eastern history, the professor used Dad as an example of the Kingdom's complicated policies. (That's the word he used: "complicated.") Another student asked the professor to explain what he was talking about. "Ah, I'd forgotten that this all happened before your time," the professor chuckled before giving a sort-of-accurate summary of Dad's disappearance. "A very unfortunate situation," the professor concluded. Another student raised his hand and said the guy (meaning my father) sounded like an idiot. "I mean, who goes to a dictatorship and criticizes the leader?"

"I agree it wasn't a very wise move," the professor said.

I sat in silent shock. Elena wasn't in this class with me—I didn't know anyone. The sense of aloneness was terrifying. It felt as if my genes had vaporized into atomic particles. The words on the dry-erase board blurred into scribbles. The desktop suddenly felt unstable. The conversation began to sound like an industrial fan. I shut my eyes and gathered my senses. I wanted to say something, but for all I knew the discussion had finished already. When I snapped back to attention, I heard the professor parsing the meaning of "dictatorship" in making a case that it might not technically apply to the Kingdom. "It's more nuanced than you think," he said. Nobody argued with him. Dad had become an abstract criterion, a bit of strange trivia, in a random professor's quest to sound reasonable. I couldn't square my father's actual life with this pitiful destiny.

To the extent that anyone even remembered him, his existence had become raw material for self-righteous contemplation. I went from afraid to infuriated. Who was this man to judge my father? He had no idea what motivated my father, what my father was thinking when he walked onto that plane. I didn't even know, not really, and certainly not well enough to discuss in a classroom. I hated that his blood, my genealogy, belonged to other people.

Before Elena and I returned to Charlottesville, I squeezed Mom for more information. (It could be years before she felt like talking about family again.) I asked what she had meant about Dad's namesake.

"He was named for his grandfather. You know that."

"Right, but why was Dad so worried about not living up to him or whatever?"

"You know the story."

"No I don't."

"Nobody ever told you?"

"What do you mean 'nobody'? Who the hell else would I have heard it from?"

"I assumed your father told you."

I rubbed my temples with my index and middle fingers. "I. Was. A. Child. Even if he told me, I obviously forgot."

"No need for the theatrics. There's no story really. Like basically every other firstborn boy, he was named for his grandfather. The original Farid was a war hero who was captured and executed. He possibly escaped. And that's it."

"That's it? That's it? That's a tremendous story, Mom! Like, war hero how? Executed? Good Lord."

"You can google him. Farid Baqir. B-A-Q-I-R."

"I did. Nothing came up."

"There's probably some information about him in Arabic. He's pretty well-known back home."

I rubbed my temples again. "Can you guess what the problem with this suggestion is?"

"You're in college. Take a class."

And so I hopped into Elena's Kia with an equal sense of clarity and confusion. She tore through the neighborhood. "Ready to get back, huh?" I said.

"You don't even know. What a shitshow." She went on to describe bounties of chaos. I could practically see Mom's knowing expression hovering in the overcast sky above us. Elena filled the drive home with stories of familial drama, which suited me fine. I wouldn't have been able to explain the weird drama I had encountered. Recent events felt like a rebirth, but not exactly, because in reality I was merely accessing a birthright my parents carefully obscured. It was inside of me from the beginning, though. Mom always knew the right stimuli would awaken an impulse that no policy, no form of repression, had been able to destroy.

By the time Elena asked how I was doing, I could give her an honest answer: things were astonishingly tranquil. I didn't tell her that as she was talking, I had decided to kill the Ambassador.

At that point, I had no idea how to do it. Nor was I prepared to spend my life in prison. I'm still not. That kind of confinement would defeat the purpose of my deed. I'm not trying to replace metaphor with brick and mortar. No. My story was a small arc in an unfinished revolution. Three generations of men cut down early. I was determined to preserve the lineage and revitalize our connection.

Being a model student from a middle-class suburb seemed unconducive to assassination, but I went about my new project the same way I completed my old ones. I studied. I conducted research. I listened to expert testimonies. I mobilized technology. I anticipated problems. I employed deductive reasoning. I did everything a good education taught me.

By the time we arrived in Charlottesville, the chain restaurants and shopping centers along Route 29 a facsimile of what we had left behind in Northern Virginia, I felt comfortable with my decision. Elena's reflections on our shitty world provided extra substance. Since I was a kid, she had been the soundtrack to my simmering ferocity. She liked to chide me for not listening, for my timidity in confronting the horrors of this world, but I had internalized her vigor, her compassion, her feral sensibility. She was the sister I never had, the father I had lost.

I had recovered something important during the Ambassador's lecture. The trip home eviscerated my clumsy emotional life. I was no longer the protagonist in a tedious saga of denial. I now could narrate my own desires. My entire life I moved in concert with strangers, but I was ready to find a world that could accommodate the dismal and the lonely.

See, Dad didn't tell Mom why he visited the Kingdom—not directly, anyway, and she was too upset to analyze his intimations. But he told me. Ten years later, I recovered the conversation—right around the time that the Ambassador was finishing his speech. We had gone to the Secret Place the weekend before his trip to the Kingdom. It didn't feel like just another trip to the woods. At first, Dad was distant and erratic. We crunched through the undergrowth and searched for migratory birds and tried to name the flora endemic to life before the city. It was a clear day and the avenues outside the park were quiet. No special events or demonstrations, just a mass of apparatchiks enjoying rare leisure on a Saturday morning.

At our spot, Dad wound his fingers into mine. I leaned against him and listened to the forest. A barrage of tapping, solid and symmetrical, erupted through the trees above us.

"Woodpecker," Dad said.

"I can't see it."

"He's out there somewhere."

"I want to see an owl or an otter."

"The otters are usually closer to the bay. The owls can be dangerous. They attack people sometimes."

"No way."

"I swear. They grab people's heads with their claws and then fly away. I heard about a guy who lost his toupee to an owl. Do you know what a toupee is?"

"Yeah, a wig." He didn't respond, but I wanted to keep talking. "Chase says there are poisonous snakes in the woods."

"Who's Chase?"

"A boy in my class."

"I doubt it, but there could be Copperheads live in this region."

"Those are poisonous snakes?"

"Yes, but I wouldn't worry about them. There's a cure for their poison. And anyway poison isn't all bad. It can make people sick, but it also cures things."

"It does?"

"Sure. Poison is an important part of our health."

"I think I get it. Like it's bad for you, but you can use it to kill other harmful stuff?"

He squeezed my fingers with his. "You're a really smart girl, Nancy. I'm so proud of you.

I looked up and saw that his neck had tightened and he was squinting at nothing in particular.

"You know I'm traveling this week, right?"

"Yeah." I thought nothing of it. He traveled all the time.

"I'll miss you."

"I'll miss you too, Daddy."

"Ready to get back home?"

"I guess. It's nice here, though."

His muscles relaxed and he smiled. "That's for sure."

"The people in my class say coming here is dangerous. They say that people get murdered and stuff and that the CIA hides bodies here."

"Anything can be dangerous. In fact, some of the most worthwhile things are dangerous. Do you understand what I mean?"

"Not really."

"Let me give you an example. Did I ever tell you about my grandfather?"

"No." Dad never talked about his parents or grandparents.

"Well, I'm named after my grandfather."

"He was called Fred?"

"I'm gonna tell you a little secret: my real name is Farid."

"What?"

"Yes, Farid. It means unique."

"There's nothing else like it."

"Exactly! Everyone calls me Fred because it's easier to say. Been that way since I was a kid. Anyway, Farid my grandfather was a hero. He defended his village against a bunch of invaders and they caught him and, well, it was very dangerous for him, but he did it, anyway."

"Why?"

"Because sometimes you have to choose between living and simply being alive. Do you see what I'm saying?"

"I think so," I lied.

He kissed my head. "Just remember that. It'll make sense soon, I promise."

"Are you being alive or are you living?"

"For most of my life I was simply alive, but I've decided to start living. And that means I may have to do some things that are dangerous. But whatever happens to your old man, I want you to always remember how much I love you."

I could hear him, but didn't know what he was saying. I continued leaning against him, scared and comfortable at the same time.

"Are you learning about democracy in social studies?"

"Yes."

"And what are they teaching you about it?"

"That we vote and stuff. We're free because we can say what we want and choose our leaders."

"Let me try to explain something: there's no democracy. Not here or anywhere else. People who make decisions about the world do things to help themselves, not everyone else, you see. To me, being free means honoring my grandfather's legacy. And I hope one day that you'll honor mine."

"I don't understand, Daddy."

"I know you don't, my love. I'm sorry, don't worry about it. Your daddy's just talking nonsense."

I heard something that sounded like a hoot in the near distance. "Did you hear that, Daddy?" I whispered. "I think it's an owl."

He raised his head and listened. "I don't think so. But let's walk along the creek for a bit and see if we can spot an otter."

It was a huge treat to get this extra time with Dad. We hiked along the water for about half a mile, stopping periodically near standing pools and mudbanks to check for amphibians and mammals. I was content with the biological life already in my possession, taking in Dad's thick wavy hair and the tired skin beneath his eyes. He looked like a movie star to me, a superhero in sweats and sneakers smelling of day-old cologne and damp foliage.

Elena's voice interrupted my recollections. "What are you thinking about?"

We were on campus now. I could see the rotunda from my window, well-lit and barely-regal, less impressive in person than it looks on television. Our old high school had a smaller replica in its front entrance. We hadn't gone that far, Elena and I. Linear time was outpacing our spiritual development. She offered to drop me near the dorm before heading to the sophomore lot, but I wanted to stay with her. I needed the sense of chaos she offered, and the confidence that came of her determination to change the world.

As Elena cruised for a space, I recalled the Ambassador alone on that stage from the darkness of the seating area, a spotlight shining from above making him appear both overcooked and angelic. A gorgeous man, I conceded—tall and fit and easygoing. Still young and possessing the charm of a game-show host. A perfect American accent with the occasional British cadence. Somewhere between white and Black without being swarthy and therefore eminently relatable to the urbane and educated. Even his thin-cut suit flouted the stodginess common to men of his class. He was talking about the importance of personal transformation in an unpredictable world, trying to convince us that we can control our destiny with careful attention to trends and opportunities. Above all, he kept saying (with dazzling changes of terminology), we should push for a modern world catered to our satisfaction. He was a prophet, suave and stately, dispensing the most logical advice I'd heard in ages. All I could think about was how nice it would feel to blast a hole right in the middle of his beautiful face.

Fred

AFTER WHAT SEEMED like hours—and very well could have been, if only in my addled mind—a man entered the room, stopped in front of me, and dropped a manila folder on the desk. He was about my age, with a commanding mustache and dark eyes surrounded by sallow gray skin. Extending a hand, he said, "Dr. Baqir. It's a pleasure to meet you," pronouncing the name with Arabic inflections.

I kept my hands to myself. He kept his hand extended. He was decked out—khaki uniform, leather boots, olive beret. His paunch and a chest full of medals completed the ensemble.

"Very well, Dr. Baqir," he said, taking his seat across the table from me. "I am Colonel Wassim. Can I get you something to drink? Coffee? Water?" I shook my head. "A cigarette, perhaps?" I was tempted, but shook my head again. "This will be a rather unpleasant experience for both of us if you decline to speak, Dr. Baqir," the Colonel said. I knew the experience was going to be unpleasant for me no matter what I did.

"I don't understand why I'm here and I'm horrified by the treatment I've received."

He grinned, revealing crooked, saffron-colored teeth. "That's a shame to hear. We pride ourselves upon excellent hospitality."

"I need to call my embassy." I knew it was a hopeless and likely insulting demand, but my brain was still conditioned by the logic of prestige.

"I'm afraid that won't be possible at the moment."

"Why not?"

"We need some information from you first. I doubt speaking with your embassy will be of much use, anyway."

"Not much use to you, I'm sure."

"Don't be so smug, Dr. Baqir. What makes you think your embassy hasn't already been notified?"

I chortled. "Do you seriously believe that detaining and abusing prominent American citizens is beneficial to you?"

"Dr. Baqir, let's stop with the runaround, shall we? Allow me to be direct: you have violated a number of my country's laws, and have done it with impunity. These violations carry significant punishment, up to and including execution." He paused to let the word sink in. "Your embassy is indeed aware of your arrest and has been presented with a comprehensive list of the allegations against you, as well as the evidence for your guilt. Your country is honorable and doesn't wish to interfere in our legal proceedings. So let's get down to business. Perhaps you can explain why you have so viciously insulted our humble kingdom."

"I demand to speak to my embassy. That's the only thing I have to say."

"Would you care for me to explain the charges against you?"

"I demand to speak to my embassy."

He stood and slowly walked around the desk, resting his butt on the edge in front of me. "You are in serious trouble, Dr. Baqir. I suggest that now isn't the time for insolence."

"I demand to speak to my embassy."

He cocked back his right arm and delivered a tremendous slap, the brunt of the force landing on my ear. I was shocked and disoriented, but another slap, this one on my cheek, jolted me back to reality. I looked at the floor, panting, the taste of blood spreading across my tongue. I spit out a gob of crimson phlegm and looked up. His face was hard, his eyes furious. Given my experience with the country he served, the immediate change of demeanor shouldn't have surprised me. Phony decorum had been an important part of my job, as well. The Colonel returned to his seat and rested his hands on the desk, having adequately conveyed the uselessness of nationality in the world he protects.

"Now let's proceed like civilized men, shall we?"

"C-civilized?" I sputtered.

"Yes, despite the many crimes of which you stand accused."

"I'm no criminal. I'm a public intellectual."

"You no longer belong to the class of the untorturable. You no longer work for the King. You are no longer American. Your degrees are meaningless. You are a criminal in our custody, nothing more."

"What crime have I committed?"

He took a slip of paper from his manila folder and scanned it. "I believe you referred to our king as a 'tinpot dictator.' You called one of his brothers a pervert. You claimed that the Kingdom has been consorting with the enemy. You accused us of abusing guest workers and trading in slavery. You refused the orders of a high-ranking officer. You resisted arrest. Each is a very serious offense, Dr. Baqir. You haven't behaved as a professional."

"And how is a professional supposed to behave?"

"I'm not here to argue, doctor. I am curious about a few things, however. Why is it you call yourself 'Baker'?" He enunciated the long A.

"That was always my name."

"But this isn't your real name."

"Originally, no, but it's the same name."

"Why did you change it?"

"I don't know. When my father came to the States, that's how they transliterated it in his paperwork. People pronounced it 'baker' and it stuck."

"You are ashamed of your heritage?"

"I was when I worked for your government. I'm not ashamed any longer."

He leaned across the desk and slapped me again, with his left hand this time. It didn't hurt, but I suppose physical pain wasn't the point.

"You are a disgrace to your father, to your country, to your religion."

I kept quiet. There was no point in answering. In a sense, the Colonel was correct. In moments of both obedience and defiance, I had rebelled. I never learned how to exist without disgrace. I spent a lifetime suppressing huge geographies of shame. These things I could never explain to the Colonel. He viewed the world through a prism that couldn't accommodate the kind of person I had become, one with blood filtering the words in his mouth, a prism I had worked hard to construct. The Colonel was integral to the structure. He enjoyed our banter, but he would proffer a beating for giving the wrong response. The brutal metaphors of academic life had become absolute.

"You have nothing to say?" he continued. I shook my head. He leaned back in his seat and removed a small stack of papers from the folder. He perused it for a few seconds and seemed satisfied. "You must sign this," he said, sliding it over.

The writing was in Arabic, which I could read only at an elementary level. I tried to make sense of the bullet points—a list of infractions, I assumed—but they were written in legalese.

"I don't really know what it says."

"But I thought you speak our language," he said in Arabic.

"Yes," I replied in Arabic, "but I never studied it."

"Shame on your father, then."

I threw the packet across the table. Its pages flapped into his lap. "Your mother's cunt," I told him, in our language.

He glared at me, licking his mustache. I braced myself for more slapping. But he walked out of the room without looking at me. I rubbed my left cheek. I could tell it was discolored and swollen. I made note of each act of abuse. So naïve was I in the moment that I still imagined some kind of recourse would be possible. It again felt like I was in the room for hours. Eventually a couple of guards led me downstairs to the same cell. It had been a long time since I ate or drank. My tongue felt like cardboard. Soon after, the cell door creaked open and somebody put a tray on the floor. In the darkness I could make out a glass of water and some kind of soup with a triangle of pita bread. I crammed the bread into the soup and ate it in one bite, slurping down the rest of the broth straight from the bowl. It was pure unholy gruel. I washed it down with the water.

Immediately I felt nauseated. I curled up on the mat and tried to sleep away the feeling. I crawled to the bucket and tried to hold steady as my intestines spat liquid. Then I flipped onto my knees and vomited, partially overshooting the bucket. This went on for hours. By the time I could rest, the stench in the cell was overwhelming—shit and vomit and sweat competing for primacy in my senses. It became a cycle, the output of my illness producing new material to make me ill. Whenever I caught a hint of air in my nose, off to the bucket I crawled. I could taste the smell in my mouth, dry and raw with acid. My difficulty breathing maybe saved my life.

I managed intervals of feverish sleep before the cell door opened. Whoever was on the other side went into a fit of coughing before gathering himself and saying, "Pick up that bucket. Let's go." When I lifted the bucket, fresh sewage spilled on either of its sides, making a sound similar to the Colonel's slaps. I felt dreck on my toes as I inched out of the cell. A soldier, mouth pressed into the interior of his elbow, pointed down the corridor. In the next room, another soldier told me to follow him down a hallway that felt like a tunnel. He opened a utility closet. "Empty it," he ordered. I bit my lips and tilted the bucket over an uncovered drain and rinsed it using a hose attached to a ceiling pipe.

Then back to the cell. The exercise had exhausted me and the cell smelled no better. I vomited within five minutes of returning. My cheek swollen, my stomach in tatters, my body depleted of fluid, I felt extremely close to death. I can't think of a night in my life nearly so miserable. And so I was in no condition for conversation with the Colonel when the soldiers next came for me. I could barely walk up the stairs to his office. My captors kicked and prodded me to no avail and finally dragged me by my upper arms. I used the rest of my strength trying to stay upright in the chair.

I had always thought of slapping as a psychological tactic. It's something you do to a man in order to humiliate him. Thus emasculated, you've defeated him no matter what happens next. But my experience with the Kingdom's security forces taught me that slapping has a practical component, for it's a terrific way to deliver pain.

The Colonel didn't even sit down before striking my cheek. After I fell off the chair, he pulled me upright by my hair and kept slapping me until I tipped over again. On it went until I passed out. I woke up on a cot, my face pulsating, still without any idea if it was day or night. When I went to feel my cheeks, I noticed that one arm was attached to an IV. They had decided to keep me alive. I fell back asleep.

This time, I didn't wake up on my own. A soldier removed the needle from my arm and led me back to my cell. The space still reeked of vomit. He slammed the door and returned a few moments later with a pitcher of water. I drank from it slowly, waiting for an eruption, but it stayed down. I took a few more sips and stretched out on the mat. If there was no chance of escape, then I preferred to die quickly. I thought about whether it was possible to leave. The Colonel didn't seem the type to fall for flattery and I wasn't willing to try. My attitude toward him was immaterial, anyhow. If I were to make it out, it would be because of strong external pressure. And I had no way of knowing what was happening in the world.

I avoided thoughts of Lara and Nancy. Instead I remembered moments of illicit pleasure. Such memories were abundant. Many came courtesy of the Kingdom: escorts during European junkets, diplomatic wives after public lectures, cocaine in elaborate palaces. It was a good life, the stuff teenage boys dream of, but it wasn't lost on me that surviving the Kingdom's brutality and partaking of the Kingdom's pleasures both required me to actively forget my family.

More than anything, I remembered Nyla, my favorite regret. I met her when she came to the Institute as a summer intern before her senior year at Georgetown. She was petite, with the sort of slinky clothing and unblemished face common to girls from comfortable Third World families. Among horny men like me, all of her actions fell into the category of charming. I quickly invented reasons for her to work closely with my office.

I don't know when Nyla became aware of my attraction. Our affair seemed to just happen. Hundreds of tiny events, meaningless on their own, put it into motion. For weeks, she rejected my ostensibly platonic invitations to tea or lunch, uninterested in the mentorship I offered to provide. In the end, the Institute's guests and affiliates sparked her interest. She saw the people I interacted with: members of Congress, TV hosts, foreign dignitaries. I guess it occurred to her after a while that college mating rituals might be fun, but they were also a career hindrance, at best irrelevant.

Or maybe I was projecting my cynicism onto her. Nothing about our union made sense. She had grown up in the Kingdom, first of all, although she wasn't a citizen. Her parents belonged to the very large community of expats plying a trade in the constellation of kingdoms surrounding the Persian Gulf. Her age was a big enough scandal, but she was also Christian and one of my subordinates. She would be disgraced and probably disowned if her family found out. I would suffer a similar fate. Only the elite are modern enough to accept a middle-aged man fucking his intern.

Funny thing, though. After a time, our tryst became a relationship. Our bond deepened beyond intercourse and we spent hours in conversation. My affection for Nyla caused more worry than our physical relationship. Sex can be written off as an aberration, but adulation is a commitment. I found myself confiding in her, things I never told Lara, or things Lara had forgotten. Nyla's advice was normally banal, but merely having the attention of somebody so young and attractive was a perfect antidote to insecurity, and always the answer to my problems. She opened up to me, as well, which only highlighted her youth and the comfort of her upbringing. I liked being absorbed in issues alien to my condition as a father and husband. Nyla was perfectly situated between daughter and wife.

My feelings could have been an expression of lust, but it seems to me that thinking about a person in moments of indescribable suffering suggests something more substantive. Even at the height of our sexual activity, I began to think of Nyla as an intellectual creature. She appeared to have done the same. It ended up subduing our desire. I didn't like the change, but accepted it as a natural occurrence. I could never separate libido from notions of success. Anyway, I knew the diminished physical activity would probably save my marriage.

My brain had changed, though. I became more liberal in my thinking, more philosophical about norms and dogmas. Why the hang-up about age difference? How can chemical appetites be squared with social etiquette? What kind of species are we to require so many constraints on pleasure? I came to realize that furtive sexual desire explains everything about human conflict. What better illuminates the fragility of respect? The limits of friendship? The conditional nature of prosperity? The mores and orthodoxies of civilization? Nyla made me happy and alienated in equal measure.

I told her so one evening as we dined on tapas on the southwest waterfront, far from my usual crowd.

"Is that a good or bad thing?" she asked.

"Both," I said. "That's the crazy thing about it. I don't know where this begins or ends."

"What begins or ends?"

I was suggesting that we either needed to ditch each other or do the unthinkable. Just by having dinner, we could adversely impact dozens of lives, and yet I secretly wanted her to consider escalating the impact. "Our friendship," I said. "I mean to say that everything about us is tenuous and all the more so the more familiar we are with each other."

She nodded. "I understand."

"And yet ... what even is life without you?"

"I can't answer that for you. But for me, life is life no matter who I go to bed with."

I knew then that she had rejected me, crushed the fantasies I so carefully presented, and had done it with perfect diplomacy. I wanted to congratulate her for being a model intern. She wasn't dumping me, though, just reminding me that my age wasn't negotiable. Her rejection stayed in my mind the duration of the summer.

The summer in turn would fill me with discontent. The Institute had an account at the Mayflower Hotel and I would book a room there and text Nyla the number. A few moments later she'd knock on the door. Sometimes we'd be together for ten minutes, sometimes past midnight. It depended on what I had arranged with Lara. Nyla slept in the room after I left. She shared a two-bedroom apartment with three roommates in Foggy Bottom, so it was a treat for her to enjoy the night in an upscale hotel five minutes from work. At the Institute we found ways to be together, in hallway exchanges, espresso breaks, and lunch dates in which other invitees abruptly cancelled. I'm sure people whispered. In office buildings, you can perceive whispers better than announcements delivered in thirty-point typeface. My suspicion was borne out when I began fielding complaints about Nyla. She was sloppy with this, she failed to do that. I can't blame them. Nyla's brand of social climbing will always foster resentment, and my way of conferring rewards has been known to destroy morale. In the end, our relationship did little damage. Illicit activity was understood to be part of our organization's mission. I was an asshole, but not a hypocrite.

Had things gone differently at the Kingdom's gala, I would have seen Nyla's family the day after my abduction. It's been a few years since our relationship ended, but we remained friends and I maintained an interest in her career. She graduated to lower management in an environmental nonprofit before nabbing a gig with the World Bank, an institution that has a way of identifying applicants with the right pedigree. We chatted on occasion, which satisfied my professional libido. She had become a colleague with important connections. When she learned of my trip to the Kingdom, she notified her parents, who insisted on hosting me for dinner. I was scheduled to meet one of her siblings in the lobby at 5:00 PM the day after my speech. When I was arrested, it bothered me that Nyla's family would think me rude. I fretted over my perceived rudeness more than anything. So often blemishes illuminate the rot.

Everything I suffered in custody felt like adequate punishment for being a horrible person. Maybe I started going insane in that dark, wretched cell, listening to the hollow thump of my skull hitting the wall behind me. Sitting alone with my insecurity presented a situation I had worked hard throughout my life to avoid. I deserved everything, but I was a victim. I was a coward, but I had acted bravely. I was imprisoned, but unconfined. The ambiguity disturbed my sense of time and place. The Institute had been replaced with a tiny cell that felt more capacious than the entire world around it.

Nyla could no longer stir my libido, but she put me in mind of a time when I was young and energetic, of robust body, of vicious ambition. Was it really these same hands that once felt her hair, her shoulders, her cheekbones, this same mouth that articulated such feral desire? Now I boasted a broken, deadened anatomy trapped inside a landscape that felt borderless and claustrophobic all at once. I tried to think of the people who occupied this strange geography before it was my turn, but they were merely protoplasm, blobby and anonymous, just as I would be to those who followed. I had finally made it home, only to die from the effort. And the goddamn tragedy of it all was that there was no other way to complete the journey.

It could have been an hour or three days when I was summoned back to the interrogation room. The Colonel again made me wait. When he arrived, he smiled and greeted me as if we were friends having tea. "How's your health?" he said in Arabic. He could see the emaciation shrinking my features and the facial bruises he delivered with his own hands. Yet I didn't detect sarcasm in his tone. He was devoted to etiquette.

"Is this a serious question?"

"Yes, of course."

"Then I'll give you a serious answer," I said, knowing that the interchange wasn't supposed to work this way. "I'm quite unhealthy right now. In fact, I feel close to death."

"That's a great shame, Dr. Baqir. I've been trying to help you with that problem."

I stifled a laugh. However much, or little, life I had left, I never wanted to be slapped again. "If you want to help, I beg of you to let me get back to my family."

"I understand. Family is the essence of life. I assure you, I understand. We can put the process into motion once you sign the paperwork, perhaps remove you from this temporary accommodation."

I tried to puzzle out why it was so important that I sign the document. Already I was imprisoned and people were looking for me, including people of influence. What difference would it make if I signed a false confession? I figured that the Kingdom wanted a confession for propaganda purposes. They would flood social media and cable TV with my admission of guilt and explain that they have a modern legal system to sort the consequences. I know. Because until a few days ago it would have been my job to spin that point as part of a vigorous defense of due process and democracy.

If I signed anything, I wouldn't see the light of day for two or three decades. Maybe earlier if my government and the Kingdom had a diplomatic contretemps. As long as they were allies, nobody of real power would consider my life valuable enough to risk the Kingdom's money. I was sure that not signing would be worse, but I was willing to accept tremendous physical pain in order to undercut the Kingdom's spin. Confessing would make all my recent decisions pointless.

"What process?" I said.

"The process of getting our misunderstanding resolved." Why wasn't the guy in politics, I wondered, then remembered that politics is exactly what he was into, with a little genetic luck helping him along.

"You still haven't told me what I'm signing."

"I allowed you to look over the paperwork."

"In a language I can't read. In a foreign country. Without a lawyer."

"That is why you must sign. You will then receive a lawyer and a right to answer to the charges."

"A lawyer?"

"Yes, of course."

"What you're asking me to sign is a confession, correct?"

"In a manner of speaking."

"If I'm confessing, why do I need a lawyer?"

"Dr. Baqir," he said, leaning the back of his head into his hands and grinning, "you have a most American attitude about these matters. Surely a man of your education understands that not every country's criminal justice system looks the same?" I assumed it was a rhetorical question, but he seemed surprised that I didn't answer. "We have a very sophisticated process," he went on, "and I'd hate for you to proceed alone. There are religious matters, for example, along with our civic code."

"Hold on. Are you saying I've violated some kind of religious law?"

"Many of them, in fact." He sounded excited, which I found chilling. There was no reason to continue the discussion. The Colonel was setting me up to commit more crimes just by talking.

"I refuse to sign anything without first discussing it with a lawyer. My own lawyer. One that I select."

His grin widened. "Are you certain? I must advise you that your current plan of action might result in, um—how do you say?—detrimental consequences."

I was too tired and scared to consider the connotations of the phrase. I was half-dead already, but even in that state I didn't understand the depth of my captors' depravity. I didn't care to understand it. Something inside my brain was alive. In order to survive professional life, I had to inhibit emotion. By that point it was an impossible task.

"Are you hungry?" the Colonel said.

"A little bit."

He left the room and returned ten minutes later with two bowls of rice and lamb chopped roughly into large chunks. The meal looked similar to minsaf. "Eat," he said. "My wife made it."

I nibbled at first. The sauce had a piquant flavor and the lamb, which I normally dislike, was tender and garlicky, with a hint of cinnamon. I looked at the Colonel, stuffing spoonsful of rice into his waterlogged mouth. He was boyishly content, all his needs fulfilled in that spartan room: nourishment and intimidation. It was the strangest meal I'd ever eaten.

"You like?" he asked with a mouth full of pulverized meat. I nodded. "My wife will be very pleased that such a famous guest enjoyed her food."

"Famous, huh?"

"You were a very important man in America, no?"

"I suppose I was."

"Things are different here."

"No shit." After thinking on it a moment, I changed my mind. "Actually, both places are quite similar."

I expected him to get angry, but he looked amused. "Do tell, doctor."

"I have plenty of experience with both places. They have the same basic rules. I never had to change my behavior for either one."

"You rather abruptly changed your behavior."

"Yes, and it upset both places. Whatever differences you imagine are superficial."

"We have a different religion, a different history, a different language, and a different culture."

"Superficial. Your Kingdom is just a pygmy version of America, a satellite of America doing its bidding. That's the only reason it exists."

Now he was angry. "It's no wonder you're in prison, you son of a dog." The insult he delivered in Arabic before returning to English. "You've betrayed your history, your people. You're a disgrace to your ancestors."

Another flash of temper, an impulse to frankness, had endangered me, but I caught a thrill from the sense of freedom it created. I didn't want to argue with the Colonel, for I recognized some truth in his accusation. He wouldn't understand the notion of shame in the same way I did. He thought he was punishing me, but in reality he was crucial to my redemption. I couldn't allocate all my energy to him, though. I needed more time in my cell to dream of escape. Provoking the man who fed me wouldn't help.

I kept the empty bowl on my lap, hoping that the Colonel wouldn't risk breaking it. The joy of eating had dissolved from his face, replaced by a severe deportment. "You will sign the documents," he said.

"May I ask you something, Colonel?"

He waved a finger at me. "You've insulted us enough, Dr. Baqir. Even a patient man such as myself has limits."

"I've no intention of insulting you," I said. He nodded for me to proceed. "I'm just curious. Here we are, dining like two gentlemen. You've been considerate enough to offer me homemade food. And yet the power disparity between us is grotesque. I am a prisoner. You are my captor. You've slapped me around. You can have me killed anytime. You're free to go home whenever you want. I'll die in your custody. Doesn't the entire arrangement feel weird to you? How do you carry on with somebody you're torturing as if we're old friends?"

He thought about it for a few seconds. "Because I am a man of honor."

"Excuse me?"

"I am a man of honor, Dr. Baqir. I have obligations to my country, my people. I fulfill those obligations whether they're pleasant or ugly."

"Even if it means making another person suffer."

"I don't make the rules of this place. I carry out my duties. I have treated you respectfully. It is you who has behaved shamefully."

"You don't seem to understand what I'm saying."

"I don't have fancy degrees like you, Dr. Baqir, but I assure you I understand your meaning."

"It's impossible for me to treat you poorly. I'm the prisoner. You're the warden."

He leaned forward and smiled. A grain of rice was stuck in the left side of his mustache. "The world is not so simple, my friend."

"This world, right here, is. This world. This room."

He shook his head adamantly. "Everybody works for somebody. Even my king. Even your president. There is none of these fancy ideas you college people like to discuss. Those things are just for talking. In the world, here, your country, wherever, there is only—what do you call it? Coercion? You either deliver it or receive it. That is the real life, doctor."

"Okay, that's a theory about how the world works, but that doesn't really answer my question."

"This way of life must be practiced with good manners. Otherwise there is no civilization."

"I see."

"Are you ready to sign?"

When I didn't answer, he left the room, giving me a reproachful glance on the way out. Soon I was back in the cell. Despite appearing to be random, the schedule was logical. I was made to suffer in the stinking darkness with the promise of a new cell after I signed the confession. I didn't meet with the Colonel at regular times because the Colonel kept irregular hours. When he was around, and felt like leaning on me, I was sent upstairs. Otherwise I was in a space designed to induce nightmares and mobilize an instinct for either suicide or self-preservation. Making someone shit in a bucket that he then has to empty is a good way to communicate his status in the world.

When the soldiers next came for me, I prepared for another rap session with the Colonel. I neither enjoyed nor dreaded them. I knew I couldn't convince him to act humanely; he was duty-bound by a notion of honor that required suffering. Appeals to empathy don't persuade civilized men. The only thing I could hope to get out of our meetings was an abstract sense of intellectual satisfaction, but even there the Colonel had proved a formidable audience, a man surprisingly insightful about the clutter in my brain. I wouldn't have expected a low-level nepotism case to be so sharp. Then again, perhaps he was confined to this ignominious post on the edge of the desert precisely because of his intelligence.

But they didn't take me to see the Colonel. Instead I was led to an open room that looked like a workshop. One of the soldiers handcuffed me and walked me to a rough wooden table holding a medieval-looking apparatus. Two vertical steel slabs were set about a foot apart with a grooved cylindrical pole connecting them at the bottom. A crank jutted from one of its sides. Before I had a chance to comprehend what was getting ready to happen, the soldier grabbed me by the hair and slammed my forehead into the pole. The other soldier turned the crank. I could see the slabs of steel moving closer in my peripheral vision.

I whimpered when they made contact with each side of my skull. I screamed for the soldiers to stop but the crank kept moving even after my head was firmly mounted. Pain shot through my cheeks down to my lower back. As the slabs persisted, steel grinding against steel on the pole as they met resistance from skeletal bone, my eyes started squeezing out of their sockets. Just as I was certain they'd pop out and my skull would implode, the soldier let go of the crank. I want to describe the pain, convey just how awful it was, but the right combination of words doesn't exist for that purpose. The inability to adequately describe pain is probably humankind's most redeeming feature. All I can say is that my brain sent distress signals to every extremity with a nerve ending, turning my body into a clamor of agony.

"The Colonel says this will help you think more clearly," the soldier at the crank said in Arabic. They left the room. I was hunched forward, my head in a vise, forced to stand as my legs insisted on collapsing. My arms thrashed to release the cuffs. My body had been partitioned into competing impulses, each at odds even as they responded to the same source of torment. I couldn't think of anything but death. I tried to envision Nyla, then Lara, then a series of memorable encounters with women I knew only as images. I finally tried to summon strength through Nancy, but thoughts of her made things worse. Only the prospect of oblivion provided any relief.

How long was I in the vise? I simply don't know. Even now, in the vast hell of my outdoor tomb, I can't think about it. I remember hearing footsteps amid the racket in my brain before somebody loosened the slabs from my head and I collapsed in a fit of misery and relief. I found my voice and began screaming. One of the soldiers delivered a kick to my abdomen. The other booted me in the ass.

"Shut up," said the one who had kicked me from behind. They pulled me up, intensifying the pressure on my brain, and tried to get me to walk. I wasn't up to the task, incapable even of being carried. No matter how adamantly the soldiers cursed my father and my religion, I couldn't follow their orders. After a few halfhearted smacks, they dragged me by the wrists. By the time we reached the stairwell, I managed to get on my feet. I didn't want the back of my head whacking each step on the way down.

Back in the cell, I roared away the pain and humiliation until my throat felt like an incinerated forest. But I was determined not to sign anything. Before falling asleep, still afraid my eyes would burst out of their sockets, I reprimanded myself for being so open about the pain, because I knew deep in my heart, in the same place housing my abrupt need to rebel, that if they took me back to the vise I'd put my name to anything they wanted.

Nancy

HOW DO YOU kill somebody? I never thought I'd seriously consider the question. It wasn't a moral quandary. I was trying to work out how to actually complete the deed without getting caught. Hollywood makes it look easy. In mob films, people get shot on the street in full daylight. The killer walks away or steps into a waiting car. I wasn't going to ask Elena to be my getaway driver and it didn't seem wise to plug a famous diplomat and then take a stroll.

I spent the rest of my sophomore year in deep contemplation about the criminal justice system. College was supposed to prepare me to successfully take on challenges in the world. The university would disapprove of my methods, but I was certainly fulfilling the spirit of its mission. In itself, killing is an easy project. There are hundreds of ways to produce a dead human being. Getting away with it is the sticky part. I could shoot the motherfucker: quick, to the point, reliable. Not difficult to get a gun, legally or black market. I could run him over with a car, stab him in the rib cage, club the back of his skull, push him off a bridge into the Potomac River. Each option was attractive. I merely needed to figure out which one was viable.

While I was immersed in the nuances of murder, Elena became omnipresent on campus. She was involved with the African Student Association, Black Lives Matter, the Anti-Fascist League, the Campaign for a Living Wage, Students for the Prevention of Sexual Violence, and other groups seeking to make UVA more tolerable. She had a biweekly column in *The Cavalier Daily* and served on the committee that selected musical acts and speakers. After a while, she quit nagging me to join her, but her enthusiasm was replaced by tension.

"I'm worried about you, Nan," she told me.

"I'm fine."

"But you're not doing anything."

"Ugh, Elena, stop it. I'm doing plenty. Just because it's not what you're doing doesn't make it useless."

"Well, I was hoping you'd be more sensitive to the kind of realities I face on this racist-ass campus."

"I *am*."

"But not enough to put in any labor."

We had many such conversations. I always lost the argument because I couldn't explain to Elena that I was very much laboring on behalf of a better world. That labor took form in the appearance of depression. Over and over, she told me I needed to be a better ally, but I didn't think I'd be any good tagging along for shows of moral support. I had decided on my own brand of activism that I needed to protect her from. That was the worst thing about my decision—it made me secretive around my closest friend, who in turn thought I was a dormant hunk of apathy. Otherwise I liked planning destruction at my own pace. Furtiveness offered tons of opportunity. I didn't have to deal with dissenting views or conflicting sensibilities. I just needed to act.

It's not that simple, of course. But still. There are benefits to going it alone. Groups are never really groups because they're never unified; they're more like crowds. That's how I think of myself, as an individual in a crowd. I wasn't even on a team of two with Elena, not really, because in important ways, life and death ways, we weren't on the same side. We belonged to the same team in principle, and wanted very badly to share the same kind of future, but our understanding of process was monumentally different, so much that in a random encounter we might view each other as threatening.

If someone had given me a reason to spare the Ambassador, I would have dropped my plans, but everything I heard about him only reinforced the probity of my effort. In the spring semester of my sophomore year, I received a weird email in my university account:

Dear Nancy:

Please excuse my writing out of nowhere. It must be bizarre
(though I hope not disorienting) to receive a message from a
stranger. It feels weird to send the message, too!

Anyway, I knew your father pretty well. He's still missed by many.
What happened to him is a terrible injustice. I was thinking about
him the other day and remembered that he had a daughter who
would be around college age today. I don't know much about
what happened to him, but I have a bit of information that you
might find helpful. If of course you even want to hear it. If you
do, I'd love to meet you whenever you can get to DC. My number
is below.

I know you don't know me, but I really hope you're happy and
thriving. I hope to meet you soon.

All best,

Nyla Ghannam
[number redacted]

After I decided that Nyla Ghannam wasn't a con artist—an internet
search had pegged her as a pretty big name in Washington—the normal
thing would have been to ask Elena her opinion, or even Mom, although
her response would have been predictable (I'd long ago learned to
read Mom in subtext). Something about Nyla Ghannam felt exclusive,
intimate, so I kept her message to myself.

I didn't reply for a while. She probably didn't expect one. I went about
my days as a regular student, somehow enlivened by the spectacular ennui
of my surroundings. The place was gorgeous, with hilly green lawns
and Georgian brick structures, its prestige derived from an expensive
performance of antiquity. Between classes, waves of near-monotonous
students invaded campus walkways and corridors, faces focused on
phones, their disaffection calibrated like an exquisite instrument. I could

always pick out kids from the other side of the state, from the southern marshes and the mountains, because they were more reluctant, more watchful, than those from the DC suburbs and the Northeast, who carried their sense of belonging naturally.

My parents met on campus. I sometimes tried to imagine the place as it existed when they were students. It didn't take much imagination because UVA worked so hard to appear timeless. The technology had changed, the restaurants, the sprawl encircling town, the buildings housing professional schools, but the core of campus was aggressively Jeffersonian, as it had been for two hundred years. I like to think that the old patriarch would have supported my plans. Perhaps only if its target were a more barbaric ambassador.

What was Mom like as a student, at my current age? I couldn't picture her personality in a college-aged body. She must have been more outgoing even if only to maintain status. I'm sure she was aware of her beauty, which she commanded as a kind of asset to exhibit or withhold depending on the situation. Dad would have recognized the elusiveness of that beauty. He was smart enough to be patient and ditch the idea of charming her. He'd have to impress through perseverance. And then he'd have to convince her that he was worth the trouble, or that the trouble was actually a good thing. Her parents would be skeptical of an Appalachian boy, no matter how ambitious or genetically suitable, but his own father surely approved the pairing from heaven. It happened somehow. I don't remember their relationship as being warm or passionate, but it was steady and secure. That's exactly what Mom wanted from it. She never pursued another man after Dad's disappearance and if she had a sex life I knew nothing of it.

She was still beautiful—her face smooth, almost silky, with charcoal pupils surrounded by plush black lashes; her mannerisms fierce and graceful; her body slender and well-toned, arranged perfectly according to the needs of her audience. But the last few times I saw her, I noticed that she was changing, not just physically, but in attitude, as well. She was more contemplative than usual. There was something tired about her movements, and often her language. She could have been preparing for death, but Mom was neither old nor depressed. Maybe being an empty-nester was harder than she expected. Should I get her a dog? (A cat was out of the question; Mom already had too much of a feline personality.) I could see Mom digging a bichon frise: small, adorable, classy. Doesn't need much walking. Perfect for cuddling in bed. Or maybe a golden retriever, which could give Mom the illusion of being protected. They're supposed to be smart, so it would be protected from Mom.

Or I could go live with her. At the time, it was a fleeting thought, too ridiculous and mortifying to seriously consider. Most everybody who left Northern Virginia for college ended up back in the area, usually in the same suburb they left, living the kind of life they inherited from their parents. To me, it seemed like an awful destiny. Yet eventually I too would move back home. My family had its own revolution to complete, except ours was all about destroying cycles of monotony.

I eventually replied to Nyla. I was wary of this woman, but I had a feeling that meeting her wouldn't be a waste of time. I was skeptical about any breakthroughs, though. If Nyla had critical information, she could have shared it with my mother, or with the media, a million times. Either her information was tepid or she and Mom had reason to stay apart. I carefully tested Mom on the phone, asking her if she knew of a person called Nyla. "No. The last Nyla I knew was in high school." Then she did exactly what I hoped she wouldn't: "Why?"

"Oh, no reason," I said, hoping my nonchalance didn't sound rehearsed. "She gave a talk the other day and it sounded like someone you might know."

"Gave a talk on what?" Mom was starting to venture past the script I'd practiced for.

"The usual crap."

"What usual crap?"

Fuck fuck fuck. Why wasn't she dropping it? I had to think quickly, one of my lesser skills. "The economy of Gulf nations and US foreign policy."

"How much of that crap are they pushing at UVA? And they have the nerve to keep asking me for donations."

Relief. Mom's brain had wandered to another subject, an indignity, the best kind to keep her preoccupied.

"Right?" I said. "They're so obsessed with money. It's pretty sick."
"Anyway, I'm curious to hear more about this Nyla person."
"Um, yeah, nothing really. I thought maybe she ran in your circles."
"I don't have circles. What are you talking about?"
"Jesus, Mom, do you have to pick a fight every time we talk?"
"What fight? I'm asking questions."
"I don't know why you're so, like, fixated on this person."
"You asked me about her. Don't ask me about something and then expect instant answers. I'm not a library."

I was the one who picked the fight, but it was Mom who had given me the know-how for that sort of effort. I couldn't tell if she was merely curious or if she was pressing me for information about a person she knew by the name of Nyla. Not telling her about the email was the right decision.

So I lied to Mom when I came home one Saturday morning, without Elena, and said I had a workshop in DC that afternoon. I was careful not to arouse her curiosity and promised I'd be home for dinner. That was good enough. Mom didn't much care what I was up to if I planned to be around for a while before heading back to Charlottesville. She dropped me off at the Metro and half an hour later I was leaving the station at Farragut West, a straight shot, to walk the few blocks to Gregory's, an upscale coffee shop and juice bar on Connecticut, next to the Mayflower Hotel and about two miles from where we used to live.

I'd replied politely to Nyla but took care not to show any enthusiasm. I framed my reply as a show of good manners and a concession to her interest in meeting. She responded the same day and after an exchange of numbers we'd set up this tête-à-tête. I was totally nervous and didn't understand why. The meeting would probably be awkward. That was reason enough for nerves, but there was also the remote possibility of life-changing information.

I pegged her as the type who shows up late as a matter of principle, but I recognized her as soon as I walked into the shop. She was seated at a two-top, busy with her phone. She looked up when I came in, but didn't seem to think I was Fred's daughter. I got in line so I could assess her a bit longer. She was gorgeous, which disoriented me: her hair was ironed into a shoulder-length coiffure somewhere between bronze and copper; her face was youthful and olive-hued, with minimal makeup. Her black skirt-suit was expensive. Nobody could mistake this woman for a damsel. My outfit of vintage tee and tight jeans atop stubby thighs had the same effect.

I ordered a peppermint tea and wondered if I should wait for her recognition. She was preoccupied by whatever was happening on her device, though. She reminded me enough of Mom that I was afraid of being judged a slobby, boyish lesbian. Sooner or later, I'd have to find out, so I walked over and stood in front of her table. She looked up and said "Yes?" Just as I was about to introduce myself, her face changed from seriousness to surprise. "Nancy? Great to see you. God, I can't believe I didn't recognize you." She stood and reached out as if to solicit a hug before changing her mind and extending a hand in greeting. I shook it and said it was nice to meet her.

"Sit sit." She gestured at the chair next to me. She had a slight accent, but clearly she'd known English for a long time and used it as her primary language. Her face was friendly, but there was also something remote about her. She didn't open up to people. It was part of her attractiveness.

"Uh, so." I didn't know what to say. "You knew my dad, huh?"

"I did," she smiled, "a long time ago. When I was in college."

"Was he your professor or something?"

"No, no, I don't recall Fred ever teaching. I interned for him at the Institute."

An intern? Ugh. She wouldn't know a thing about Dad. Already the meeting had been a waste of time.

"I remember he used to talk about you all the time," Nyla continued. "Cool."

She sighed. "Anyway, I don't know if you know this, but he was scheduled to be at my house the day he disappeared."

"No. I'd never heard of you until your email, to be honest."

"Well, you were young. Maybe your mother knows about it."

"I don't think so." I caught a hint of strain on her face.

"Why don't I tell you a bit about myself?"

"Sounds good."

She was a project manager at the World Bank—there's the suit explained—and got her professional start at the Institute. Dad had been instrumental in connecting her with important people around town. Despite their age difference, they were close friends. (I searched for a hint of suggestion in the word "friends," but couldn't detect any.) She wasn't married, had no kids. She grew up in the Kingdom—her father was a civil engineer for a government-owned public works company—but hadn't been back in years. Her parents moved to Canada a few years after she graduated college.

"And my dad was supposed to be at your house the day he went missing?"

"Yes. Well, my parents' house, the one I grew up in. I was still here. I had arranged for him to visit them. He was pretty annoyed, but I'd told my family so much about him that when they found out he'd be close by they insisted he come over. You know how it is." I didn't really know because getting roped into dinner at a stranger's house was exactly the sort of thing Mom tried to insulate me from.

"Do you know what happened to him?"

She didn't, but she could make some strong inferences. Here's what she knew: her older sister had gone to Dad's hotel lobby at an appointed time. Their father was going to send a hired driver, but the sister, Rose, was a fan of Dad's and insisted on scooping him. Rose arrived at the hotel on time—the Ghannams are a punctual clan—and waited about half an hour before getting worried. She had the front desk call up to his room a few times, but nobody answered. She asked to go up, but they refused to disclose his room number. A manager agreed to check on him. The room was empty. The bed had been used and there was an open laptop on it, but no sign of Dad. The sliding door to the balcony was open, but it was impossible to leave or enter the building from it. His pants were on the floor next to the bed and a cold, almost empty cup of coffee sat on the nightstand.

Rose began texting Nyla, who in turn began texting Dad. He never responded. Nyla was angry, thinking Dad had flaked. She told Rose to go home and forget it. Their mom had prepared an elaborate meal they could still enjoy. As Rose was leaving, a bellhop, looking scared, summoned her over and told her to wait outside, away from the entrance. She walked to an empty nook in front of a service door. The bellhop joined her and explained that he had been working the previous night and during a cigarette break saw a man being escorted out the back by police officers. The man's head was covered. The police put him into the backseat of an SUV and drove away. Perhaps this was the man Rose was looking for?

Later that evening, I searched online for the hotel where Dad had stayed, trying to virtually recreate the scene. There was a room like the one he had occupied, spacious and well-appointed, with vague Eastern décor—a round brass lamp, a porcelain tea set, a throw with tribal characteristics. The lobby was spacious with a high ceiling, adorned in oatmeal marble with ashy inlays. Outside, near the spot where Rose probably waited for the bellhop, was a parking lot filled with rows of thick squat date palms, their crowns pregnant with reddish branches. I couldn't find photos of anything that would pass for a back exit or a loading zone, so I lost Dad's movements somewhere in the lobby.

Rose rushed home to tell her parents. Their father told her to forget about it. He didn't want anyone finding out they were to host Fred. Rose couldn't let it go. The next day, she returned to the hotel. No word about Dad. The room was still in his name. She went to a police station and inquired about him. They were ignorant of his whereabouts, offering to open an investigation. She assured them it wouldn't be necessary. She tried some government offices, carefully and delicately, but if anyone had information, they weren't sharing it. A handful of people living in the Kingdom made inquiries with their contacts, but Dad's fate remained a secret.

"And that's really all I know," Nyla said. "I wish I had something better for you, but I thought you'd at least want to hear this."

"I did. I do. Thank you. It kind of affirms what my mom and I knew. You know, the government snatched him and killed him. We'll probably never find out exactly what happened."

"They definitely snatched him and there's a 99 percent chance they killed him, too. Fred's experience fits a pattern. He's not the only one. He was the most high-profile, though. I'm still shocked that they did this to a well-known American. And completely got away with it."

"How could that happen?" I found myself warming to Nyla, on the brink of opening up. "I mean, I remember people just abandoned us after a while, but I don't understand how the government just let him, I don't know, die or whatever."

She closed her eyes and shook her head. "I know. I'm sorry. Right around that time the Kingdom was involved deeply with the US and nobody wanted to upset the relationship. The King and his underlings knew it, so they felt comfortable pushing the envelope. I always thought they used Fred to test the Americans' sincerity."

"What do you mean?"

"It was a challenge. 'Okay, we're working together. We're investing billions into your economy. We're doing your bidding on foreign policy. Try and stop us from disposing of this nuisance.' That's how I imagine it went down. In the end, the Americans thought there was too much at stake."

"That's so fucked up."

"This government lets its client states do whatever they want as long as they stay in line. Trust me, Fred knew that. I doubt he had any illusions about being rescued. Sorry if this is hard for you to hear. Please stop me at any time."

"No, this is helpful. I've been thinking the exact same thing lately. Especially about how many people suffer because of it. I wish there was something we could do about it."

"I do, too."

"So you think it's hopeless? We should just try to get whatever we can out of a rotten world?"

She smiled. "I wouldn't put it that crudely, but I don't know what other choice we have."

"God, you sound like my mom."

Her smile went away. I wondered if she knew Mom and hated her. (Hating Mom was always a possibility.) "Oh? Is that a bad thing?" Hmmm. Now she was soliciting complaints about Mom. I declined.

"Can I ask you something while I have you here?"

"Sure." She looked nervous.

The nervousness gave way to relaxation when I said, "Why do you think my dad went all radical? Like out of nowhere?"

"I don't think it was out of nowhere. He always had it in him, held it inside. That's not unusual for us, right?"

"I guess not."

"Here's what I think: I think that your father lived according to a certain American ideal of a responsible family man, but always had this impulse to do something great. He finally realized that he wouldn't achieve greatness in his job, no matter how successful he was in it."

"I remember him talking about his dad and grandfather. Before he disappeared. He told me that he wanted to make them proud."

"I'm sure he did."

"Do you mean … never mind."

"I mean he made them proud. But I'll bet they would have told him to go easy and focus on his career and family. I can't say, though. I didn't know them. And I didn't know Fred like that."

"He seemed possessed, almost."

"I've been there. I don't know a single person from our country who hasn't had that inner dialogue."

"Yeah."

"How about you, Nancy? What do you think of all this?"

"I've had the inner dialogue. It makes me feel, I can't find the right word … alienated?"

She nodded. "You can always talk to me about it, okay?"

"Okay. Thanks." I had run out of things to discuss. I wanted to know more about Nyla, but worried about being intrusive. I went for it, anyway. "Are you happy? Working for the World Bank, I mean?"

"I can always try to get you an internship. It's the least I could do for Fred. It would open lots of possibilities for a bright girl like you."

Had she misunderstood or was she redirecting? And how rude would it sound if I told her what I really thought of her employer? "Oh, thanks, I'm not really looking right now, though."

"You sound so corporate," Nyla laughed. I laughed along with her.

There was a warmth to our meeting even amid the bustle spilling into the coffee shop, people taking a break from the relentless business of governing. They all looked the same, like Banana Republic mannequins, used the same gait, spoke with the same inflections, and pretended to be busy with the same harried expression. In and out like ants building a granular colony. For so many years Dad was among them, part of their odd, all-powerful society, until he decided to seek a different world. He discovered that you can't just up and leave. I wouldn't make the same error.

Nyla peered at my empty teacup. "Are you hungry? Can I get you a snack? Or another drink? They have fantastic smoothies here."

"No thank you."

"Well, I hope this has been helpful to you?"

"Sure, yeah. I don't know how to explain it. It's all so fucked up."

She stood and gently squeezed my wrist resting on the table. "You have my number. Use it if you need me. It was great meeting you. It makes me really happy to see that Fred's little girl grew up to be so smart and beautiful." She left before I could respond. It felt like my opportunity to get information from Nyla was over. She'd made her appearance, satisfied her curiosity about me, and would no longer be available short of an explosive new discovery. She wouldn't become my mentor and had no intention of assuming any motherly responsibilities.

Neither did my actual mother. I had decided that if Nyla told me something new I'd share it with Mom, but all she offered was a different perspective on Dad. The meeting was important, though, because it solidified my understanding of Dad's attitude at the end of his life. That attitude was now completely in my possession. No, I wouldn't tell Mom. But I hoped to provide her a moment of happiness.

Things at UVA deteriorated in the final months of my sophomore year. I wanted to be a writer, but college seemed anathema to the desire. I was growing bored of dating apps and literary theory. Formal education felt designed to deaden the kind of sensibility I wanted to cultivate. The stimuli around me worked in reverse, absorbing rather than producing energy. I was interested in abrupt transformation, in ruptures and breaches and schisms, anything that might put a hiccup into the earth's rotation. Even now, especially now, after the decd, I often remember something Nyla had said: "The Kingdom's security forces were known to drop people off to die in the middle of the desert. It was their way of saying that it would be impossible to live without all the technology and comfort they provided. They turned a desert into an advanced civilization. Cross them and back to hell you go." My purpose is to generate the possibility of life in that hellish world.

I occasionally hiked in the parkland around Charlottesville. Elena never came, declining every time with the same chortle, and I didn't care for anyone else's company, so I made my way along dirt trails winding through granite ridges and hardwood forest. Hiking wasn't an escape; it kept my mind busy. It was a good activity for scheming the Ambassador's demise. It also gave me time to question and reconsider. Mostly I wondered if Dad would have approved of my choice. I couldn't come to an answer. The exercise required too much speculation without enough concrete knowledge. Society would find no way to justify it, not legally, not politically. Everything I'd learned about being a conscientious citizen was clear: you don't kill politicians, even if they do horrible things and even if they directly cause you suffering. I found the mentality unconvincing, disgusting really. Common sense didn't concern me. The Ambassador represented at least three regimes that inscribed pain into my genetics. Isn't relief a form of morality? Why should I follow ideals of decorum that only help people with power, people who kill and torture in the name of safety?

Out in the foothills, it all made sense. It was inside classrooms and libraries that I questioned my sanity. I loved the randomness of the gnarled green underbrush alongside the walking paths, plush and prickly, inviting but practically impenetrable. I never felt alone out there. I saw hundreds of squirrels, less curious than those in my old neighborhood. Elena had emailed me an article about the large population of bears in Appalachia, but I never encountered one. No bobcats or copperheads. I did spy a couple of foxes and raccoons, which are surprisingly intimidating in person. If I went near a creek or pond, I always looked for otters, despite Dad's belief that they tend to stay near the coast. Once, while I was taking a rest, a skunk shuffled across the trail right in my direction. I considered getting up and running, but I didn't want to trigger its spray. It came up to my sneakers and sniffed around my ankles. I froze and tried not to breathe, but soon relaxed. The skunk had no intention of spraying me. I watched it with exhilaration. It was beautiful—flawless markings, acute and diametric, a lush, shiny coat. I was stunned that a skunk, the most fearsome animal in the forest, had put me at peace. We regularly smelled them in town and they always elicited a disgusted expression or comment. How unfair, how superficial, we had been in our hasty judgments. The skunk soon went on its way, leaving a faint smell of musk in its wake. After the encounter, I made it a habit to rest and wait for another to come along.

Much of the time I focused on coursework. I had more or less decided to return home, but I wanted to leave campus in good standing. I was always a serious student. The idea of slacking on homework didn't register with me. Studying had become an impediment, though. Nothing in my classes offered any help for a pupil trying to figure out how to kill the prominent representative of a repressive kingdom. It was all theory and praxis around a polity that insisted on my disappearance. I no longer cared to make sense of absence as a social condition. Existence, I understood, required bloodletting—it always had, and yet teachers ignored the obvious correlation, legible in nearly every society on the planet, because it was a thoroughly inappropriate topic in spaces of higher learning.

Then there was the matter of Elena. As her star rose so did her disappointment in my recalcitrance. We struggled to maintain love as different aspects of the world seized our attention. Getting out of the suburbs had introduced possibilities neither of us anticipated. Those far-away geographies that followed us to America kept calling us back. Where it was easy to be the closest of allies in high school, with its transparent norms, allyship was more complicated in college. Too many options existed for self-exploration. While I felt constricted and unsatisfied, Elena embraced the challenges and possibilities. I envied her boldness, her sense of duty, but I had no civic obligations to satisfy. The problem was that I had also rejected social bonds, a choice that always causes tension among friends and families. Elena knew I was betraying her. I wish she also knew that my betrayal was the greatest act of love I could possibly offer.

Elena fought more with her parents while Mom and I had settled into détente. It was bound to happen because they spoke every day. The bickering sometimes felt serious. I remember one Saturday her parents came to visit. They brought her father's cab, which amused some of our friends. Elena wasn't embarrassed or anything, but she didn't like learning about other people's shortcomings through reference to her family. Her parents insisted on taking both of us to a nice dinner. Elena tried to convince them to have a picnic in the outdoor amphitheater, but they wouldn't hear of it.

"No ma'am," her father said. "We're going to a good restaurant. That's final."

"Dad, I'm trying to eat healthy. I don't want rich food. We can buy whatever we like on the mall and enjoy some fresh air." It was true. Elena had become self-conscious about her weight at college. I thought she was more beautiful than ever, but Elena was prone to lifestyle trends and diet fads.

"I came all the way down here to eat a bagel?"

"You don't have to get a bagel," Elena shouted. "Get a cheeseburger for all I care."

"What? We don't have Five Guys at home? I can get a cheeseburger anytime."

"Name me a single thing you can eat here that you can't get at home."

"It's not the same. We insist to treat you. Quit being stubborn and learn how to accept a nice gesture."

Here Elena's mother stepped in. "It's all right, Robel. A picnic sounds very nice." Then she turned to Elena. "Darling, your father was very excited to do this for you. He saved for weeks before this visit."

"Fine, let's go to a restaurant."

"I'll stay behind," I said.

"Absolutely not," said Elena's mother. "You are family. You'll join us."

Elena was on the brink of tears; her parents were giddy. We ended up at Prime 109, a few blocks from the amphitheater. *just don't eat?* I texted her. It would save her the calories and make a point. *I can't say no*, she texted back. I understood her meaning: she lacked the discipline to abstain, a problem she had struggled with since our days at TJ. Steak was a good meal for the body-conscious, but not at a high-end restaurant. We were treated to baskets of buttered bread, oysters soaked in bechamel, wedge salad drizzled with gorgonzola, cuts of dry-aged strip with bearnaise. And of course dessert (in this case flourless chocolate cake). The bill was probably worth three days of her father's salary, which appeared to make him happier.

As we walked the mall afterward, Elena looked miserable. Her mother kept pointing to antique trinkets in store windows. Elena gave halfhearted approval. Her father flounced around the brick promenade, nodding at strangers and smiling at children, the prerogative of any satisfied patriarch. When they left, fussing over Elena despite her obvious distress, she crawled under her blanket and wept. I stretched onto the mattress next to her and ran my hand along her forehead. We fell asleep next to one another, cherishing the safety of our loneliness. I woke up thinking about all the times since high school that Mom left me to choose my own dinner, which always made me wish she loved me in a different way.

Soon after, I would throw away most of my stuff, pack the rest, and board a bus to Northern Virginia. I still haven't returned. I often think of that night when, in the aftermath of unwanted largesse, Elena and I, pensive and silent, pressed our shoulders together on a twin mattress and willed away untold lifetimes of shame.

Fred

LIGHT FILTERS THROUGH glass panels in the widening gap between concrete and sky. I'm carried toward refractions of sunshine on a bounded horizon, the descent of heaven into our tunnel, or the ascent of hell onto earth. I lean against the escalator railing to the right, one among dozens in a single line, a few hurried passengers climbing past us to the left. The curved concrete enclosure surrounding us is stained with years of spit and soot and spilled drinks. I don a jacket and tie, a man of means and influence, at home on Dupont Circle. As the escalator reaches the aperture, the light turns off and the commuters disappear. The world smells like shit and vomit again.

Such were my days in the Kingdom's dungeon. Eating was traumatic, but I forced myself. Thinking was painful, but my environment offered nothing else. My mind kept forcing itself to Nancy and the pain she must have been feeling. All my failures in fatherhood haunted the cell, but Nancy still managed to provide the space with a persistent, immutable beauty. She was the life inside this void. I envisioned her grown up, flummoxed by her old man's choices. Maybe she'd understand. Maybe she'd even approve of my ruinous decision to become a better person. I wish she could know my regret for having so often chosen professional gratification over her company. Those choices had made it so that I couldn't atone without losing her forever.

She was a peculiar and introspective child. I confess that I suspected something was off about her. She could be almost robotic, yet she was a deeply feeling person, animated and even impulsive in private spaces,

shy and contemplative outside the home. It gave me hope that she'd
survive my absence. It even gave me hope that she'd one day understand.
Being in captivity amplified memories of the times I did spend with her.
I remember the day Lara needed me to babysit when Nancy was three. I
wasn't happy with the arrangement. Tending to a toddler fell under Lara's
share of the household responsibilities. On that day, Lara hadn't cooked
a lunch so much as prepared an assortment of snacks fit for a party much
larger than two: a huge dish of hummus, fūl (smartly garnished with
parsley), tortilla chips and salsa, crackers and cream cheese, little smokies,
tabbouleh, artichoke hearts, cheese cubes, berries, pickled vegetables,
and a basket of whole wheat pita bread. I sat beside Nancy at the kitchen
table and brooded as she munched on chopped strawberries. "Daddy, I
want to write a book," she announced. Fucking great. I would be hours
behind in my work.

Nancy drew a series of pictures on construction paper and told a story
about each one. I arranged the pictures in sequence and transcribed her
words, then folded and stapled the papers. She called the book *Cat Goes to
Sleep*, about a feline named Blaze who naps whenever the sun comes out.

> During the day the cat goes to sleep
> At night the cat goes outside to play
> The cat is orange
> When the sun comes up the cat takes a nap
> When the sun goes down the cat wakes up
> The cat has four feet
> The cat likes playing in the dark

Nancy was thinking about cats because I had told her about all the
strays on a campus where I had recently given a talk. It had been a long
journey, with six-hour layovers in both directions, and I was gone nearly
a week. I gave interviews in both English and Arabic and met with various
NGOs and public intellectuals. The Kingdom had put me in contact with
various people at the US Embassy and we spent hours talking policy. I
worked hard to cultivate personal and professional relationships. That
was the parlance I used to describe the transactions, in any case.

Campus administrators treated my visit as a big deal. I dined with the president and the chairman of the Board of Trustees. They urged me to emphasize the importance of civic responsibility. Sloganeering about revolution and other unrealistic scenarios apparently was a problem on their campus. The students needed intellectual structure and reassurance that they could be invested in the system.

"We also deal with the problem on the other end of the spectrum," the president said. "Apathy. Kids from rich backgrounds who think the world is their oyster. All they care about is money and status."

"That can be dangerous to any society," I said.

"Quite right. We need leaders. Those best suited for leadership are frittering away their talent."

And so I gave what I liked to think of as a rousing call to action. There are elections here. Vote! There are groups working to improve society. Donate! Dozens of foreign governments offer grant programs. Apply! There are political parties speaking in your name. Join! I talked a bit about my family's history, how we went from refugees to productive members of a democratic society. That achievement required sacrifice and hard work, but we never complained. We kept our eye on the ball and swung for the fences. I considered it proof of a quality argument that both undergrads and administrators loved the talk. The following day, I met with a small group of graduate students, as a favor to one of my friends on the faculty. They weren't excited by the speech I had given. (I must have missed their scowling faces amid the applause that filled the auditorium.) I wasn't prepared for their outspokenness. The students I interacted with in the United States would have considered it rude (or career suicide) to sharply question a visiting dignitary. They smiled at first, were friendly in the typical way of people from their country, but the conversation quickly became serious.

"Professor," one of them said, transitioning the group from banter to confrontation, "I found your presentation of American democracy to be interesting, but from our vantage point there is little that is democratic about your country. For us it is a symbol of destruction."

I was familiar with the vantage point. I repeatedly heard my grandparents make similar arguments in our kitchen in Blacksburg.

I couldn't answer with boilerplate because the audience was tied to emotion, not logic. They peppered me with questions about a host of misdeeds and aggressions, about war and military rule, about theft and corruption. I answered calmly, feigning empathy for their complaints. These were kids at an elite private university; millions of their compatriots were locked on the wrong side of its gates. They'd soon enough figure out the nature of their trade, unless they were prepared to starve, a thought that informed the smirk I wore as I endured the students' performance. Inside I was upset, though. I didn't like being made into their enemy, especially because it kept occurring to me how much my father would have enjoyed the discussion.

Once home, I skipped the drama and told little Nancy about the cats lounging along the low wall on the busy street just outside of upper campus, happily awaiting scraps from restaurant owners and sloppy pedestrians, or shading themselves beneath sprawling banyan trees, each the idle monarch of its own little territory. Nancy wanted to hear more about cats and Lara was content to hear nothing at all. Their reactions helped me make sense of the experience of travel. It was a lonely activity no matter how many people I encountered. Nancy and I were able to transform that experience into something coherent. I can't remember feeling more at peace than the afternoon my little girl told me stories about a lazy cat.

The cat never would have fallen asleep in my cell because it was continuously dark. It was nice to get out of there, even if to be abused, but my eyes were so accustomed to the dark that it hurt when they adjusted to light. Florescent bulbs were especially unpleasant. So I had mixed feelings the next time they brought me out. As usual, the guards half-dragged me until I could get my eyes and muscles working again. They took me to the same room where I waited for the Colonel. I noticed something different this time: there were two chairs on the other side of the desk.

When the Colonel came in, I could hear a set of footsteps behind him. The Colonel walked around to my left. Another man stopped next to me on the right and extended his hand. "It's lovely to see you again, Fred," said the Ambassador's son.

I made sure I wasn't hallucinating before giving him a nod. It was him, all right. Tall with broad shoulders, friendly and composed, in stylish jeans, a tailored jacket, and Italian loafers. I didn't take his hand. He smiled and sat next to the Colonel.

"Dr. Baqir," the Colonel said with exaggerated friendliness. "I've been told you were given some time to think about our last conversation." I glared at him. The Ambassador's son chuckled.

"I'm sorry to run into you in such unfortunate circumstances," he said.

"Did you come all this way just to see me?"

"Of course not. I have business to attend to before my return to Washington. But when I learned that you're here, I couldn't leave without visiting you."

"My arrest was a surprise to you?"

"Naturally. But the Colonel got me up to speed."

"I explained your reluctance to sign any papers," the Colonel said.

"That's one reason I'm here," the Ambassador's son said, "to impress upon you how critical it is to begin formal legal proceedings. I want to emphasize that it's to your benefit."

"But I haven't committed any crime."

"To the contrary. You believe that what you did shouldn't be considered a crime, but it is indeed criminal. It's a very serious crime, in fact. We have all the evidence we need for an easy conviction and a harsh sentence. Your cooperation will perhaps mitigate some of the King's anger."

I was never leaving the Kingdom's custody. If I didn't sign, they could lie and say I did, but it would be a risky move because they'd be admitting I was in their possession. If I signed by having negotiated a reduced sentence, then they wouldn't let me out alive. I knew way too many secrets. I could torpedo the palace with a single gossip column, and get rich doing it.

"I've told the Colonel numerous times that I don't even know what it is I'm supposed to be signing," I said.

"I'd be happy to clear it up for you in as much detail as you like."

"I made the same offer," the Colonel interjected.

"I'm all ears."

"May I be frank with you, professor?"

"Go ahead."

"I'd like to explain what your problem is."

I interrupted with a chortle. "Maybe that I'm being imprisoned and tortured by a hereditary dictator and his lackeys?"

He laughed as if I'd told a knock-knock joke. "Yes, I can see how that might upset you. But let's think past your current situation for a moment. Your problem is that you've become doctrinal."

"Did you learn that word at Harvard?"

"I did, actually. I also learned that being doctrinal is bad for a career in diplomacy. I've always avoided it, learned to understand problems and conflicts based on their specifics. Otherwise, I'd miss too many nuances. That's what landed you here, professor."

"With all due respect, mister Ambassador, what landed me here is criticism of your government."

"Tsk tsk, Professor Baqir. I'm not the ambassador yet. My father is nearing retirement, though, and it's expected that I'll accede him. They're watching how I handle this situation, of course."

"I thought you knew nothing about it."

The Colonel lit a cigarette and offered me one. I accepted. The Ambassador's son waved his hand and continued talking. "No matter. At this point I'm involved, and I'd like it to end well for all parties."

"Then let me go. I'll pack up my office at the Institute tomorrow and we'll never have to see each other again."

"It's not that simple. There's the problem of your turn to the doctrinaire, unfortunately."

"I still have no idea what the hell you're trying to say."

"A doctrinal man uses dogma as a form of emotional comfort. You can't expect him to make rational choices. Why, he might even be willing to get imprisoned in a foreign country just to make a point. It's impossible to imagine a circumstance in which you don't give us trouble. You are too devoted to a cause. It's like a religion for you."

"This is very true," said the Colonel, nodding.

"Don't pathologize me. What about your devotion to the King?"

"It's quite different," said the Ambassador's son. "The devotion is mutually beneficial. For you, a nation is an idea. For me, it is an instrument."

I considered what he was saying. Despite the fact that his job was to pander through illusions of being learned, I sensed real sincerity in his tone. My devotion to a set of ideals passed down from ancestors, to unorthodox notions of freedom, didn't correspond to the demands of professional responsibility. He could please his father by merging political fealty with personal success. I had no such luxury. I had to choose between conflicting expectations. My choice led to this conversation, pleasant on the surface but saturated with violence. The Ambassador's son couldn't allow me to complete my transformation. He had to kill the possibility in order to ensure his own survival.

As it happened, I'd heard the word "doctrinal" before. Lara had said it to me when we first started seeing one another in college. We were walking down The Lawn, in the direction of Homer, and I had asked her why she seemed so down on her culture. "Everyone back home is so doctrinal," she had explained.

"Doctrinal? That's a serious word."

"Really, Farid [it would take months before she called me Fred], you people in the diaspora—that's what you call it, right?—can be very stupid."

"What did I say?"

"It's not what you said. It's what you suggested. Why wouldn't I know a big word?"

"No, I meant you're making a serious criticism of our culture."

"Wait until you meet my parents."

She turned out to be correct. They had a million hang ups—about my finances, my aspirations, my nationality, my linguistic capabilities, my lineage. Lara more or less severed contact with them, but there was no specific fallout. It kind of just happened, a byproduct of emigration and marriage. Whereas my parents kept me adrift in Appalachia, Lara's demanded tribute and attention. I could describe Lara in a hundred different ways, but "doctrinal" would never make the list. She could be both idealistic and pragmatic. It depended on what best fit the goal of being left alone. She was at ease in Washington society, and generally enjoyed the lifestyle, but had no illusions about the nature of that world or what she had to sacrifice in order to be accepted.

I apologized to her for overstepping. I could tell she liked the idea of a man who apologizes. "It's fine," she said, after a while adding, "I'll tell you right now, though. If I ever have a child, I'll never be doctrinal."

There I was, a few decades later, being accused of the trait most likely to have wrecked my marriage and I couldn't argue with the accusation. Lara was certainly working nonstop to locate me, bulldozing through any wishy-washiness she encountered. I also knew that she was furious and unlikely ever to forgive me. In a strange way, I was enjoying my chat with the Ambassador's son. In my job as director of the Institute, I was unaccustomed to candor. "By thinking of the nation as an instrument," I said, "aren't you disrespecting your king, all your people, really?"

"I'm surprised you'd think that," he said. "My attitude is the very foundation of our society. And yours, too, I might add. We're not allies simply because of mutual economic interest. We share important values, as well."

"And you, Colonel? Surely you have an opinion."

"I told you, Dr. Baqir. I am a simple man, a military man. I follow orders. The world is difficult enough without heroes."

"So that's it, huh?" I said. "I have to be imprisoned and tortured for what? So people can take whatever they can get out of the world?"

"I agree that it's most unfortunate and I wish it didn't have to be this way. But civilization depends on it, professor."

The Ambassador's son then excused himself, explaining that he had another appointment. "I cannot impress upon you how important it is to sign the paperwork," he told me on his way out. The Colonel spread his hands as if to say, "There you have it." I was nearly in tears as I shook my head. The Colonel slammed his fist against the desk and left the room. I still suffered pain throughout my nerve endings. My back and chest were sore. I was a rag of a person, battered and terrified, my humiliation manifest in torment and malnutrition. But I would sign nothing, no matter how overwhelmed I became by the sadness of my refusal.

Sometime later, the guards returned and summoned me to get up. Instead of taking me back to the cell, they walked me down the corridor to an empty room with a drain in the floor. I could see faint stains on the concrete around the drain, and a few on the walls. In a panic, I tried the door handle. It didn't move. I pounded it with the side of my fist, screaming for it to open. The lock felt impenetrable. The door was heavy against my shoulder. Even if I managed to leave the room, where would I go? I was in a well-guarded compound far from any crowd into which I might disappear. I gave up and sat in the corner. Trying to think about anything else only reminded me how terrified I was of what might come through that door.

It was two different guards, distinguishable from the others only by girth. They wasted no time with small talk. One of them grabbed my hair and dragged me into the center of the room. The other kicked me in the lower back. On it went until I felt like an onion sack. They kept kicking and I kept trying to escape, rolling along the floor until I ran out of space. I managed to sit up. One of the guards connected with my chin, sending a rope of bloody saliva from my lips to the wall. The beating removed my mind from my body. I could hear the thumps and the grunts and smell the awful combination of sweat and cologne, but I was almost a spectator to the violence. The guards got tired and left. I assessed the damage with my fingers. Everything from my jaw to kneecap screamed in distress, but all major bones seemed to be intact. I had protected my skull well enough. But my body had become a topography of contusions, welts, and lacerations.

They made me walk back to the cell and left me with a bowl of fava beans and bread. I had trouble chewing so I let the food sit on my tongue until it was soggy enough to swallow. My abdomen wasn't ready to accept nourishment. I crawled to the bucket and vomited a few handfuls of blood and bile. I knew the end was coming. I could feel it. My body invoked feelings of death; my brain was coming around to the reality. I was neither worried nor comforted. I had come to a simple recognition the way I might have come to understand that bad weather will cancel a flight. I would soon be killed. The main concern was how much I would suffer until the moment arrived. They knew I wouldn't confess. I suspected that the beating was a kind of catharsis for them, a way to express frustration that they couldn't pass me along to the next agency and get on with the usual laziness.

In the next increment of time—hours? days?—the Colonel dropped his guise of friendliness. I was dragged into his office twice more and asked if I'm ready to sign. I said no each time and was put back into the cell. My body wasn't recovering well in its damp, cold environment. I needed a mattress and pain medication, fluids, a bath. When I cleaned the bucket in the utility room down the hall, I also hosed myself, but still felt filthy. Maybe, I considered, they're being strangely considerate, helping me to welcome death by delivering misery. The Colonel was impatiently waiting for instructions on how to dispose of me. I had become everybody's inconvenience.

I could no longer prevent myself from thinking of happy moments, of peaceful days, of beloved women, but the memories came with flashes of regret worse than any physical pain I had suffered. In recollections of joy, I couldn't ignore how awful I had often been. The regret always landed on Nancy. My hiking buddy. My emerging author. All I wanted was to hear her tiny, innocent voice telling inane stories about school drama and superheroes, but mostly I remembered that voice pleading for company. My absences back then were the expression of my rottenness; now I was trying to redeem myself by disappearing. My father would have spent hours each day in Nancy's company. He would have made Lara smile. I couldn't fulfill that legacy. I had surpassed him in every way that didn't matter.

One scene in particular pulsed through my broken anatomy. Nancy was little, a hazy timeframe that spans preschool to second grade, and wanted to play a game of Monopoly. Not now, darling, I kept telling her. Later, later. She didn't believe me. She knew what later meant. It was a word to her as definitive as "maybe" is to most children. I usually brushed her off without a problem, moved on to some task or phone call or lunch date without a second thought, but that morning her voice was sad and pouty. She had opened the board on the dining room table and chosen our pieces—the car for me and the kitty cat for her. I tried to reason with her. In just a little bit, darling. Try to understand. I *have* to get this thing done. What was it I had to do? I don't know. I only remember my girl's devastation. She's an awkward child and on that day she was even more beautiful in her awkwardness, her looping curls falling to either side of a dark, pudgy face. Her eyes were glazed in sadness and I knew that I'd never get the same chance to indulge my daughter. She'd always remember the moment, and someday I'd regret my callousness. What choice did I have? Important people needed me to profess. I left Nancy sitting alone at the table.

She didn't deserve anything I had bequeathed to her. But now, at the very end, the callousness of youth became my own inheritance. In my cell I could hear the sound of Nancy's chair backing away from the table as she returned the board game to the cabinet. A scratch and a squeak. Light footsteps. The click of a metal latch against a magnetic clasp. Goddammit. Goddammit. I repeated the word as I whapped the back of my head against the wall. Thump thump thump. Sharp jolts into the cortex. Sunken tremors inside the concrete. *Goddammit.* This time, at least, my absence would be justified.

Nancy

I WAS AWARE when Elena arrived from Charlottesville for the summer. She lived close enough for me to see her car parked along the street in front of her townhouse. Her bedroom window was visible from mine. We spent lots of time in childhood trying to invent a system of codes and signals, but distance and a bad angle made it impossible. I'd give her time to settle in and sort through family affairs and then pay her a visit. But I was hoping she'd come to me first.

It was my fourth day home and I had no intention of returning to college for the fall semester. I didn't want Mom to find out until it was necessary. In mid-August, when I'd normally be preparing to leave, she'd ask why I wasn't packing and I'd nonchalantly explain that I'd requested a semester's leave. I was in good standing. My accounts were paid up and my GPA was close to perfect. Mom would go ballistic, but I had time to think of an excuse that would calm her. "I'm burnt out" wouldn't work. Neither would anything about finding myself. It would have to be something practical, and something that wouldn't subject me to ridicule. I'd read her mood as the moment approached.

Whatever I came up with, it had to thoroughly conceal the truth, which is that I had an esoteric job to do in DC. I thought of that job as an off-the-books internship. I wouldn't get credit for it, but it would provide great opportunities for real-life experience, the selling point of actual internships that don't come with pay. Like any other intern, I needed money, so I scoured high-end restaurants in Georgetown and Foggy Bottom. Waiting tables would keep me in cash, essential to my task. I got lucky and nabbed a gig on the floor at Filomena.

"Filomena?" Mom said when I told her. "Are you serious? Your father and I used to eat there."

"Yeah, all the big-shits in DC eat there."

"Do they still have that room with the old woman making pasta? When you go down the stairs?"

"I haven't seen anyone there yet."

"I always hated that room. It was like one of those old circus shows where they put people from the colonies on display."

"Huh?"

"Back in the days of the British Empire they used to take people from Africa and show them off like animals. They did the same with Indians here in America."

"What the fuck?"

"It's true. Google it." I don't know why the phrase cracked me up, but I peeled into laughter. "What's so funny?" Mom said.

"I don't know. Nothing. Just...'google it.' You're so hip for an old woman."

"Old woman? Ya binti, I choose to live a quiet life, but if I wanted, I could have a dozen men buying me diamonds."

She was right. Mom had the looks and personality to pull it off. She didn't need traditional beauty, though she had plenty of it. She could get by purely on style. I wasn't so lucky. At best, my sense of style produced mild curiosity.

"Anyway," Mom continued, "I always thought it was creepy. Like that poor woman didn't have anything better to do than make pasta in front of strangers."

"I'll try to get the story for you."

"I already know the story. I don't care what they say. I didn't like eating there to begin with. It smells like feet. And it's too crowded."

The restaurant did smell a bit like feet. And it was definitely crowded, even on weekday nights, with an urbane clientele. I made good money, but I worked for it. Half the customers were assholes and most of them were demanding. I had to tend to their every need without interrupting urgent conversation, which to them meant talking about anything at all. They were into privacy, leaning forward and whispering whenever I came near, but got pissy if I kept a distance. They needed me to know they were important people, but I wasn't allowed to share in that importance. The trick to good tips was deploying visibility and invisibility into a seamless fantasy of taste and discretion.

Once I waited on a six-top featuring a US Senator. He dominated the conversation and the other diners listened to him with great attention. The table had gone through four bottles of wine before the entrees arrived. It was an easy party to serve because the Senator wanted to be heard and liked giving orders. He spoke in an upper-class Southern accent, which I thought was exaggerated; his belligerent demeanor didn't fit with the image he cultivated as a silver-haired gentleman. By the time the table got to dessert, the Senator was thoroughly soused. "Hey boy," he yelled at me as I was tending to another table, "go on and fetch me a double-espresso."

"I don't think it's a boy," the woman across from him giggled.

"It damn well looks like a boy," the Senator said. "Hey you! Boy. Whatever you are. Come on over here for a second." I stood a few feet back from the table, frowning. "Don't be shy. We ain't gonna bite." I didn't move.

"Okay, enough of this silliness," a man next to the Senator said, unconvincingly. "Let's finish up and get out of here."

"By golly we have to solve this mystery. Don't be so hasty." The Senator then addressed me again. "You supposed to be a girl?" I nodded, caught between wanting to smash my tray on his head and running into the kitchen. The Senator flashed a quintessential campaign smile, all shiny white teeth with drab lips stretched into nothingness. He leaned over and slapped my hip. "I'll just have to take your word on it," he said, roaring with laughter. "That's a boy's ass right there." The rest of the table laughed along with him. I begged another server to close out the tab and sneaked to the back of the restaurant where cooks and dishwashers took smoke breaks. Nobody was there. I leaned against the metal door leading to the kitchen and hotboxed two cigarettes.

"He's a good tipper," the other server sneered when I got back onto the floor. Fuck both of them, I thought. There was only one reason I wanted money. If the Senator had known that reason, he wouldn't have tipped a nickel. I was more motivated than ever to succeed at my internship.

Sometimes Mom was still up when I got home. "Why are you going all the way to Georgetown?" she asked one night. "There are plenty of expensive restaurants in Virginia. With parking."

I was hoping Mom wouldn't raise this obvious point. I could go to Merrifield, Tyson's, or Old Town and find dozens of fancy eateries with well-tipping customers. And I hated Filomena. The tables were too close together and the décor was dark and gaudy. Georgetown had no Metro station; the closest was in Foggy Bottom and our townhouse wasn't anywhere near the orange line. I could ride up to Rosslyn and walk across the Key Bridge, but it was a pain in the ass—easier to just drive and pray for a parking spot on one of Georgetown's crowded residential streets.

"I really wanted the experience of working in DC," I said. "I know Virginia through and through. I thought it might be rewarding to spend more time in the city, meet new people and stuff."

Mom looked skeptical but accepted the explanation. In reality, I didn't care about anything other than location. Working at Filomena put me in proximity to the Ambassador. It could have been any other joint, so long as it offered a reason to spend time in the neighborhood. Mom wouldn't know when I was actually working. And she'd never pay the restaurant a surprise visit. The pasta lady in the window would make sure of that. (I did see her sometimes, by the way, and agreed with Mom that the setup was creepy.) I would spend the next eight months learning the Ambassador's routine. He was often gone, so the task wasn't easy. But like every mover and shaker in DC, he frequented the same few spots. Dining and drinking choices were as much a part of a person's political identity as party affiliation. I gradually learned his patterns. They weren't uniform, but he was consistent enough to be tracked if somebody had the time to do it. During my research, I learned where various other dignitaries liked to hang out. This map of social life among the DC elite was more valuable than any college degree.

I'm getting ahead of myself, though. There was still the matter of my falling out with Elena. I didn't want to go through life without her. I could do without her acceptance—her ignorance about my plan was essential to its success—but I didn't feel like I could retain my humanity without her friendship. Always I remembered her as that brave child undisturbed by Mom's suspicious glances. She would do great things in the world. Anyone who knew Elena could see it. But nobody would know she had inspired me to action. What is activism in essence but a seemingly random series of unseen consequences? The anti-fascists in Charlottesville had learned that lesson. So had my father. You can't inoculate yourself from violence in our society. Not as an activist. Not as a civilian.

It became clear that Elena wasn't coming over and I wasn't interested in a battle of wills, so a few days later I knocked on her door. It was a half-measure because I saw that her car was gone, as was the taxi. Elena's mother was alone and I wanted to see her. I missed her badly. She answered the door and gave me a long hug, then ushered me into the kitchen. She stirred and seasoned a stew as I sat on a barstool at the island.

She dipped her pinky finger into the pot and gave it a lick. "Tell me about school."

"I mean, it's fine. I'm doing well."

"That's all? It's fine? Getting information out of you girls is like pulling teeth."

"Elena did well this semester, too."

"That's what she says. But nothing more." She made a zipping motion across her lips.

"And how are you doing, Ms. Berhane?"

"Ms. Berhane! Again with this! How many times must I tell you to call me Mariam?"

"I know, I know."

"Honey, you're grown up now. I don't want you to think of me as an authority figure." She paused for my acknowledgment. "So what's going on between you and Elena? You don't have to look surprised. I know you two had a fight."

"I don't know." It was a lie. We had again argued about my dubious allyship, although it felt less like an argument than a reckoning that had been a long time coming. Only this time I had responded more aggressively than normal.

"Have you ever considered that I'm trying," I shot back after Elena accused me of apathy.

"Trying? Fuck out of here."

"Don't be so condescending, Elena. We all have different ways of doing things."

"That's fine. But you're not doing anything."

"Why do you fucking care?"

"Doing something is a part of who I am. Understand?"

I understood. She felt rejected, that there was a part of her I didn't care about, or had no interest in knowing. What I took to be nagging and condescension was actually an appeal for empathy. By that point, Elena's hurt had turned into anger. I eased my tone. "I do understand. It's the thing I most admire about you."

"There's some shit about my life in this country that you'll never understand."

"I know." And I fully intended to create the possibility for something better. Affliction as prelude to good fortune. It wasn't something to be discussed, only undertaken.

We did our normal half-ass ritual of conciliation, but the tension didn't abate. By that point of my life, I had accepted the utility of abrupt endings. So I got my shit in order, finished my exams, and left. Elena didn't ask me to stay.

I wanted her mother's affirmation that I wasn't a horrible friend. Being thought insane or rotten by the Berhane women would have been the only thing to stop my plan. In the end, it was to my benefit, not theirs, that I kept it a secret.

"Elena told me you left without saying anything."

"I guess that's true. But, like, she knew I was leaving."

"Whatever has you mad at one another isn't worth it. A friendship is something to nurture and cherish. It requires care, like a fine stew." She chuckled and gave me a spoonful to taste.

"Delicious."

"Stay for dinner? Elena should be home in an hour or two."

"I'd better not."

"She'll be happy to see you. Believe me. Tell Lara to come on over, too."

"My mom?"

"Of course."

"Um, I don't want to be rude, Ms. Berhane, but I don't think my mom would ever come over here. You know how she is." She grinned and then began laughing. "Oh my gosh, I'm sorry," I said, embarrassed by my blather. "I didn't mean to suggest that my mom dislikes you. She's just… stubborn and doesn't like to socialize."

"Baby, I'm not offended. I'm laughing because I know what your mother is like. She's sat right where you are plenty of times."

I was confused. "Are you being metaphorical?"

She laughed again. "Metaphorical? Do I look like an English major? I'm being—what's the opposite?—literal? She literally sits where you're sitting now and tells me about herself."

My confusion intensified. "My mom? No way."

"She does! She's been coming over a lot. She's an amazing woman, your mother. You're very lucky."

I understood what she was telling me, but it didn't make any sense. I wasn't sure how I felt about it, anyway. Elena's mother was my friend, not Mom's. My relationship with each parent had always been compartmentalized and I didn't want them to overlap. "Yeah, that's a pretty big surprise," I said, doing a poor job of hiding my disappointment.

"Good. So invite her over."

"To be honest, I'm worried that she'll make things with Elena worse."

"Don't be silly."

"With all due respect, Ms. Berhane, you don't know my mom all that well. Believe me on this."

"What did I tell you to call me?"

"Mariam," I said, ashamed.

"I think your mother really wants you to repair your friendship with Elena, that's what I think."

"This is so weird," I giggled.

"Lara is rough on the outside, but she's a heck of a woman. She's been through a lot. Her heart is soft."

"It is?"

"Oh, Nancy, don't be silly. You know good and well how devoted she is to you. And she was really helpful when I decided to work."

I was upset. Already this collision of distinct worlds had damaged my position with Elena's mother. "Wow, congratulations. What are you doing?"

"I drive a school bus."

"Are you serious?"

"Yes," she laughed. "Robel drives for a living, so I figured I should do the same thing, only bigger."

"Do you like it?"

"It keeps me busy, you know? But when I see the students it makes me miss Elena. I still can't believe she's halfway through college. I stayed home to care for her and when she left I didn't really have anything to do. Robel is easy. He entertains himself. Besides, I told him that I'm not doing this old country crap. We're in America. He can cook for himself and do his own laundry. McDonald's is just down the road."

I laughed along with her. We both knew that no matter how adamantly she bucked old norms she'd never allow anybody in her household to eat a Big Mac. "How did my mom help?" I said. "She doesn't know anything about driving."

"She encouraged me, gave me advice, that sort of thing. You wouldn't believe how excited she was."

"Do you go to TJ?"

"No no," she chuckled. "I work Lake Braddock, which is nice. It's such an easy commute and I can come home in the middle of the day."

"It's kind of bizarre picturing you driving a big ol' bus."

"I know, it's very weird. But Elena is all grown up. I always thought raising a good child would be my way of making a difference. Thank God I succeeded. I hope I did, anyway. [She winked.] Now this job, I don't know, it's kind of like my way of contributing to the world. Do you know what I mean?"

"I know exactly what you mean. I'd better get home now," I said, giving her a quick hug and running off before she had a chance to stop me.

Mom still wasn't home. I fucked around on social media and waited for her. Why was she even gone on a Saturday? I accosted her as soon as she walked in the door. "Where have you been? I need to talk to you."

"Can I at least put my things down and change?"

She took her time—on purpose, I was sure. When she finally came to the living room, she said, "You should have told me you weren't planning on having any food ready. I could have picked up something on the way home."

"No need. We were invited to eat at Elena's."

I could see the makings of a smile at the edges of her mouth. "Is that so?"

"Yep. I thought it was super-interesting that you were invited."

She snorted. "I've been invited to more dinners than you've eaten your entire life."

"Not at Elena's house."

"What's with the interrogation? You're making it sound like I did something wrong. Was I not supposed to become friends with Mariam? Excuse me, but I never got the memo."

"I don't know. It feels duplicitous."

"Don't be petulant, Nancy. Mariam is perfectly capable of knowing two people in the same family."

"It's not that." My tone was growing excited. "Ugh, I knew you wouldn't even try to understand."

She shrugged. "What should we do for dinner?"

"Where were you, anyway?"

"Not that it's any of your business, but I was at the office. I got overloaded with work and wanted to finish before the new week."

"That sucks."

"So are we going to Mariam's?"

"I told her no."

She looked surprised. I'd spent a decade coming up with excuses for having dinner at Elena's house. Now I had declined the opportunity. I could tell Mom was thinking about making me go. Expressing displeasure about her friendship with Mariam had backfired—Mom probably had no interest in going there until she realized it would bother me—but if Mom nagged me to go, it would also backfire. So we ordered Moby Dick. After it was delivered, we sat next to each other at the small, round kitchen table, as we'd done thousands of other times, and sorted through steak and chicken kabobs.

"Mom, seriously," I said between mouthfuls. "How did you become friends with Elena's mom? I honestly thought you didn't like her."

"When did I ever say that? When did I ever say a negative thing about her?"

"Oh my God stop being so defensive. I didn't say you talk shit about her. I said you don't like her. And don't start pretending that you've always been lovey-dovey or whatever. You totally ignored her the entire time I was in high school."

"Here, eat more steak." She spooned two chunks of kabob onto my plate.

"She told me you were really helpful when she decided to go back to work."

"I tried."

"She admires you."

Mom started cleaning up the table. "Well. I admire her, too. It's brave to go to work at her age."

I rinsed dishes and handed them to mom, who put them in the dishwasher. We then sat in front of the television mounted against the living room wall and scrolled through a menu of streaming services.

"What are you in the mood for tonight?" she said.

"Ozark?"

"Too heavy."

"Money Heist?"

"Too unrealistic."

"Outlander?"

"Too disgusting."

"Great British Baking Show?"

"Perfect."

We took in a few episodes, resting against opposite arms of the couch. Mom wasn't a talker in everyday life, but she rarely shut up when watching TV. She critiqued the appearance of each candidate's dessert, analyzed their voices and mannerisms, and opined about which one should be sent home. She was the world's most judgmental telestrator. She also made snide comments about Paul Hollywood, but I could tell she secretly liked him. I relaxed on my end of the couch and nodded along.

Until I got the job at Filomena, these were our typical nights. Mom would go to bed at around ten and I'd stay up a few more hours, munching on high-calorie snacks and doing research. The Ambassador was surprisingly public. He liked to be seen around town, fancied himself a proud citizen of the city—no entourages or limousines, just quiet meetings with people similarly attracted to the camera. The Ambassador was a regular person of the upper class. He traveled often and did lots of outreach, visiting high schools and colleges around the region. He didn't show up on cable news frequently, but he made an appearance every now and again. Propaganda was usually reserved for the Institute and the Kingdom's other intellectual properties. He seemed to have an open invitation to the White House and Capitol Building. None of this information put me any closer to acting, but it fueled my desire. He was right there, just a few miles away. And I could track him anywhere, for I was merely a ghost in Washington's social life.

On weekday mornings, Mom would be gone by the time I woke up. She usually left me a nice breakfast: pitted Castelvetrano olives, yoghurt, Afghan flatbread, za'atar, sliced apples. Mom had always taken breakfast seriously. I ate fruit and protein almost every morning during my thirteen years of school. No Frosted Flakes or Cinnamon Toast Crunch or the other sugary stuff American kids get. For the longest time I was jealous, but I now realize that the foundation Mom set allows for my unhealthy lifestyle as an adult. She still made comments about my weight and ungirly appearance, but seemed too tired anymore to put much effort into the nagging. Our routine that early summer mostly consisted of passive interaction. Mom had moved through the ranks of middle management at George Mason and had no interest in theatrics. She wanted to eat and watch television, which allowed her to argue without anyone talking back.

We were cycling into a role-reversal. I hadn't become the parent, per se, but she had forfeited much of her standing as the mother, which for me meant more peace and quiet. It was strange to see her aging. I developed feelings of tenderness for her that shocked me with their intensity. What if Dad hadn't disappeared? Would we still be living an exciting life in the city? Would Mom have grown even more imperious, more glamorous, rather than maturing into another middle-manager ground into tedium by the suburban routine of work and slumber? I could forgive Dad because I grew to understand his mentality. I would never forgive the Kingdom.

One afternoon I decided to make Mom a big dinner. She would be either annoyed or elated. It was impossible to predict. She wasn't much on symbolic gestures, but she was also growing tired of fast-casual dinners. I had never cooked—never really had to—because Mom had always done enough prep work throughout the week to whip together a decent meal each day after work. Since I left for college, though, she put in less effort, eating from big pots of leftovers or grabbing something on the way home. It occurred to me how similar she was in certain ways to Elena's mother and it finally made sense why they became friends. They had to alter eighteen years of habit all at once. Who else but another empty-nester can you talk to about that kind of thing?

I kept my expectations realistic, but I didn't want to make something out of a box. I decided on a veggie stir-fry—healthy and basic. Making rice seemed easy: two parts water to one part rice. Rinse rice. Boil. Cover. Simmer. Evaporation. Voila! As the rice cooked, I chopped broccoli (in awe of how many stems exist on a stalk), carrots, green beans, and mushrooms. I tried to grate ginger, but ended up with mush and sore forefingers. Good enough. I diced up a spongy chunk of tofu. I had trouble following the recipe I'd pulled up on my computer screen. It looked easy when I found it. Putting it into action was harder than I expected. Sweaty and disheveled, I poured soy sauce and sesame oil and tried to keep the rectangles of tofu in one piece. Every time I took a sample, the taste was off, so I dickered with salt and garlic powder.

I checked the rice. Water still in the pot. I turned up the burner. The frying pan with vegetables was beginning to smoke, so I set its burner to low. I pulled a box of P.F. Chang's spring rolls from the freezer and put them in the microwave. I was setting condiments on the table when Mom came home. "What's this?" she said, a hint of suspicion in her tone.

"Come, sit down. I made you dinner."

"You made me what?"

"Dinner. Don't be a smartass."

"Why?" She looked genuinely confused.

"Just wanted to give it a try."

"Should I be scared?"

I was on the edge of tears and slammed a bamboo stirring spoon onto the stovetop. "Go to Chipotle if you don't like it."

"Okay, okay, calm down. Jesus. I'm just surprised, that's all."

"You don't have to be mean about it. I was trying to do something nice for you."

She lifted her head and gave a few hyperbolic sniffs. "Let's see… smells like Chinese."

"Sort of. It's a stir-fry."

"All right, let's give it a try." She sat down while I served her a plate. My heart sank. An inch of rice was stuck to the bottom of the saucepan. The rest of it was dehydrated. In the skillet, the broccoli looked pathetic—soft and droopy. The tofu hadn't held its form and half the sauce had dried onto the surface of the pan. I spooned some rice onto a plate and topped it with vegetables. I made my own plate, dodging the mushrooms, and sat across from Mom. She eyed the food warily and then took a large bite. I took a smaller one.

It was awful. There was no crunch to the tofu or vegetables and the entire thing was too salty. The sauce—what was left of it, anyway—didn't really moisten the rice; everything on the plate had an unpleasant texture. I looked sheepishly at Mom. She was taking bites as if everything were fine.

"You don't have to pretend, Mom."

"It's fine."

"No it's not," I said, putting my head in my arms.

"Look." She took another bite and patted my arm. "I'm still eating. See?"

Her attempt at kindness, with the same tone a second-grade teacher uses on a child who just botched a simple arithmetic problem, put me over the edge. I could feel tears dribbling onto the bridge of my nose. Soon my shoulders were convulsing as I tried to control my breathing. Mom stood and rubbed my neck. "Come with me," she said.

I didn't want to move, but she lingered beside me with her hand extended. She led me to the couch and sat me down so that my head could fall onto her lap. Wiping my tears with her thumb, she said, "Nancy, the food tasted like shit, but I've never had a meal so special." This only made me cry harder. "It's okay, darling, it's okay, habibty." She stroked my hair, letting her nails graze against my scalp.

"I really wanted to do something nice for you," I managed between sobs.

"You did. What does the quality of the food have to do with it?"

"Making a nice dinner was the whole point."

"You did make a nice dinner. It tasted bad, but it was nice. Very nice."

I sniffled and sat back up. "I'm sorry, Mama."

"Don't apologize, darling. I'm proud of you." She walked back to the kitchen and finished her plate.

"Can I order Paisano's?" I asked, sending her into a fit of laughter.

We spent the rest of the evening watching Food Network and eating cheese pizza. Mom kept giving me pointers. "See how she's turning down the heat for the garlic? It burns faster than onions…. Look, he saved a cup of the pasta water. Now if his sauce gets too thick, he can lighten it up…. The trick is to add just a little salt at a time. You can always add more, but if you add too much the entire meal is ruined." For the first time in ages, none of it annoyed me. Despite my failure, I felt at peace, like I was a little girl again. Our reversal of roles had a limit.

I had intended to try cooking again, but then I got the job at Filomena. It didn't leave much time for reconciliation with Elena. I was in DC exploring various neighborhoods even on my days off, although Mom thought I was working (she never questioned how many hours I was putting in). Elena was gone whenever I was home. I wasn't always ready to talk, but I was tired of our silly fight, our needless separation. I saw myself as timid and Elena as stubborn. From her vantage point, I could have been the stubborn one. She had no idea I wanted to talk. I assumed that she wanted to talk, as well, but I was scared of being wrong. I half-expected to run into her in DC sometime. All the action was there. I looked out for Nyla, too, but she apparently had a different set of haunts than the ones I was stalking.

I should have known the parents would interfere. With Elena's mother off for the summer and mine looking to revive her devotion to bossiness, interference was a foregone conclusion. Maybe that's why neither Elena nor I made a move; we both knew it would be done for us. When Mom asked about my next day off, I refused to divulge my schedule. I needed the freedom to move around according to the Ambassador's timetable. But Mom persisted until I fessed up. I couldn't pretend that I worked seven nights a week. (In reality, I only worked about thirty hours.) I knew she was setting up something with the Berhane household even though she acted like her interest in my schedule was simple curiosity.

And so we walked down the street one evening and knocked on their door. Elena answered and stood to the side.

"What a surprise," her mother said, hugging us both.

"I was telling Nancy that we need to come over and congratulate you for finishing your first year."

"Thank you. How sweet. And so lucky that Elena's home."

Elena rolled her eyes and said, "Pathetic."

The mothers ignored her. "Believe it or not," her mother said to mine, "I'm just finishing up a nice dinner and there's plenty for everyone. You must join us. I insist."

"Absolutely not," Mom said. "We wouldn't think of imposing."

"No, no, you must. Really. I'll be insulted if you don't."

"We certainly don't want to insult you. Are you sure it's not an imposition?"

"Of course not! It's an honor."

"Well, if you're sure, I suppose we can stay. What do you say, Nancy?"

"I agree with Elena."

Elena's mother started telling mine about what she had cooked, beginning with analysis of the produce at various stores and the prices therein. Mom pretended to care. I sat at the kitchen island, trying to abstain from a facepalm. Elena stayed in the living room. I walked over and sat next to her on the couch. She didn't acknowledge me. I looked at the same family pictures I'd seen thousands of times—black-and-whites of ancestors in traditional clothing or posing awkwardly in suits and dresses, the photo clearly a big event at the time. They were everywhere, these photos, on end tables and hanging from walls, in rustic frames that accentuated their dignity. The room was filled out with colorful fabrics and ornate crucifixes.

Elena wasn't making a show of ignoring me, but her face was tense. She finally spoke. "I was worried about you. Did you even consider that?"

"No," I said.

"Well, I was…am. I didn't want you to be lonely or depressed, just sitting around the room. I don't give a shit how woke you are or whatever. I didn't want you to be alone."

"But I didn't feel lonely or depressed. I was okay. I'm just introverted."

"You could have told me that instead of copping an attitude."

"I'm sorry, Elena."

"It's fine." It occurred to me that Elena might not want to make up on principle, because she didn't want to validate our mothers' scheme. We returned to silence until her mother called us to eat. After half an hour of small talk about traffic, food prices, and the impending arrival of Amazon's new headquarters to the region, Elena stood and said, "Excuse me, Ms. Baker, I don't mean to be rude, but I have a date I really need to get to. It was wonderful seeing you."

"Oh? A date-date?"

"Nah, just some friends."

"You can't stay a bit longer?" her mother said.

"I wish I could. This was lovely, though. Let's do it again?"

I snorted and everyone stared at me. Elena smiled before turning around. The plan had worked, sort of. Elena would keep on doing her thing and I would disappear into the noise of Georgetown. I wouldn't see her again until after my rendezvous with the Ambassador.

My pursuit of him began slowly—lots of walking without much purpose, lost in the stone and pastel of the neighborhood's architecture. I developed a crazy understanding of space. Nothing was pointless, everything mattered. Nooks, side doors, benches, lightposts, alleyways, parks, dumpsters, walking trails, shrubbery (with or without foliage). Even the ugly, empty trench of the B&O Canal had its uses. I could see how the city was designed and built over the course of decades, centuries, and how its design allowed generations of homeowners to build power. I didn't remember much about Cleveland Park, never went there anymore, but it was different than Georgetown. The vibe was similar, but each area features a different layout. Georgetown has a busy commercial district and butts against the river. It also has a hilly campus with lots of trees and green spaces, but not many options for getting in and out. Cleveland Park has some quiet streets with single-family homes and is close to Rock Creek Park, which, with a little know-how and exertion, can lead somebody all the way to Maryland. I couldn't think of any reason why the Ambassador would go to Cleveland Park. It would have been easier to murder him in my old neighborhood.

I tracked the Ambassador by proxy, relying on his public schedule and social media feeds. Getting to him at a speech or media event would be near-impossible, but I wanted a sense of his movements and habits. What part of the day did he like to schedule certain things? Where did he eat? Shop? (Did a man of his status even buy his own groceries?) Drink coffee? Whom did he socialize with? Or avoid? Did he frequent prostitutes? Keep mistresses? Which hotel did he use? Or did he rent a bachelor's pad?

I decided to follow him. I didn't want anyone to see me near his house, so I waited outside a venue where he was a guest. (It was shockingly easy to find his address online.) The Ambassador finally appeared long after most others had left and got into a black sedan that had been waiting for nearly an hour. The car dropped him off at Le Diplomate. Two hours later, he left the restaurant and got back into the black sedan, which took him to a wine bar in Georgetown, down below M Street, the quiet area. The bar was a quick walk along the canal from Filomena. I learned that he frequented the wine bar. Le Diplomate was also a regular haunt, as were Fiola Mare, on the riverfront, and Il Canale, a brick-oven pizza joint a block east of Filomena. I also saw him at the Old Ebbitt Grill, near the White House, and Charlie Palmer Steak, on Capitol Hill. Standard DC power spots. He never came to Filomena when I was working, which made me wonder if I transmitted a dangerous vibe.

The Ambassador didn't keep a fixed schedule, though. Well into what should have been my fall semester, I knew that he sometimes visited a gym in the morning, never for more than an hour, and seemed to avoid all outdoor activity. No jogging, mountain biking, kayaking, none of that stuff. He ate out for dinner three or four times a week. He often spent the entire day in his embassy, but it wasn't unusual for him to lunch with men (almost always men) who looked very important. He traveled, but never locally: no trips to Virginia or Maryland and nothing beyond the corridor between his house and Capitol Hill. All travel was international, with short trips to New York and San Francisco or to a university so he could dispense advice about the importance of democracy. If he did any philandering, he was extremely discreet about it.

I only got near him once, when he was walking down 31st Street to Fiola Mare. I knew where the familiar black car would drop him, so I decided to follow. When he reached the restaurant, I continued along the walking path next to the river. He was tall and elegant, charismatic really, with a calm, almost gentle face, the same russet color as his razor-bald head, exactly how I remembered him from the year before. He was thin, but it wasn't a frail thinness. I could tell he was strong; his posture said as much. It was easy to see why the Kingdom had installed him as Ambassador. He appealed to every American myth of grace and masculinity.

At the onset of the holidays, I had the outline of a plan. The details were a constant source of worry. I would have one chance to complete the task without spending my life in prison. And I was firm that it would just be the Ambassador. No bodyguards. No mistresses. No bystanders. I was driven by a singular question: how could I get close to him? I couldn't befriend him. He accepted friendship according to criteria I had no hope of meeting. I couldn't seduce him. He would be attracted to a more womanly partner. The answer came to me in flashback. I couldn't gain access to DC's most exclusive spaces as my father's daughter, but I could do it as his son.

Fred

IT'S OKAY, LOVE. It's okay, darling. I got you. Daddy's got you. I cup my hand beneath her mouth. Blood fills my palm. I can smell the residue of Dr. Bonner's and Mr. Bubble in her hair. She looks tiny in moments of pain, struggling to breathe, to comprehend what just happened.

I gently lift her upper lip to see if her teeth are still there. I see them, baby pearls awash in red. She screams. I remove my finger. It's not your fault. It's not your fault. Daddy's going to take you to the doctor now, okay. I carry her to the car, her blood dribbling onto my shirt, and strap her into a booster seat. I park illegally near an urgent care office and rush her inside. We wait in an examination room without windows. I fill out insurance forms. She sucks on a popsicle the nurse had given her. She's lucky, the doctor explains; she won't need stitches. The mouth, it bleeds a lot, makes a wound seem worse. Look, it's already stopped. Her upper lip is enormous. She'll get to eat lots of ice cream the next two days.

She's embarrassed. I can tell. She doesn't want me to tell her mom what happened. It's not your fault, I keep repeating. This wound, this disfiguration, it's my fault. I was supposed to be watching you, but I got lost in my email. You were climbing on the kitchen island and I didn't notice. Mama had had enough of my delinquency and put me in charge while she met friends for lunch. But I didn't understand how an innocent psychology works, didn't realize that at your age you knew no better, that like all children you'll poke around and climb. It was my fault, you see. Because I didn't care. I wouldn't entertain you. You got bored. And so you wanted to see the world from a different vantage point. I was sick with guilt, terrified, as I waited for you to fall asleep so I could get back to work.

Thump thump thump. The back of my skull echoed against the wall. I was trying to stop my brain from dispensing memories, but they were the only type of thought I could manage on the threshold of my demise. If I forced away Nancy, in came Nyla and I was remembering scenes from the Mayflower, sitting next to her on the bed.

"This is really weird," she had said the first time.

"A little bit."

"You're my boss. And so much ... I mean, you know, the age difference."

"Why concern yourself with social conventions? They're an affront to human nature. Isn't our primary mandate as humans to enjoy the rare opportunity for pleasure? We have the power to offer one another bliss, literal bliss, simply by responding to our brain chemistry. We can't get the same feeling from anything else. Just our bodies. By sharing touch. That's all. It's quite remarkable. Miraculous."

"I know." She fell back onto the mattress, a half-smile highlighting a puzzled expression. "I know."

I stretched beside her, putting my hand on her stomach. "In this room, this world, you can be the boss."

Thump ... thump ... whack. Now I was trying to knock the shame from my mind. For even as I was arguing nonsense to Nyla, I was thinking about Lara and more unpleasant notions of pleasure. Only it wasn't exactly nonsense I was preaching to Nyla; it was more a lesson in the finer points of professional conduct. The sermon only became embarrassing after ejaculation. My line about being the boss, so horrible in hindsight that I wish I couldn't remember it, served its purpose and eased our transition onto the billowing comforter that smelled of flowers and chlorine. After that night, it became easy, the trysts and encounters just another mating ritual haunted by the possibility of conception. Once we could be naked without feeling inhibited, thoughts of age and status went away. Our relations—her father, my wife, the entire goddamn apparatus of civic life—became sources of anxiety and excitement. I could be killed or divorced and found in either possibility a source of titillation. Being with Nyla was also safe. Getting caught wouldn't threaten my career.

My thoughts never stopped at Nyla. I couldn't recall my lust for her without also remembering Lara. What drives a man to unfaithfulness? We like to give all kinds of biological explanations—procreation, temptation, evolution—but in my case it was something more. Nyla was an appeal to nostalgia, an exquisite source of youth, a hedge against mortality, and most important an antidote to the boredom of prosperity. I couldn't separate her from Lara because my love for Lara was real and Nyla supplied the illusion of virility that Lara refused to offer. Throughout the affair, I thought of Nyla as life. Not life as managed by demands of civility, but teenage fantasies of pleasure and passion. Life in its purest incarnation. I suppose I loved Nyla, too, but mainly as a reflection of my narcissism. That seems to me the real reason for man's infidelity.

It's why I came to understand after my arrest that principle is possible only in isolation. It was true in just about every example I could think of. Often the isolation was involuntary, but either way it struck me as a prerequisite of virtue. Everything I'd been taught about good citizenship nurtured the idea that only power could provide salvation. It was all based on the depravity of competition, a kind of common sense synonymous with profiteering. Only in that dank, empty cell, riddled with shame and regret, did I ever think of myself as a decent person. I didn't know what difference this realization would make, but I was glad to have enjoyed the feeling at least once before dying. I wondered if Nancy would one day understand my conundrum, if she might even be proud of me. I curled into the corner of the cell like an imperious house cat. For the first time in ages, I slept heavily.

A kick on my shin jolted me awake. Two guards had entered my cell and ordered me onto my feet. I couldn't be sure how long I had slept. It could have been a full night or a catnap. I got on my feet and waited for the guards to cuff me. I was sick of the routine. Seeing the Colonel again would be its own form of torture and I didn't think I had enough fortitude to endure more of the physical variety. Once more, moving into light was dreadful. It seemed to enter through my eyes and burn the interior of my entire body. The guards led me upstairs but we didn't stop to see the Colonel. Nor did they take me to any other room. Instead we went outside, where the sunlight nearly blinded me and felt like a wool blanket on my skin.

"Where are we going?" I asked the guards in Arabic.

"To your mother's ass," one of them replied to the other's laughter. They walked me out a side door and pushed me into the backseat of a black SUV, perhaps the same one that had taken me to the building two, three, four weeks ago, maybe more. Whatever the case, it was long enough for my body to have become taut and pasty. The mere fact of being outdoors was enough of a shock to constrict my airways. I allowed myself a moment of hope. Would they take me to the US Embassy? To meet somebody with enough power to release me? To the airport so I could be deported? The hope started to diminish when a man in the front seat, different from the original officer (although nearly identical in appearance and attitude), handed one of the soldiers a sack to put over my head.

I was back into darkness, reliving a suffocating trauma. Soon after we started moving, I smelled the subtly sweet odor of imported Gauloises. My hope went away altogether when nobody offered me one. About five minutes later, the man to my right lifted the sack and pressed the cigarette into my cheek. I screamed and tried to move my head away, but the man on the other side whacked my skull with the heel of his hand. The heat from my breath made the wound burn harder. Sweat poured down my neck. I could feel it mixing with discharge from the lesion.

Where were they taking me? We weren't near civilization. No stoplights. No voices. The road sounded empty. It didn't feel like a highway. I took an assessment of my condition. My cheek was in serious pain, but it wouldn't slow my mobility. My muscles felt undernourished, though. My will to survive was also weak. I would submit to death with any more torture. I would quit eating in further isolation. But I would survive if given the opportunity. I owed that much to Nancy and Lara. My father, I recalled, had died gracefully. He fought the disease until it made no more sense to resist. That decision outlived him. I too had a descendant to consider.

I wanted to sleep. I loved sleeping in cars, a habit I inherited from my father. When I was a kid, it wasn't easy to do when he was driving because he talked so much. I learned to just shut my eyes midway through his ruminations. When I woke, he'd start back up again. I always thought of him as a mindless yapper, but after his death I came to realize that he was deeply curious and possessed a tormented interior life. He talked so much because he wanted to understand everything. He would be unmoored from a sense of morality without making sense of the world's physical and intellectual properties. I also suspect, in retrospect, that he was trying to please his father, to ease whatever guilt his father may have felt for not being around. See, Baba, I turned out okay. I'm smart. I can take care of myself. I'll pass it all along to your grandson.

Looking back, I don't know if my mother was introverted, that category I kept reading about on the internet, or if she was simply content in a controlled environment, but she didn't often venture out with us. She preferred tidying the house, reading books in French and Arabic from the university library, and hosting long, intense conversations with my grandparents, which I liked to join in silence after school. They were vivid and stubborn. I watched with fascination. I could make out an entire world in those arguments, something that never happened in school. Usually my mother and grandmother ganged up on my grandfather, but no matter how loudly they bickered, it didn't seem to affect their feelings about one another. Just as quickly as they started shouting, they reverted to calm discussion about travel schedules and dinner plans.

So my mother stayed behind when my dad decided to take me to Washington DC. My father tried to convince her and his in-laws to come, but they refused. "I'll only go to spit on the White House," my grandmother said. My father quit pestering her after that.

It took around four hours to get to DC from Blacksburg, but nothing was ever straightforward with my father. He wanted to stop everywhere along the way: Natural Bridge, Lexington ("there's a delicious Southern restaurant I read about in the *Roanoke Times*"), Luray Caverns, Shenandoah National Park. When he took me and my mother to DC when I was a kid, he explained, he missed all this stuff and he wasn't about to do it again.

"George Washington's initials are the most boring thing about this place," he said of Natural Bridge before badgering two rangers who explained that we weren't allowed to walk across the top of the rock. I pulled him away before they lost their patience. I nearly froze in Luray Caverns, but my father was fascinated and explored every nook exposed to light. All I wanted was to be above ground with my friends, shooting hoops or playing soccer. Anything but listening to my father's analysis of stalagmites. After driving a short stretch of Skyline Drive, the day was over and we weren't near DC.

We booked a motel room in Front Royal and my father immediately fell asleep on the suspiciously narrow queen bed. I slumped into a scratchy armchair and turned on the TV. Some X-rated movies came up on the menu. I'd seen a few moments of porn at one of my friends' houses during a slumber party and couldn't stop thinking about it for three days. The action almost seemed cruel but it put sensations in my stomach that I couldn't get from anything else. Everything was in shadows and closeups and was provocative enough to deliver concrete imagery while leaving more advanced fantasies to my imagination. My friend's older brother bought us magazines from the adult section of the video store, but my father discovered the stash and made a show of throwing them into the garbage can. I would never outgrow those sensations, though I can no longer conjure them in my condition. I wanted to watch one of these movies in the motel, but couldn't do it with my father nearby, no matter how heavily he slept. I watched the NBA playoffs, instead.

In the car the next morning, finally on our way to Washington, my father asked, "What time did you get to sleep last night?"

I had perched on the edge of the bed, as far away from him as possible, a little past midnight. "Around ten," I said.

"Fine." He was broody and laconic. He got that way occasionally. I could see an elevated vein running from the midpoint of his neck into the wispy hair below his ear. Nobody knew why he got this way. It happened randomly, or so it seemed. And then it would pass. It was hard to imagine my father as capable of violence—I don't remember him ever striking me—but during these rare episodes the possibility was slightly less outlandish. My mother never seemed concerned. She could always feed him back to happiness.

That morning, his silence terrified me. I waited for him to make observations about the shape of the ridges in front of us, the Civil War trivia, the cows and horses grazing in the rangy green farmland on either side of the highway. He gripped the wheel tightly and kept his eyes in front of him, saying nothing.

We were nearing Manassas when he spoke. "I'm in pain today, my son-son."

"Did you sleep funny?"

"It's not that. Bas walla those pillows were terrible, weren't they?"

Back to normal. Just like that. I knew he was inviting me to ask why he was in pain, but I didn't want to. The question felt too intimate. He decided to explain, anyway.

"Here's the thing about your old man. I went through certain things when I was young, not much older than you are right now, and they come into my mind sometimes."

Now I was curious. "What things?"

"Just things. Ugly things. I tell you, my boy, I was so happy yesterday. What a special time to spend with you! Running all over God's creation. I was singing in my head when I went to sleep. And, you see, when I'm this happy, sometimes bad memories come." He paused for my response, but I kept quiet. "So I woke up very upset," he continued, "because I'm afraid somebody will try to steal my happiness."

"It's not like a pack of gum. You can't just snatch it."

"Ah, but you're incorrect, yaba. It can always be snatched. It's an object, worth more than any bar of gold."

"No it's not. It's a feeling. It doesn't even exist."

He sighed dramatically. "That's what they want you to think."

"Who?"

"Bad people." He was losing me. I was used to it. His ruminations always managed to be simultaneously abstract and specific. "Bad people," he repeated.

"Dad…"

"Here, let me tell you a story from back home," he intervened before I could finish, ignoring my groan. "There was a shepherd who had a very nice flock, but he had a problem. A leopard kept eating his sheep. The shepherd tried many things to protect his flock. He guarded them at night, but the leopard waited until he dozed off. He put up scarecrows, but the leopard wasn't afraid. He built a fence, but the leopard jumped over it. So one day he decided to confront the leopard. 'Why do you keep stealing my sheep?' he asked the leopard. The leopard was surprised. 'Why do you keep trying to prevent me from eating?' the leopard replied."

I waited for the story to continue, but that was it. "So...it's okay to steal sheep if you're hungry?"

Another dramatic sigh. "This happiness you feel, it has to be shared. If somebody has to be unhappy to make you happy, then you should think about what you're doing. Sometimes you have to be the one who suffers. Do you see what your Baba is telling you?"

I nodded. But I didn't see what he was telling me and wouldn't understand it until avatars of the Kingdom put my head in a vise. Only then did I figure out that my father's story wasn't about the shepherd or the predator, but the flock. They got slaughtered no matter who ended up happy.

My father wasn't much interested in DC's conventional landmarks. "Why would I want to climb a million stairs inside a boring white phallus?" he said of the Washington Monument.

"What's a phallus?"

"It's like the things you saw in those magazines I confiscated from you and your friends."

He was equally unimpressed by the White House. "Everything in this town is white white white," he said, drawing glances from passersby. "They need to paint the trim. What do you think, yaba? Maybe some red, black, and green, huh?"

"Sure, Dad."

He preferred the Smithsonians, which I hated. They had some cool exhibits, but the crowds scared me and I could never find a place to rest. I couldn't understand how my father ran around from display to display, building to building, without getting tired. The half-cooked tourists in tube socks and Tevas came in waves, yapping and ambling and snapping pictures. My dad, swarthy and unkempt, somehow managed to fit in with them. He chitchatted with anyone who showed interest in his discourses about bones and fossils.

Otherwise, he was interested in neighborhoods. We explored residential streets and parkland, stopping by the National Zoo. At some point we probably walked past what would one day become my office. I enjoyed this part of the trip. The zoo was too crowded even for my dad, but most neighborhoods were sparse and peaceful, with mature oak trees and neat little gardens. Maybe it was then I got the idea of being a big man in Washington. I don't remember any epiphanies, but perhaps the place got under my skin in a way that drove my ambition. Whatever the case, I wasn't out of high school when I decided that I'd someday experience the life of this peculiar city.

I was close to dozing off, memories of the time with my father calming my soul, when I was jolted to consciousness by the smell of cigarette smoke. It was coming from my right and I prayed that the soldier would throw his butt out the window, but a few moments later the side of my hood went up and I felt a searing pain about an inch below the original blister. I roared and thrashed my head around to get the embers off my face. The soldier to my left smacked me with the heel of his palm again. I felt a gloppy liquid dripping from the first wound. The second one was more painful. I could no longer think of anything but my ailing face. I tried listening to sounds from the outside. It would be good to get clues about where I was going, but I lacked the right skillset for the task. All I could discern was a rush of wind.

Nobody in the car spoke. I kept my mouth shut, too. My impulse was to argue because I saw in argument a kind of life drained from me by isolation, but saying anything likely would have gotten me a beating. Occasionally, the man in the front passenger seat gave a quick order to the driver—"don't miss the turn"; "watch that truck"; "go faster"—but the driver never answered. They behaved as men on an unpleasant but necessary business trip. But there was also a sense of anticipation and respite. They were finally being allowed to relieve themselves of a nuisance.

After a while (short or long, I couldn't tell), the car exited the pavement and appeared to be driving on sand. I started timing the journey in my head. I couldn't be exact, but we drove for many miles in what was obviously rough terrain, the SUV lurching and dipping and swaying in a world of unsolid footing. I could picture the scenery: endless mounds of sand that were tan or yellow depending on the angle of the sun. I'd been in similar places as a guest of the Kingdom, enjoying off-roading in the dunes before retiring to dinner in a well-appointed Bedouin encampment. I didn't expect any oasis this time around.

We finally stopped. The SUV was parked at an angle. I had slid against the man to my left. The odor of cigarette smoke wafted inside the sack. Social conditioning kicked in and a heavy sweat enveloped my neck. This time when the sack came up it wasn't to extinguish a cigarette. The guards took it off altogether. I lowered my head to my knees so my eyes could adjust to the light. It was intensely bright. Nothing organic or artificial grew from the sand to provide shade. A cloudless blue sky adorned an infinite desert. The sheer volume of the openness made me dizzy. In any other circumstance I would have found it beautiful.

Only one of the guards got out of the car with me. He pushed me to the ground from behind with his foot. The sand irritated my skin and eyes. And there it was. The solitude, the emptiness, that had colonized my lust, fully realized in this florid desolation. No foliage. No animal tracks. Just me on the frontier of eternity. Without a word, the soldier returned to the SUV. It drove off in a fog of dust.

Nancy

THERE WERE ONLY two consistencies in the Ambassador's life: he liked the wine bar in Georgetown, down below M Street, and he rarely walked anywhere. He had a driver/bodyguard, a bald, thickset Black man who always scowled, even when greeting his employer. How devoted was he to the Ambassador? Would he really risk his own life to save this rich foreigner? Probably not, but I couldn't be sure. Anything involving the driver was out. I wouldn't entertain anything more unpredictable than the Ambassador himself.

I planned the operation much longer than I needed to, but I was in no great hurry. If something happened to this ambassador—a plane crash, a promotion, whatever—there would be a new one to kill. The position mattered more than the person, although I was pleased to discover that this ambassador was an attractive target. He had a direct history with Dad, but I also tabbed him as a drunk and a fabulist. That he was so lovely, so urbane, increased my confidence that he was the perfect target. His inner rot would expedite my task.

During this period, I thought about Dad a lot. Would he accept my actions? I'd been asking that question from the beginning, but I finally decided that it didn't matter. Maybe that's not the right way to say it. Dad's approval mattered, but his disapproval wouldn't affect my decision. My love for him, for what he would have been, wasn't contingent on his blessing, in any of his incarnations. Besides, I knew that I was the most logical person to negate his disappearance from the world. I had become what he was changing into when he disappeared. Dad didn't know how to change, that was his problem. He was afflicted by what he understood to be an impulse. Because it didn't go away, he came to think of it as a sickness. (He wasn't really wrong; according to most standards of normalcy, he was clearly unwell.) But then the sickness started to look like a cure. At that point, he pursued the cure with typical ambition even after realizing that death was actually the prescription. Had he learned to be less ambitious, he might be alive right now—living a different type of suffering, for sure, but able to act out his own struggle.

I was motivated by a similar desire. But I wouldn't be impulsive. I overcompensated by becoming too cautious. I was learning about oppression and inequality and the other heavy things Elena discussed with her activist friends, but my education was mapped onto the landscape of a city obsessed with power. Because the Ambassador was an important man, wealthy and famous, he was almost always out of reach. It wasn't just that he enjoyed the luxury of a chauffeur. People were always around him. He could create social life out of nothing, just by appearing. It was an extremely valuable asset in a place where attention is a prized commodity.

Killing somebody in Southeast DC would have required little planning. I'd get a gun, find the person, and finish the job. Right in the middle of the street. Maybe the cops would investigate the crime, maybe they'd chalk it up to gangland violence, file it away with the other unsolved cases. Nobody would say anything. The act wouldn't have been recorded. It would be just another anonymous addition to the dark-but-charming violence that comprises the city's authenticity. On the other end of town, where I operated, most residents aren't anonymous—their social classes provide a secure identity. The crowds in Georgetown and Dupont Circle aren't considered surplus and so individual life is ratified, valuable. The attitude is reflected in the infrastructure. Cameras are everywhere. Police. Feds. Spooks. Private security. Killing is strictly unidirectional.

It took me a while to solve this puzzle. I had long fantasized about putting a hole beneath each of the Ambassador's eyes. Quick and satisfying. I couldn't plan it in a way that seemed possible. Gunshots are too loud, even with a suppressor on the barrel. (I spent a lot of time reading about guns.) I could conceivably shoot the Ambassador and run away, but I couldn't count on an empty sidewalk. Someone was always around, even in the sedated areas down by the Potomac. And if I got to him in a quiet spot, something I couldn't plan for, dozens of people would hear the gunshot. It wouldn't take long for police to arrive. I needed to be well out of the area. I finally thought of an option with a good balance of effectiveness and efficiency.

After I decided on a course of action, I took great pains to make myself untraceable. The busyness honed my sense of purpose. It would have to be done in or near the wine bar, the Ambassador's most frequent hangout. He was never alone, of course, but that wasn't a problem. His friends' shock would help my cause.

So I set about putting the event in motion. I look back fondly on that period. Overwhelmed by anxiety and hope, I invited the entire human community into my project. I'd always envied that quality in Elena, the dogged impulse to justice, and for good reason, I discovered. Nothing was quite like the feeling of singular purpose. Suddenly I was doing something immeasurable. In a world of order and precision, that felt important.

I lost enough weight to pass for a gentleman. Then I drove out to Leesburg and bought a suit and dress shoes from the men's department at the Brooks Brothers outlet, paying cash. I went to Maryland for a fake beard and a tasteful fedora. I didn't want anything traced to my address.

I used the dark web to acquire the most essential item, which required a trip to New Jersey. On the way, I bought a track suit and baseball cap. I would do the exchange as a man, dressed casually, a dry run to see if I could pull off masculinity. It was pretty easy to do when I wasn't trying, so I figured the trick was to act naturally. I turned up at the Rockaway Mall—"Townsquare," they called it—about half an hour early and waited at the edge of the parking lot near Macy's, as the guy (I assumed it was a guy) had instructed me.

His username was doctortoxic and I found him by nosing around a forum on contraband. I was too paranoid to use my own laptop or our modem at home, so I bought a cheap PC that I planned to dismantle and dispose of in parts and found a quiet café in Rockville with good Wi-Fi. Over the course of two days, doctortoxic walked me through a bunch of morbid options. Everything was cryptic and suggestive but he picked up on what I wanted to do and promised to satisfy my needs. Our deal arranged, I rented a car and drove north to meet him. He would discover that I wasn't from the area, as I had claimed, but there was little chance he'd be surprised. If I wasn't a cop and brought the right amount of cash (a large chunk of my savings) then I was pretty sure he wouldn't give a shit where I came from. I didn't give him my number. I was supposed to wait for him to approach me.

He tapped the passenger side window right on time. I didn't want to let him in the car, so I started the engine and rolled the window halfway down. His face was pasty, with acne scars and a thin goatee. "You have the money?" His accent was vaguely Slavic. I nodded and handed him an envelope. He put it inside his jacket pocket without checking the amount. After looking over his shoulder he dropped a prescription bottle onto the passenger seat. Before I could say anything, he was walking briskly toward the mall.

Did he know I was a woman? He didn't seem taken aback or unusually suspicious. His demeanor was about what I expected given the circumstances. The exchange was quick. He probably wouldn't remember me well enough to describe. Dude in track suit. Mid-twenties. Short curly hair. Beard. A bit chubby. Darkish skin. Maybe Mexican or Italian or Pakistani. (A significant portion of New Jersey, in other words.) Driving back to Virginia under a white sky garnished with puffs of silver and gray, I began to feel confident. I could be a man. I could access sites of power. I could be a murderer. I was finally doing my part to sustain life on the planet.

I stored the prescription bottle within layers of junk in my closet. Men's formal clothing hung on the rack. I'd picked up various items in different stores. The goal wasn't simply to pass for a man, but to look like a regular guy of the professional-class DC variety. That meant dark suits, well-cut but not too fancy or stylish, and English instead of Italian shoes. Or pastel V-neck sweaters, preferably cashmere, with pleated slacks for casual outings. I never found occasion to wear my fedora. It was too out of place. I'd have to experiment with various hairstyles. I needed to be adequately preppy, but not of alien stock, just another go-getter surviving the grind. The Ambassador and other representatives of the world's potentates were the ones who dressed with class.

I visited the wine bar in disguise one evening after working a lunch shift at Filomena. If I couldn't be convincing in my new identity, then it was better to find out early. I was nervous walking in, but steadied myself and sat at the bar. The space was small without feeling claustrophobic. Square tables with a lacquered black surface were set apart a few feet from one another. Booths and two-tops covered the majority of the floor. Across one wall, a long bar of polished mahogany rounded into floor-to-ceiling wine racks. The lighting was dark enough to encourage relaxation without inducing slumber. Cameras weren't visible, but I had no doubt that customers were being recorded.

A bartender in a black tuxedo vest approached. "What can I get you this afternoon?"

I hadn't thought about what to order. Stumbling around would kill any pretense that I was a regular guy looking for a bit of calm after a long day at the office. I gathered myself and asked in a gravelly voice what he recommended. He gave various options.

"House red will be fine."

"Yes, sir. Coming right up."

I drank two glasses before paying out in cash. I didn't like wine, still don't, and couldn't discern the tannins and undertones that were supposed to make the house red so enjoyable. The drink had undoubtedly helped my mood, though. I could finally understand the appeal of fancy alcohol. It didn't need to taste good if it mobilized the drinker's endorphins.

I returned a few days later at the same time and repeated the routine: a request for recommendations followed by two glasses. This time I sat at the end of the bar, near to where the drinks came out for delivery to tables. It became my usual spot.

My third time there, the bartender, identifying me as a potential regular who might be encouraged to keep tipping 40 percent, started making chitchat. He asked what I do for a living, a predictable question. I told him I'm a consultant, an equally predictable answer. In DC, being a consultant can mean anything and normally halts further inquiry. If people keep asking, all you have to do is put an industry to the term: "I consult for the aeronautical industry" or whatever. IT is another good answer. "I work on IT for the Pentagon." Half the white-collar-types in this town are up to some shady shit and so it's no big deal if you get tabbed as a spook or some kind of operative. It's more respectable work than what the poor bastard serving you is doing. Thus I became Matt the consultant, with a realistic fake ID and upmarket prescription frames constructed of thick black plastic. I devised all kinds of banal stories about office stress. The low tenor of my voice became natural when I was in disguise. I never stayed long. I wanted to maintain the appearance of a man enjoying a few moments of peace before returning home to his wife and baby.

Mom noticed my absences. "Have you found a boyfriend, girlfriend, whatever?"

"Why do you care?"

"Because you're gone all the time. And you're skinny all of a sudden. I'm hoping it's for a good reason."

"Would a girlfriend count as a good reason?"

"That depends on the girl. I never wanted you to fritter away your time with a loser."

"I'll be home more soon, I promise."

She looked skeptical. I wasn't accustomed to this version of Mom, the one who wanted me around. After years of working in university administration, her sense of purpose had been whittled to a simple pleasure: privacy and downtime. To my chagrin, and probably to her surprise, her ideal state of relaxation included me. She had sacrificed her vision of an optimal life—a professional woman who lunches with the elite—for the tedium of raising a healthy daughter in the environment most conducive to that goal, even if it meant moving into an ersatz version of the city. The mother of my childhood would have preferred connections to a solid education, but could no longer imagine the possibility of being connected to anything but mendacity. She learned to defer her fantasies for a responsible course of action, to transform herself into a good immigrant. But I had gone from academic superstar to college dropout. She was second-guessing her decision, had been since August rolled around and I was forced to tell her that I wouldn't be leaving. She had refused to accept any explanation as valid.

I wanted to tell her that she needn't worry, that she had achieved the greatest kind of success as a mother by having raised a daughter who cared deeply about healing the world, deeply enough to act, to sacrifice, to potentially suffer. My effort needed to remain a secret. Mine was a form of activism absent of vanity. It was something visceral, an attempt to disrupt the business of harm and alienation. I couldn't tolerate the loss of my sensibility, my identity, to prominent individuals who purport to represent me. I wanted to connect with forces of life that didn't correspond to the timeline of my physical existence. The grandiose language I'd read in my father's articles, heard in so many classrooms and coffee shops in Charlottesville … all that stuff supported a kind of logic its champions considered unsuitable in practice. The yawning space between diagnosis and prescription confused me until I embraced all the talk of change and then it seemed obvious that everyone, deep in ignorance and denial, tacitly supported a bloodletting. Dad's life had taught me that it was impossible to make change without breaking skin.

As with Elena, I'd have to endure Mom's disappointment. It was part of the process. I knew it had to be that way, but it didn't make their simmering disapproval easier to bear. Ignorance of my capabilities was the perfect camouflage for my activity. I was a model student, a timid consumer, the kind of person who avoids upheaval. But I had learned on the hip of an expert. It was Mom's flight from trauma that organized my sense of purpose.

Her father died a few months after I returned from college. I couldn't believe it when she informed me that she wouldn't be returning for his funeral. "They do it quickly," she had explained. "He'll be in the ground before I get there." Why, I wanted to know, wasn't she going to visit her mother and siblings? She had no explanation. She didn't feel like it.

"There's a reason," I said, "and I wish you'd just tell me."

But there was nothing to tell. Long ago, when Mom had decided not to return, it included not returning for events like death. I was the focus of that decision. Our family, our people, had suffered generations of trauma. It was baked into our DNA. Mom wanted to halt the transmission of those genes. Dad did, too, until history caught up with him.

A day or two after her father died, Mom muted the TV and said, "He wasn't an especially nice person, if you must know."

"He was nice to me." I had good memories of my grandparents.

"Jesus, Nancy, you knew him for a month," she snapped. "He was small-minded, racist, stuck up. I don't know what to tell you."

"So do you just, like, hate everybody?"

"I don't *hate* anyone. I simply choose not to put myself in negative situations."

There it was. All I needed to know. For Mom, the world only made sense in fantasies of escape, first into the layers of DC society and then into suburban anonymity. She deserved to exist, though, to enjoy a civic life that offered something more than anxiety. Her exile seemed elective, but it was in fact a legacy. When people she once thought of as friends expelled her from their circle, she was forced to relive a trauma, the same trauma imparted by her parents. I wanted to open the possibility of joy and indulgence. The Ambassador represented a sanctified class of people who stood in the way.

The Ambassador came in one afternoon when I was drinking at the bar. He wore a beige cashmere overcoat with black buttons atop a pastel green sweater and stonewashed Gucci jeans. His calfskin loafers were a shade darker than the overcoat. He was with a much younger woman—an intern, I thought, or maybe a reporter. They sat in the booth closest to the door, the Ambassador with his back to me. I pretended not to pay him any mind. He ordered Scotch, unusual, I thought, for a wine bar.

"What kind of whiskey is that?" I asked the bartender after he set down the glass.

"Laphroaig. A favorite of politicians."

"Oh, you get politicians in here?" The bartender grinned. "As if I don't see enough of them at work," I added hastily.

"That guy over there," he said, motioning with his chin toward the Ambassador, "is some kind of big-shot. Comes in here a lot with the guys from Capitol Hill." I listened with interest as he listed various congresspeople and media personalities and explained which of them were shit for tippers. The Ambassador was generous. "Always orders the Laphroaig," he finished. "A hell of an aperitif."

On my way out, I tried to assess the Ambassador in my peripheral vision. He and the woman were leaning into one another, but not closely. Their conversation was casual. Neither of them seemed animated or intense. He didn't notice me. She gave me a small glance and immediately lost interest. I couldn't wait to see him again. Parked nearby the bar, illegally, was a black sedan. The driver was probably inside, napping or tinkering with his phone.

Waiting was my top priority, but I couldn't wait too long, either. I wasn't afraid of losing nerve. I didn't want any more footage of me as a woman or man circulating in the area where the Ambassador would die. The timing came into place as my knowledge increased. In pursuing someone's death, I gave myself new life. I missed college sometimes, especially on difficult nights in the restaurant, missed the excitement of hook-ups and the thrill of good grades, the party scene and the late-night chats with Elena, but it felt like a lost world. If I ever went back to finish my degree, it would no longer be as a traditional student. I'd have a different set of priorities and a darker understanding of the world than my younger counterparts. I wouldn't be there to learn, but to graduate.

One afternoon as I was getting ready for work, Elena texted.

hey what are you up to these days?

still waiting tables in georgetown. how's school?

same old.

do you like your roommates?

they're okay. whatever. I wondered how long we could keep it up before one of us broke. Amazingly, it was Elena. *not as cool as you.*

are you not coming back for real?

not this year. miss you tons, tho.

miss you too.

After the exchange, we didn't chat regularly, but we kept in touch. She never talked about visiting and I never asked. Seeing her would have disrupted my routine. I had become so reliable at work that I earned some leeway. I preferred lunch and the late dinner shifts and the manager in charge of scheduling usually obliged. It validated all the lessons I'd learned about success in the United States: flexibility, sacrifice, resilience. Go above and beyond. Be a team player. As long as those lessons satisfied the right people, the ones who need think tanks and ambassadors, then they'd remain common wisdom.

By February, everything was in place. I only needed to sit in my usual spot at the bar and wait for the Ambassador. He was in town and didn't seem to have any travel plans. I was confident that he'd turn up sometime during the week. If he didn't, the plan would stay the same.

I was nervous, constantly envisioning life on trial and then in prison. Physical and emotional suffering scared me, but I hated the idea of giving up anonymity. It was an asset that, once lost, was impossible to recover. Your image belonged to strangers and in a sense so did your destiny. They could fuck with your ethics, your relationships, your actions, everything, in essence, according to their own requirements for entertainment or satisfaction. Most activists need a limelight, but the anonymous ones are most devastating. I could do so much more in this condition.

I finished my lunch shift on a Monday and then headed to the bar in disguise after wasting a few hours on the waterfront. The river was murky with stagnant puddles of organic material grown from the runoff of food residue and lawn chemicals. The structures of advanced civilization stretched along the banks: glass and steel towers, handsome condos, boxy office buildings, university spires, boat docks, food stands, walking trails. Beyond the shoreline, the current moved strongly, creating divots around rocks and trestles. It was a peaceful scene, the very picture of misery. A bluish cloud gathered in the sky and began spitting fine snowflakes into the wind. They reminded me that my fingers and nose were freezing and so I walked back up the hill, invigorated by everything I'd seen.

The bar was about half-full. I sat in my normal spot and waited for the Ambassador. I didn't want to break routine, so after two drinks and a bit of dilly-dallying I returned to Virginia. Instead of going home, I knocked on Elena's door. I pushed away the idea that it might be the last time I see her mother. She acted like it was the first time I'd ever visited. After hugging me and examining my streamlined face, she ushered me into the kitchen. Elena's father was on the couch, watching CNN. "Hello, sweetie," he waved.

"How are you, Mr. Berhane?"

"I am Robel and I am fine."

"You're not working tonight?"

"I did morning shift. I may do Lyft for a few hours. I'm tired of hearing about these jackals," he said, pointing the remote at the TV.

"Just stay in and relax," Elena's mother said. "Enough work."

"Says you," he grumbled before turning to me. "Almost forty hours a week she works. She's the one who needs a break."

"And I don't waste time with the news when I finish," she said. "I do useful stuff at home."

We sat at the table. "I don't want to keep you long," I said. "I know you have to work early."

"You're not working tonight?"

"Lunch shift."

"Is it a good job?"

"Yeah, for the time being. I'm making good money." She smiled, but I could tell she wanted to nag me about returning to UVA. "Can I ask you something weird?"

"Oh my. Elena always says we're weird, so I can probably help."

"Well, it's just...I don't know how to explain it. Basically, when did you know what you wanted to do with your life? Like, are you happy with how it turned out? Because you always seem really happy but your life isn't the sort of thing they put in movies to show happiness."

"What do you mean?"

"Okay, it's like this. You drive a bus and then you come home and cook dinner. You live in a regular townhouse. You're not rich, you don't have a glamorous life. Stuff like that. I want to know why everything that's supposed to make me happy is either impossible or feels like it would make me a crappy person."

"I understand now." She paused and pursed her lips. "I consider myself happy, yes. I see it as a question of scale. I got everything I wanted from life. I thank God every day."

"Serious question. This is what you wanted?" I motioned around the room.

"It's not just a place to sleep. It's a home, with food, and for many years with a daughter. Let me tell you, child, you and Elena don't understand how good this is."

"I guess not. It seems so boring."

"That's the point, yes? I grew up in the countryside. My parents moved to Asmara—that's our capital—when I was ten. We all worked, slept in two rooms, fourteen of us. Sometimes there wasn't food. But I thought the city was magical. It had all these old beautiful buildings, like Rome. I wanted to live in one of them, in my own room, with my own maid."

"But that never happened. So you didn't get what you wanted."

"Something better happened. I got married to Robel and we came to this country. We tried for years to have a baby and then Elena came. That made me happy."

"So, a baby? That's supposed to make me happy?"

"Lord, no. You're not listening to me, child."

"But you just said that Elena made you happy."

"Yes. Elena. Not a baby. Not some thing, some idea. A real person. My daughter. And I could give her food and a safe place to sleep. I could give her a room, just to herself. A good education. I got everything I wanted because I saw wisdom in God's mystery."

It was about God, then. Not the answer I wanted. There was no God in my life. I had to navigate a world of flesh and ambition. "Do you think I should start praying?"

"If you want to pray, you pray. But don't waste God's time with nonsense. He's not Santa Claus."

"Honestly, Ms—Mariam, sorry—I appreciate what you're telling me so much, but I can't really think about babies and God. I'm not—"

"You're not listening, Nancy." It was a rare tone for her, urgent and slightly aggravated. "Do you think Lara is pleased with her life?"

"I don't think she used to be, but it kind of seems like she is now."

"Yes, she is. And it's not because of you, is it?"

I laughed. "Probably not."

"Is it about God?"

"Definitely not."

"That's right. She understands that she achieved her main goal. She wanted to be free and she made it happen."

I could see that. Returning to the funeral would have resulted in another death. There was a kind of brutality in her decision, but also a straightforward moral calculation: social convention was sometimes more harmful than offense. Mom's initial vision of freedom almost certainly looked different than what it became, but she had made her own life, on her own terms. Dad's disappearance made it possible.

Elena's mother took my hand. "You have to decide what you want the world to look like. Then you do what it takes to make it a reality. Do you see what I mean?"

I left Elena's house more motivated than ever. What her mother told me resonated. This world wasn't exclusive to the cynical. But look at Elena's mother, stuck inside a school bus all day, or mine, lounging around the house after eight hours of paperwork. Why should people have to abandon social life for a sense of purpose? Why do we need God to embrace us or family to disown us in order to exist peacefully?

It excited me to imagine completing Dad's transformation in order to release Mom of her obligation to sorrow. I refused to include the Ambassador in my vision of a decent life. I had been deprived of a necessary love and when I thought long enough about it, I could see that it was only the beginning of the Ambassador's depravity. Nearly everyone was dreary, robotic, constricted. We got some parkland amid blocks of private architecture, some aging infrastructure, some cut-rate provisions amid high-minded talk of being exceptional. We were the décor, providing a bit of spice to the civic landscape. Or else we were the service.

My anger wasn't visceral or irrational. It was a logical reaction to observing my surroundings, seeded in the halls of TJ and ripened during two years at college. It took me a long time to realize just how isolated I'd been most of my life. And yet Mom would describe a lively home life, a la Elena's, as a kind of isolation. As would people in those crowds at frat parties and football games. I wanted to act on the anger, not the loneliness. Lonely students crowded spaces that promised relief—concerts, lectures, marches, anything that combined enjoyment with purpose—but those spaces were implicated in the same system the attendees wanted to reject. The nation pretends to welcome us, but we're mostly surplus apportioned into tiny, insulated republics with discrete cultures of ennui and disappointment.

I tried to remember the times my entire family was together and came up with only one memory that didn't involve a restaurant or social function. It must have been a Saturday or Sunday and I don't know why my parents were content that morning to sit around the table entertaining me. Usually I ate breakfast with one of them—cereal with Dad, French Toast or an omelet with Mom—while the other worked or did something outside the house. But on that morning they sat across the table and asked questions about school and friends and encouraged me to share fantasies of my adult future. I told them I had learned how to make snowflakes out of paper and offered to show them. Mom grabbed scissors and three sheets of typing paper. I ordered them to cut out a large circle from their sheets of paper and showed them how to fold it into a triangle.

Dad started drawing what looked like a square with rounded edges. "You're doing it wrong, Daddy," I said.

"She's right. Your circle is terrible."

He chuckled. "Well, I don't know, Lara, yours isn't exactly Copernican."

"Here, I'll do yours for you," I said, taking Dad's paper.

"This is a very complicated project," Dad said.

"No way, it's easy," I said.

"Daddy's not very good with his hands," Mom said. "All that education for nothing."

"I didn't get my PhD in snowflake-making," Dad snapped.

I couldn't understand why Mom laughed so hard in response, but it didn't matter. I was happy that my parents were in the same room, smiling. Their professional obligations had deprived me of typical domestic patter. Everything in our lives was arranged in Google alerts. On that morning, we seemed to exist beyond schedules, united by ridicule and genetic material. A few years later, when Dad tried to put us back together, he managed only to bequeath loss and separation. Now I again had to take over his work.

The next day, a Tuesday, I waited for the Ambassador. A lump arose in my throat every time I saw the door move. I developed the habit of picking at my facial hair. In came a trio of lawyers, a few grad students, some State Department types, a young couple on a date, but no Ambassador. I paid my tab in cash and drove home.

Mom was at the stove. "Hey," she called out when I closed the door. "I'm making molokhia. They got some in at Grand Mart."

"Cool, give me a second." I went upstairs to my room and changed into pajamas. I was hoping to order pizza or some other junk, but mom would disapprove. To her, molokhia was the ultimate comfort food. Mom ladled me up a bowl and tossed a bag of pita bread on the table.

"How was work?" she said.

"The usual."

"No bad-tipping big shits today?"

"They come for dinner. Lunch is for tourists and old people."

"Things have changed. The restaurant used to be part of your father's lunch rotation."

"I don't like to think about Dad in that world."

"He didn't either, apparently."

"Can I ask you something weird?"

"I guess. Maybe you won't like the answer, though."

"Well, it's just … it's been more than ten years. Why can't you forgive Daddy already?"

She slurped a clump of soggy leaves off her spoon. "Why should I need to forgive him?"

"I don't know. Maybe because he's dead? So what good is it to stay mad at him?"

"Why do you think I'm mad at him? Fred had his own ideas. He made up his own mind. Khalas. He doesn't need my forgiveness."

I tapped my spoon against the bowl. "Don't you kind of understand why he went rogue? His grandfather, his parents. That stuff runs deep."

"Who are you telling?" Her tone was excitable. "My family didn't experience the same thing? I know how deep it runs, believe me."

"So why blame Dad, then?"

"Good Lord, Nancy, you're so thickheaded. You ask a question and then don't even listen to the answer. I'm not mad at Fred. I'm mad at the bastards who took him. I wish he would have gotten the chance to become the person he was trying to be. I'm mad that none of our so-called friends appreciated his courage. Instead they treated us like a disease. I'm mad because he knew it would happen and left me to deal with it alone."

"I don't think he meant to leave you alone."

"He knew it was possible. But what could I do about it? I'm mad at myself for understanding his thought process."

"Obviously none of it was your fault."

"No. I'm at fault, too, we all are, those of us who refuse to give up the idea of going home."

I finished my food in silence while mom took her bowl to the sink and put on water for tea. She leaned against the counter and smiled at me. "In this version of the world, Nancy, we can't be normal. We're not allowed to be, I mean. We can't relieve ourselves of our burden without getting into trouble. That's just the way it is."

"Why not make a different version of the world, then?"

She shook her head sadly. "Your father got killed trying to answer that question."

"But history didn't end with him."

"I don't know," she shrugged. "I did everything I could to sever you from our history. I thought it would be the only decent way to raise a child in this country. Why pass along the pain? The anger? All the crazy infighting? But it must have been in our genes, because here you are, raised like a regular American girl, and you're asking the same questions my generation did."

"Everyone asks these questions. It's all we talked about at UVA."

"I suppose I should have known," she said, ignoring my comment. "Some things we can't just forget, no matter how much we try."

I helped Mom with the dishes, using our usual system: I rinsed and she stacked. After we finished, she went to bed. I wasn't in the mood for television, but I was too anxious to sleep. I tried to write, but all I could think about was my project and I didn't want to put anything incriminating on paper. I read some of the true crime articles at Longform.com. They were pretty inspiring until law enforcement or internet detectives managed to piece things together. I reminded myself of how many articles were never published because nothing came of the investigations.

Mom was gone when I woke up the next morning. I dawdled around the house until well past noon. Worried about being immobilized through self-pity, I headed to Georgetown, put on my disguise, and walked around the residential streets, wondering if this would be my last day of innocence. I ended up in the wine bar at the usual time. It was crowded for a Wednesday. Lots of people wearing lanyards. There was probably a convention nearby.

I was surprised that some of the conventioneers introduced themselves to the Ambassador when he came in a few moments later. He activated his million-dollar smile and chatted with them for a moment before rejoining his party, three men, all youngish, dressed casually. The Ambassador looked relaxed, especially graceful in dark-wash jeans and a fitted suit jacket. They sat in the third booth from the entrance, closer to the bar than normal. The Ambassador, as always, faced the street. I tried to behave normally—according to the rules of my abnormal condition—but I couldn't stop my foot from shaking or my hand from twirling the hair on my chin.

I needed to watch the Ambassador closely without making it obvious. Throughout the planning, I presumed that I would be on camera. Being recorded was inevitable. I'm sure the wine bar had at least partial surveillance. The trick was never to give anyone reason to check the footage. I had to assume that authorities from at least two countries would study the wine bar's tape if my plan worked. If my caution paid off, I'd be just another befuddled customer with no connection to the event. The conventioneers were a brilliant stroke of luck.

In my peripheral vision, I watched a waitress take the order at the Ambassador's table and saw her tap it into a touchscreen. I tracked the bartender—not my friend, another stroke of luck—as he took down a bottle of Laphroaig from the shelf. He poured one glass, neat. I could feel my heartbeat between my ears. The bartender set a bottle of red on the landing and placed the glass of Scotch next to it. The waitress was busy with another table. To my left was the narrow corridor that led to the restrooms. The conventioneers made the place louder than normal. Their din would provide a fine preamble to chaos. Outside, winter gloom at the edge of dusk settled onto the neighborhood. The darkest reach of the bar emitted a bluish vapor of fluorescent light. The waitress left the touchscreen and headed toward the landing.

I had waited too long, overwhelmed by the surroundings. Just as a sense of failure spread into my brain, somebody called for the waitress and she turned around. I reached into the inside pocket of my blazer and removed the capsule, breaking off the top underneath my leg. A man exited the bathroom and started walking to the seating area. I timed my movement so that he would pass me right as I was within reach of the Scotch. As he passed, I muttered "pardon me" and squeezed against the end of the bar, facing the drink apron. I widened my shoulders and poured the powder into the glass of Scotch in a swift, jerky motion, pivoting immediately toward the restroom. I stood in front of the mirror, eyes bloodshot, elbows shivering, and tried to recognize my expression. But I was blank, beyond command of sensuality. I simply existed without definite feeling, in a unique, precarious universe. I tidied my beard and left.

I got a good view of the Ambassador's table as I walked back to the bar. The waitress had delivered his drink. The same glass. There wasn't another like it that I could see. I almost collapsed with relief. Whatever happened from that point forward, I wouldn't have harmed a stranger. The Ambassador technically fit the category, but we knew one another in waves of brutal intimacy. I was the detritus of his arrogance. He was the progenitor of my rebirth.

The wait seemed interminable. I played with my phone. I smiled at fellow patrons. I ordered another drink. Just as the bartender put it on the counter, the commotion began. Few noticed the sound of a fist banging against a table the first time it happened, but when the sound continued everyone gazed in the general direction of the Ambassador's booth. Soon the Ambassador had fallen sideways onto the floor. Some people stood, morbidly voyeuristic, pretending they were gathering around to help. I didn't have a good view, but could picture the Ambassador tugging down his collar and writhing on the ground. A few guys shouted to call 911, but I figured someone had done it already. There turned out not to be a doctor in the house. Not the kind that could be useful, anyway.

"Jesus, I hope he's okay," I said to the person nearest me.

He nodded his head in concern. "Poor man."

"What a tragedy."

As the manager tried to maintain order, backing people away from the Ambassador's booth and pleading for calm, some of the patrons shuffled toward the door. I left a hundred-dollar bill on the bar and followed them out. Staying was too big a risk. Anyway, I didn't need to stick around. I already knew the bastard soon would be dead. Once on the sidewalk, I marched briskly to my car and changed into a new outfit. A woman again, I walked back in the direction of the wine bar, ignoring the sirens as they overtook me, and worked the dinner shift at Filomena.

Farid

EACH STEP FELT like a magnetic repulsion. My feet no longer wanted to touch the ground. The wounds on my body behaved as sunflowers in the burning light. I thought of my condition as voluntary, the known outcome of my own decisions, but accepting responsibility didn't ease the sorrow. It was other people, loved ones, who would survive to experience the pain of my liberation.

Delirium set in. I couldn't quit worrying about legacy. What would I be leaving behind for those loved ones? Regret? Misery? Their gift from me would be an enormous burden: the need to find an ending to my story. But wasn't I bequeathed the same burden? My legacy, I realized, would be the same as my inheritance. I couldn't stop the process of reproduction.

The world was open on all sides and yet the space around me was limited. There were no tracks to follow, no signs to read, just an unforgiving vastness with the strange capacity to feel oppressive. It was a lifetime of work condensed into a physical crisis. I forced myself to believe that vitality would survive my body. I had exercised my will, made my own decisions. I was just another victim of democracy.

Memory of little pleasures carried me to the end: housebound nights in peacetime conditions; a baby's grip on my index finger; the vaguely fetid odor of seawater; solitary mornings with tobacco and coffee. I wanted to lay down and expire, to disappear into the ubiquitous beige, but I forced myself forward. Even if they wouldn't know the epilogue to my departure, I needed my family to understand that I died before hitting the ground.

Nancy

I WAS JITTERY at work that night. It was difficult keeping my exhilaration in check. I didn't want anything to seem out of the ordinary. No angry diners. No broken plates. All in all, it was a normal shift. I was scheduled past closing and finished cleaning my station as the manager was closing up the register. We left the restaurant together and I was glad for the company, although he couldn't have protected me from the danger I faced. He commented about the number of cops and I said some VIP must be in the neighborhood.

Sleep was easy that night. I don't remember any of my dreams. I woke up mid-morning and stayed in bed, wondering if I'd really pulled it off. Terrified of jinxes, I refused to allow myself the satisfaction. I considered showing up at the wine bar again, but it would have been an amateur move. Returning to the scene and all that. Watching the news could screw up my tenuous peace of mind. As far as I saw, the world was the same as it had been the day before, with one notable exception. I had no desire to change that illusion.

I had stuffed my disguise in a Target bag and hid it on the top shelf of my closet. Soon I'd transfer it into a duffel bag, weigh it down with bricks—abundant in our complex—and toss it into the Chesapeake or Potomac. The river once featured prominently in my plans. I thought about shooting the Ambassador and kayaking down to Gravelly Point, next to the airport, where my car would be waiting. I could drop the gun in the river along the way. It was too much like an adventure novel, though. So was my plan to shoot some kind of poison into the Ambassador's ear. I'd read about a similar attempt in real life, but it didn't work. If a professional spy agency couldn't pull it off, then I didn't like my chances. It was fun reading about the ricin pellet fired from an umbrella into someone's thigh, but that kind of operation was never a serious possibility. I settled on a more modest but appropriate use for the river. It was already polluted by years of deceit.

With nothing to do, and too much energy to browse social media (I didn't like the thought of what I might find there, either), I decided to take a walk. It was a chilly day, but the sun soon infiltrated my jacket. I walked past the edge of our complex and across the overpass where a creek merged with a concrete drainage ditch, then up the hill to an intersection filled with strip malls and gas stations. I didn't need anything, but wandered around Whole Foods for half an hour. I bought two slices of pizza and walked home.

Mom came in when I was settling onto the couch to eat. "I came home for lunch. Keep me company."

I grumbled and moved to the dining room as she fished in the refrigerator for leftovers. She emerged with a container of mjuddara and put it in the microwave.

"Did you hear about the Ambassador?" she said after joining me at the table.

"What about him?" I was becoming a decent liar. Nonchalant questions, I had learned, were a good way to disarm people. Learning the skill was necessary because murder is a compound sin. You can't do it without lying.

"He's dead."

"Whaaa? For real?"

"Yep. He was in a restaurant last night and, boom, he dropped dead."

"Just like that?"

"Just like that."

"What happened? Did he have a heart attack or something?"

"I think so. I'm just glad he's dead, God forgive me."

I know it was a throwaway comment, divorced from any real understanding of the event, but it was exactly what I needed to hear.

"When do you go to work?" Mom said.

"Not for a while." I wanted to ask more questions about the Ambassador, but couldn't appear too curious. Now that I had produced the news, I was stuck being an aggregator.

"I'm thinking of retiring," she said.

"Oh? Wow. Okay."

"I've been at it a long time. You're grown, making your own money. I have plenty saved up. Why not?"

"If you're ready, go for it. Won't you be bored, though?"

"Not at all. You may be, though. I'm thinking of getting out of here."

"What do you mean 'getting out of here'?"

"Traveling. Visiting the places I always wanted to see. Maybe moving somewhere else, warmer, less crowded. I don't know. I haven't thought it out. But I wouldn't retire just to sit around the house."

"Go for it, Mom."

"I'd like you to return to college, though. You're making good money now, but you don't want to be waiting tables when you get older."

I fixed up an exaggerated glare. "I was actually thinking about going back, but now I don't want to because you'll think it was your idea."

"Grow up, Nancy. This is the time in your life when you should be thinking about doing great things, making your mark on the world, before reality sets in."

I laughed instead of continuing the argument. If Mom knew just how well she actually knew me, then she'd go into life-coach mode. I liked the rhythm we'd developed over the past few years. She didn't nag about my body or my appearance and I made a point of not provoking her disapproval. Mom's uptightness existed in proportion to her social life. Detachment made her easygoing. I never fully got the sense that she was pleased with me, though. Wanting to leave the country was a pretty good hint that our solitary life was unsatisfying.

The Ambassador's death made the news cycle and I could no longer avoid it. With the scrutiny came a hundred conspiracy theories. None of them traced to me. Most people online didn't think the Ambassador suffered a natural death, although that's exactly how I thought of it. The Kingdom, of course, raised a fuss, and its sponsor responded with spin that people with blue checks beside their names found distasteful. Each day, I became less shaky and found a new routine, one that didn't involve sneaking around Georgetown. I avoided the wine bar. If suspicion somehow landed on the people there that evening, I wouldn't be among them. They'd need to find a young, bearded man who seemed to have disappeared.

Going to the city only for work left more time for me at home. I was ready to quit Filomena. I'd already decided to finish my degree. It would open more professional opportunities, which I envisioned as critical to the kind of change I wanted to make in the world. Keeping the job until summer would minimize suspicion and allow me to accumulate cash for my return to Charlottesville, so I decided to stay on.

I began seeing one of the hostesses, Katy, a student at GW. She was cynical and unimpressed by everything and I found her to be good company. Completing my project freed up my libido. I was eager to resume the joy of intimate contact, the thrilling process of becoming familiar with a new mind and body. Katy had an apartment in West End, within walking distance of the restaurant, and I began staying over a few nights a week. Her roommates seemed not to care. They were nice to me, but I was wary of striking up a friendship. Katy was temporary. Her disaffection seemed to come from an uneasy knowledge that she would always be temporary, so she made evanescence a condition of her desire. The ritual of smoke and sex kept my anxiety in check, but it always had a mournful quality, too, a foreboding that this might be the last time I do it.

Katy wasn't like Elena, though. With Elena, time didn't simply pass; I was always preoccupied. She wouldn't let anyone waste away in a different condition. Her intensity never fell off. I missed it, the challenge, the intimacy, the provocation. Elena provided a kind of love that hooking up couldn't recreate. I hadn't seen her in many months, but we texted almost daily. The logistics of our friendship were different, but the old affection had returned. I was eager to see her again.

Soon the city began to fill with tourists in search of cherry blossoms and bowdlerized history. Neighborhoods grew more secluded as oak and willow bloomed into dense canopies that occluded low-rise buildings. The odor of hot dogs and falafel mixed with bus diesel and sunbaked asphalt to create the perfect simulation of urban grit for the cargo-short-and-ballcap set. I didn't participate in the life of the city. The tourists brought more business to Georgetown, but they were no boon to service workers. I earned more money; average tips decreased. I worked and slept and spent a bit of time with Katy and so the sum of my life was crudeness, in both industry and pleasure.

I thought a lot about my encounter with the Ambassador. I knew that I'd forever be subject to fits of unease. I couldn't be satisfied with a job well done because murder has an afterlife. It creates a particular kind of energy in the world, something insidious and civilizing, what I came to understand as the heartbeat of modernity. I left the wine bar that afternoon a bona fide member of the social elite.

News reports dwindled. My confidence would have grown into comfort had I not made the terrible mistake of ditching Katy to go home one night after work. The next day I slept until Mom came home for lunch. I joined her at the table, where she had a mug of coffee waiting for me. We browsed our phones in silence. I looked up to say something and saw, out of the bay window across the living room, a police cruiser idling in front of our townhouse. I almost dropped my mug. I excused myself and hurried upstairs. I could see a cop emerging from the car as I rounded the bannister.

I dressed just in time to hear a polite but serious knock on the front door. "Who is it?" Mom yelled, surely thinking it was some kind of solicitation.

"Fairfax County PD," the officer said.

"Come in," Mom repeated a few times. She didn't hear what the visitor was saying. Finally she got up with a sigh and answered. From my position I could see that the storm door was still closed and Mom was peeking her head through a foot-wide opening. I couldn't detect acrimony in their conversation. I frantically thought of ways to escape before accepting that it would be impossible. The windows were too high for any Walter White-type shit and I couldn't get downstairs without passing the door.

"Get down here, Nancy," Mom barked and I almost began crying because it occurred to me that she might forever regret the command.

"One second," I said before sliding into the bathroom and dry-heaving at the sink.

I walked down the stairs cautiously, measuring my steps as if carrying a laundry basket. Mom swung the door open so I could see the cop on the other side of the glass. He was holding an envelope and looked bored. I cracked open the storm door and held it with my hip.

"Nancy Baker?"

I nodded, scared that talking would make me bawl.

"I've been instructed to deliver you this summons to the District of Columbia Civil Court." He extended his arm. I took the envelope.

"Excuse me?" I managed, short of breath.

"You've been summoned to court in the District of Columbia."

"But, but… why?" I didn't want to invite suspicion, but curiosity and relief combined to activate my voice.

"Unpaid parking tickets. They've sent you repeated warnings."

"No they haven't."

"You'll have to take it up with the court, Ms. Baker. Nice day."

I watched him get into his car and drive off and I could barely stop myself from screaming with joy. When I turned around, Mom was glaring at me.

"Jesus Christ, Nancy. The police? What the hell were you thinking?"

"I had no idea."

"He says you were warned." I shrugged in protest. "Anyway," she continued, "you should have paid the tickets when you got them." She paused for further consideration. "You never should have got the tickets to begin with."

"It's DC. You know how it is."

"I thought you were paying monthly rent on a space."

"I was. But I stopped. It was too expensive and there was plenty of street parking."

"*Illegal* street parking."

"Okay, fine, whatever. I'll pay the tickets. What's the big deal?"

"The big deal is that you probably owe hundreds, thousands, of dollars. How many tables do you need to wait on for that kind of money? Don't be a dummy, Nancy."

I was mad at myself, no doubt, but for a different reason. Parking tickets are a paper trail that go directly into police computers. I was one of many sloppy motorists with a backlog of fines, but still. I should have been more careful. I wasn't happy that Mom had busted my lie about renting a parking space, either. That lie had been the basis of my argument that working in DC was a reasonable idea. I would have been happy to pay for one, but parking garages are filled with cameras. I told Mom again that I'd take care of it, but she wasn't mollified.

"Why are you so mad?" I said, aggravated, after she began slamming cabinets.

"The police just showed up to my house to give my daughter a warrant. See if you can figure it out."

"Oh come on, Mom. It wasn't a warrant. Quit overreacting." Truth is, her overreaction helped calm my nerves.

She slapped the counter with both hands. "You don't understand. I shouldn't expect you to."

"What are you talking about?"

"Being a parent. It's a prison."

"Gee thanks."

"Need I get started again on who just paid us a visit?"

"No. God no."

"Then leave me alone."

I worked lunch shift the next day and was home when Mom arrived in the evening with a sack of rice and kabobs. I sat across from her and munched on a kubideh like it was a carrot stick.

"You have a plate and fork right there," Mom said.

"I see you came home in a sunny mood."

"Did you take care of the tickets?"

"No, I had to work."

"Might as well flush the money you made down the toilet."

I didn't want a repeat of the previous day's argument, so I pursued a different one. "What did you mean when you said parenthood is like a prison?"

"I didn't think I'd need to explain a simple metaphor to a professional writer."

"Okay, Mom, I get it. You're upset. But you need to quit being so salty. I'm just trying to talk."

The thin wrinkles around her eyes and lips deepened into jagged channels intercrossing a look of defeat and exhaustion. "I'm leaving, Nancy. At least I was. Now I'm not sure. I was planning on telling you soon."

"Leaving? What? Where?"

She sniffled and looked at the ceiling. "Portugal." She returned her gaze to me and waited for a response. I waved my first two fingers into a circle. "There's a town on the southern coast," she went on. "It's called Portimao. I rented a flat there for six months. It has a big balcony and a view of the ocean."

"That's so random."

"No it's not. I was there years ago, before I met your father. I went to Europe with a group of friends and we spent some time in Algarve, in the south of Portugal. I fell in love with it. I've always wanted to retire there."

"This is a lot to take in," I said. "So for sure you're retiring?"

"At the end of the semester. I've been arranging to go to Portugal a month later."

"And you were planning to tell me…?"

"Now, actually. But yesterday ruined it. I can't go anymore. How can I? The entire idea was premised on you being able to take care of yourself. Clearly I was being too optimistic."

"It was a few *fucking* parking tickets, Mom. Get some perspective."

"I don't know what to tell you, Nancy. I know it was just parking tickets, but something changed. The whole thing feels different."

"Mom, go. Please. You have to."

"And what if something happens to you? What if you end up in jail?" She was soliciting my reassurance.

"Jail? Give me some credit. I don't think you'll ever know how hard I've worked to make sure that you never have to suffer the possibility." I reached my hand across the table and she accepted it. "I'll be fine. You have my word. I'm pretty sure I'm going back to school, anyway."

"To UVA?"

"Yeah, unless you need me to live in the house. I can finish up at Mason."

"No. Go back to UVA. You can use this place on break."

"Sell it. I can stay at Elena's when I come home."

She shook her head. "It's paid off. Wouldn't be smart to sell. All you'd be responsible for are the HOA dues and the bills. If you go back to school, I'll send the money. You just have to make the payments for me and watch over the place. I'll have Mariam and Robel look after it, too."

"Why don't you rent it?"

"Ya binti, I'm trying to enjoy my life, not kill my soul. Landlording is the last thing I want to do."

"I'll do it for you!"

"No." Her reaction was excitable, instantaneous. "We have what we need. More than enough. Do something useful with yourself."

"I'll try."

"I don't know, Nancy, I really don't. I just have a weird sense that something is off, with you, with me, I can't tell. Something, though. Like the world slipped an inch or two off its axis. I know it sounds crazy."

"A little bit," I laughed. "You're just worried about leaving. And probably feeling guilty for not telling me."

"Go to hell." She smiled and her wrinkles thinned into creases again.

I knew Mom had been restless, but I never expected her to just take off. I couldn't help but think it was my fault for being inaccessible and boring. Or simply for being. She had deferred lots of fantasies in order to take care of me and I understood what it meant for a person of her disposition. It seems to me that deferral of fantasy is the essence of a well-adjusted person. But I'm not ready to become tempered, to learn the ways of a responsible citizen.

And so the police encounter receded into the past while Mom prepared to leave forever. I knew she wouldn't come back to visit. She'd die somewhere in the past, having traveled hundreds of spontaneous itineraries. Portugal was the last place she felt possessed of love before meeting my father and she wanted to reclaim that sense of romance eliminated by domesticity. She's gone as I write and I miss her in ways that make no sense, in ways that defy my emotional moorings, my entire self-perception. I'm the rare child with empty-nest syndrome, teeming with pride and jealousy for the wanderlust of an unshackled mother.

But family remained. Elena, my putative sister according to conventional wisdom, filled a paternal role in Mom's absence. She appeared on my front porch one morning before Mom had left, flipping the doorknocker until I woke up and staggered downstairs. I was so surprised, so happy, that I couldn't hug her; I simply fell into her shoulder. I tried to mumble a question or two and she interrupted. "Spring break."

I made tea as she sat at the island and described the goings-on at college. It was classic Elena and I could have narrated the stories, but they were delightful coming from her mouth. I told her about Katy and Elena figured it would last another two weeks, tops, and then I'd be prowling dating apps again. She noted how different I look, skinnier, somehow more masculine but with a girlish vibrancy. It was true, I told her; I felt satisfied, unburdened. When I said I'd be returning to UVA, she chattered about where we would live and promised she'd enroll in grad school so we could stay together. She hung around until I had to get ready for work and I swore I'd take a day off.

On my day off, we decided to skip the usual suburban diversions and go for a long walk. The day was clear and cool, the landscape capped by a shade of blue specific to the equinox. We walked up the main road outside our subdivision and onto a paved trail that descended into a wooded area, the first shoots and sprouts of the season providing light decoration to the bare scenery. We stopped on the fenced-in bridge spanning the commuter tracks and read padlocks inscribed with messages of love. Elena gestured to the wooded surroundings. "Just like being in Paris." Most of the locks were inscribed by the same person. "This girl fucks around more than you," Elena said.

Just past the bridge, we left the paved path and followed a dirt trail to Lake Accotink (which was a lake in the same way that our subdivision was a version of Georgetown). Circling the reservoir took a few hours and we did it without hurry or purpose. The shuffle of newly-awoken insect and avian life filled the air around us.

"Seriously," Elena said as we walked past the visitor center, "is that all you've been doing? Waiting tables?"

I wanted to tell her. It would have been the only time to do it, isolated in a moment of apparent trust. The trust was conditional, though, because

I knew that telling her would change everything and then our lovely walk might become a punishment. We would leave our friendship behind to be swallowed by the emerging wilderness.

"Pretty much," I said.

"I don't get it, Nan. Like, what are you searching for? Or what were you running from? Was it me?"

"A little bit," I said. "I didn't feel like I could keep up with you, so I just kind of ran off. I wanted to see how I fit in the world without you."

"That was so unnecessary."

"Not really. Come on, Elena. You can do fine without me. You have this huge life. A million friends. Always into something interesting. You're a star on social media. My life isn't like that. I have...you. I was afraid I'd become a burden."

"To be straight up, I was getting frustrated with you, too, because you're so brilliant and I didn't want you to waste away."

"I didn't, I haven't." This is when, in ideal conditions, I would have told her. "I feel like I've accomplished a lot since leaving."

"I'm glad, Nan."

"Anyway, I'm ready to come back."

We returned to the dirt trail and headed toward the neighborhood. We kept walking down the main road until we ended up at the elementary school. We sat on the bench where we used to wait for the bus to carry us to TJ. By then it was late afternoon and I was chilly, staring at the rooftops of nearby townhouses through the buds of emerging cherry blossoms. I wondered if any other kids from the neighborhood got into TJ or if the stop was discontinued. I asked Elena and she thought we were the last two, maybe the only two. It was a nice reminder that our experience was singular. The idea of an entire culture in a universe of two was comforting, made me more secure in my recent decisions. I wanted to disrupt more of these ordinary patterns, carry out my own little insurgency.

Elena invited me over for dinner. Mom was leaving soon, I explained, and I wanted to spend time with her. Bring her, too, Elena said, a response I expected and declined to answer. Elena interpreted the silence as a polite rejection. We rose from the bench and walked the few blocks home.

I didn't see Elena again over the break, but we kept in contact. Whatever tension had affected our earlier communication was gone. We were somehow converging and diverging at once. I was satisfied with the convergence. The divergence didn't bother me. I had already diverged from the great majority of the world. I intend to spend the rest of my life persuading others to join me. Killing the Ambassador was my thesis statement.

As Elena predicted, my relationship with Katy fizzled out, in part because I dropped down to three or four shifts a week. I used the extra time to hang out with Mom and work through a backlog of novels on my shelf. Reading with an eye toward being an author rather than a critic made for a more enjoyable pastime. I began exploring how a mass of words could demarcate an otherwise illegible world, how in the hands of a determined storyteller the limits of experience nevertheless produce universal meaning. And that's all I wanted to pursue, just like when I was a child. I became fixated on authoring a tolerable existence, sublimating my libido to pen strokes and poison pills and impossible plotting.

The project almost got ruined when I went to greet a table one evening and saw Nyla sitting there. She dropped her menu when she saw me. "Nancy?"

"Hey," I said, with more pep than she probably preferred.

"You two know each other?" said one of the two other diners (both women, both roughly similar to Nyla in appearance and mannerism).

I waited for Nyla to respond. "Not really," she said. "Some time back, I was discussing the possibility of an internship with her. It never came to fruition."

Her. No name mentioned. I pivoted into an explanation of the specials. Nyla's two companions listened eagerly, looking me in the eyes, but Nyla kept focused on her menu. She glanced at me just before I left to put in their drink orders. Her expression was pensive. The pensiveness continued throughout the meal. As the group was leaving, Nyla trailed behind and caught me walking back to the kitchen.

"Everything okay with you?"

"Sure, yeah."

"Good." She put her hand on my arm. "Are you sure?"

I tried to smile casually, but my entire face felt false. I nodded.

"I'm asking," she said, "because I know you probably had a lot of feelings about...recent events."

"Not really."

She dropped her arm, gave me a long look, and walked away without a word. I was shaken the rest of the night. I didn't allow myself to think through why Nyla acted so weirdly, as if scared and disappointed but anyway obliged to nurture. I refused to consider the obvious question. It was too outlandish. Fantastical even if accurate. And yet I was preoccupied by Nyla's body language. If I kept quiet, she would be just another of those conspiracy theorists, a damning appellation in DC—worse than a liar or a cheat or a backstabber. We suddenly became intimate though a mutual need to distance. I haven't seen or spoken with Nyla since, but she's an important part of my life. I expect her to summon me on her deathbed. She'll want a confession. And she'll want to confess her secret approval.

Between the awkwardness with Katy, who had a habit of mumbling insults at me when I passed too closely, and no longer needing a pretext to be in DC, I was ready to move along, but I stuck to my plan of saving money. The time passed quickly, at least. I grew comfortable reading about the Ambassador on Twitter and Reddit. Governments had patched over their tension. The official line was cardiac arrest, an unexpected tragedy. The Kingdom's subjects weren't convinced, nor were a decent number of Americans. The CIA was protagonist of most theories, which I found funny and flattering at the same time. Rumors persisted of behind-the-scenes animosity. Commerce between the two countries continued as normal. And neither country looked very hard for a culprit, content to spin the matter as a freak accident. In the end, nobody wanted to upset the relationship.

Mom retired in May. She refused to have a party or entertain any other kind of fanfare. She and I went to eat at a French bistro in Old Town.

"This place reminds me of DC," mom complained after we had been seated.

"DC is right across the river. What did you expect?"

"You know what I mean."

Whenever Mom said that, it meant that only a fool would be unable to spot the obvious thing she was seeing. But I didn't really know what she meant. That the restaurant was pretentious? That its clientele looked like private school kids in middle age? That it was cozy and crowded and designed to look rustic?

"You could have gone anywhere when you left DC, so why did you move just outside of it?"

"It's a different place entirely. Hardly anything like DC and no reason to ever go there."

"Right, but you could have gone to Atlanta or Denver or Cleveland. Why did you stay in the area?"

"It was a long time ago. I don't really remember anymore. The schools, I believe. It turned out to be the right decision, don't you think?"

"I guess."

"What 'guess'? You went to one of the best high schools in the entire country. In DC, or anywhere else, that kind of school would have cost thirty thousand a year."

"It was just high school, Mom. The parents cared about it way more than we did."

"That's right. And I was the parent, making the decision."

"Mom, I swear…." I let the annoyance trail off. Mom was punchy. I suppose a part of her was sad about retiring, or at least whimsical, and she had always processed emotions by arguing.

"I did what I thought was best for us, for you. Do you understand? If you want to second guess, fine. But wait until I leave."

"I'm sorry. I wasn't trying to second guess. I was legit curious."

She took a sip of wine and smiled. "Listen to me. My time in this world is gone." I gasped and put my hand to my mouth. "Don't look at me like that. I plan to be alive for a long time to come. I mean in *this* world, *this* grind. I'm cashing out, as the Americans say. If you want the truth, I sometimes think your father decided to be a stupid ass because in his own crazy way he was trying to be a better husband. Sure, the schools are good, but maybe I wanted to leave without going too far."

"And now you're going to a place that existed before you knew him."

"Yes. If there's one thing I ever wanted to teach you, it's that you should work for this kind of outcome."

"What kind of outcome?"

"Going back to the beginning of the story," she smiled, reaching for a slice of bread.

She took two suitcases. Everything else stayed in the townhouse. Her apartment in Portimao was furnished. She wanted to shop locally for everything else. Already she chattered about going to Morocco, Algeria, Tunis, to oases with warm lagoons and thick groves of palm, to a lake covering ancient cities, to a verdant delta where the Nile spreads into distributaries by the sea. So many places, she mused as we traveled along the airport highway, surrounded by boxy glass buildings advertising technological aid to the government. Mom was shifty and spunky with childish excitement. Yes, she was ready, yes, she had everything she needed. No, I didn't need to come inside the ticketing area. She'd call if anything came up. I dropped her at the curb, in between two enormous concrete pillars, and after giving me a long hug she walked into the building without turning around. It was a devastatingly anticlimactic moment. I drove home feeling like I had as a little girl when it dawned on me that Daddy wasn't coming home.

I was alone and unable to enjoy the solitude. I chatted with Mom regularly and spent lots of time at Elena's. In June, I quit my job (without telling Katy) and kept reading, searching for moral clarification, or maybe sustenance. I wouldn't find it in a book. Characters can do all kinds of things that will be judged differently in real life, in spaces where words oscillate between weightlessness and gravity. I had done something horrible and that was supposed to make me a horrible person, but I had to live with a kind of loss that repeated itself somewhere on this earth every time a powerful man opened his phone, which seemed to me more horrible than any rite of vengeance. I didn't like that everything I'd been taught about being a good person encouraged subservience to a ruthless way of being in which suffering was a natural part of life. But it's not natural, is it? It's coordinated and deliberate and maintained with painstaking care—in the legislatures, in the boardrooms, in the embassies. We're obliged to be violent, forever absorbing and conveying lowkey brutality, but we don't get to choose what kind of violence will satisfy our moral predilections. That's the one thing I learned from Dad—a special little place in the world will either be completely isolated or crowded with hostility. I was mortified by what I had done, and I was also unbelievably proud.

I walked off the dread when it threatened to immobilize me. The parks were overgrown with brush and exotic grass from steady thunderstorms. When I went off trail, leaves and branches turned my skin into a slippery mess of itchiness. Humidity made the world damp and heavy, but I liked the feeling of burning away parts of my body as I huffed through the wilderness. I was officially thin, an unusual condition for me. By mid-June, I was half-unrecognizable, even, I imagined, to an enterprising fed who might notice that the man in the wine bar was an illusion. My skin had tanned into a bronzish-brown and my hair dropped into curls on my shoulder blades. I looked like a different person, but still carried myself like the fat boyish girl who dominated my identity.

With Elena's mother off for the summer, I could drop in anytime to give her updates about Mom or get updates about Elena, who had been interning for a high-profile NGO that does refugee work. She raved about the gig and all the exciting stuff she got to witness. Her mother was thrilled that she'd been assigned to the East Africa portfolio. As one of the lucky ones who made it to the United States, she explained, it was a joy for her child to give back. I floated the idea that the NGO wasn't really giving much of anything, that it seemed like a corporation, with its wealthy CEO and celebrity board. Elena's mother wasn't having it. That's how these things work, she insisted. You need the money and the connections and you had to compete with the private sector for good leadership. I'm sure Mom would have disagreed, but Mom had stopped thinking of herself as an immigrant the moment she became friends with the people who run those organizations.

I didn't share the thought with Elena. She was too excited about the internship and would have told me of course she knows that the NGO industrial complex is problematic. Elena had enough self-confidence to believe in her ability to make change from within. I held no such belief, and as a result I've always associated cynicism with insecurity.

Besides, Elena was dragging us into her new world. The NGO was having its annual gala and interns would get to mingle with the attendees, one of the great perks of the job that was supposed to replace money as an attraction. Elena had been given permission to bring two guests and I would be going instead of her father, who swore he had to work that night. Elena dragged me to Lord & Taylor to buy a dress. "It'll come in handy in the future for other stuff," she said after I told her that I don't wear dresses. After an evening at the mall, I was ready to look respectable, if not pretty, and in even greater awe of Elena's can-do attitude. She wouldn't let me waste time in the men's department.

On the afternoon of the gala, I walked to Elena's house, stopping every few steps to adjust my flats (I refused to buy anything with heels). I knocked on the door and stuck my head inside. "Come on in," Elena's mother yelled from upstairs. "We'll be down in a second," Elena added. I sat on the couch and looked at the familiar pictures, following the sound of Elena's footsteps until I knew she was headed for the stairs. Elena had her hair newly braided with a chevron pattern on each side. Her mother's hair was blown out and tied into a ponytail. Otherwise they looked identical.

Elena drove. I sat behind the passenger seat. "Slow down," her mother said as she pushed fifty going up Carrleigh. She turned left onto Old Keene Mill and started doing sixty. "Really, daughter, what's the hurry?"

"It's fine."

"We have plenty of time."

"By the time we find parking and walk to the hotel? No."

"Don't worry, Nancy knows where to get good parking."

"Sorry, Miss B, not in that part of town."

"We'll pay for a garage. It's no big deal."

Elena wouldn't park in a garage on principle. Not finding a space on the street would be a kind of failure and Elena always believed in her ability to force an unnatural outcome.

"I just don't want to miss anything," she said. "Rumor is that Obama might drop by."

"Drop by?" her mother exclaimed. "Is that something he does? He just drops by? With a pot of zigni and a bottle of wine?"

"Mom, you have no idea how these things work."

Her mother let it go. She had raised the girl, after all. She knew that arguing was futile when Elena's main tactic was to portray her as a rube. Traffic on 395 was moving, typical for a Saturday, but no guarantee. Elena lightened up. Soon we rounded an uphill curve and saw the city in panorama, the Pentagon dominating the foreground. "I had to drive for a field trip here," Elena's mother said as we crossed the 14th Street Bridge, water and limestone surrounding us in all directions, "and oh child let me tell you I've never been so scared in my life."

Elena and I both laughed. "Where were you going?" I asked.

"That crazy dinosaur museum. When I finally parked, my knuckles were whiter than the capitol building."

"My mom's such a badass," Elena said. Her mother cackled, leaned over, and kissed Elena on the cheek.

"That's a pretty great metaphor for life," I said.

"Yep," Elena said. "Especially the part about the capitol building."

We passed the Washington Monument and White House to our left. Traffic had picked up, mostly because of pedestrians taking forever to cross the street, but it wasn't crowded and I started to think Elena would find her spot. I was getting nervous. I wasn't sure what to expect, but I knew the gala was considered high-end. Tuxedos and dresses. Former presidents dropping by. Serious shit.

In the end, Elena couldn't find parking. After twenty minutes of circling, her mother insisted on paying for a garage. Elena refused. I suggested using the hotel's valet service. That way Elena wouldn't be conceding defeat; she'd merely be taking advantage of a nice amenity. Elena agreed. Her mother looked uneasy. Nobody mentioned the bill.

We left the car with the valet and strolled into the Mayflower. I could see security guards stationed around the lobby, doing a poor job of looking innocuous. The space was filled with right angles, its ceiling covered in small glass panels, its perimeter lined by square columns with gold leaves painted on their crowns. The lotion-colored tile was beautiful but common to expensive properties. I knew exactly what the guest rooms looked like without ever having seen one.

We made our way to the ballroom, following a straggle of well-coiffed humanitarians. After passing through a metal detector we went inside. It was a large room, two stories, with the same ornate trimmings as the lobby and a series of curved balconies overlooking the floor. Hundreds of people mingled in between circular tables covered in white cloths with matching flowers. A stage was set up on the far side of the room. Two bars flanked the tables, each one getting heavy action.

Elena dragged me and her mother around the room, introducing us to fellow interns and various staff. The names evaporated somewhere between Elena's lips and my brain. It was a numbing procession of uniformity. The smiles and outfits and inflections. The affectations of warmth and sincerity. The perfectly timed gestures. It was the world I knew as a child in suffocating microcosm.

I sneaked away to get some space. Elena's mother was obliged to stay with her daughter. "I can see why Robel refused to come," she whispered to me at one point, but I knew that Elena's father would have been impressed by the spirit of the gathering. I wasn't so lucky. The kind of civility on display was somehow disorienting, aggressive, mixing luxury and homelessness into a kind of elegant piety. I made my way to the second floor and leaned my elbows on a balcony.

From my vantage point, the event was a diorama filled with gussy figurines in varying tones of solid color, among whom I could easily imagine my parents, young and dark with glossy skin and curly black hair, smiling graciously as they moved through the crowd, and I realized that although both were gone, each having disappeared under mysterious circumstances, everything I needed to honor their lives could be found on the floor of the ballroom. I watched the luminaries in the crowd— politicians, activists, pundits, ambassadors—and relaxed into a smile. The prospect of earthly paradise, once so distant, so impossible, was suddenly right there in front of me.

ABOUT THE AUTHOR

STEVEN SALAITA is a scholar and writer based in Egypt. He is the author of nine nonfiction books, most notably *Inter/Nationalism: Decolonizing Native America and Palestine, Israel's Dead Soul,* and the recently published memoir, *An Honest Living.* He currently teaches at the American University in Cairo. *Daughter, Son, Assassin* is his first work of fiction. His essays can be found at stevesalaita.com

ABOUT COMMON NOTIONS

COMMON NOTIONS is a publishing house and programming platform that fosters new formulations of living autonomy. We aim to circulate timely reflections, clear critiques, and inspiring strategies that amplify movements for social justice.

Our publications trace a constellation of critical and visionary meditations on the organization of freedom. By any media necessary, we seek to nourish the imagination and generalize common notions about the creation of other worlds beyond state and capital. Inspired by various traditions of autonomism and liberation—in the US and internationally, historical and emerging from contemporary movements—our publications provide resources for a collective reading of struggles past, present, and to come.

Common Notions regularly collaborates with political collectives, militant authors, radical presses, and maverick designers around the world. Our political and aesthetic pursuits are dreamed and realized with Antumbra Designs.

www.commonnotions.org
info@commonnotions.org